*There was no turning back now; she had
to find out the truth about Tony . . .*

Emily gave a furtive glance, looking for observers. It was a foolish act. She could barely see
around her two companions—how could she be
seen? The not uncomfortable press of Tony's
shoulder against hers reminded her that there
were even greater perils than being discovered.
What Emily herself discovered during this inquiry was likely to change her life. Somehow she
felt sure that whatever step she took now, nothing would ever be the same . . .

THE GENUINE ARTICLE

MARY E. BUTLER

DIAMOND BOOKS, NEW YORK

THE GENUINE ARTICLE

A Diamond Book / published by arrangement with the author

PRINTING HISTORY
Diamond edition / March 1991

ISBN: 1-55773-478-X

Diamond Books are published by The Berkley Publishing
Group, 200 Madison Avenue, New York, New York 10016.
The name "DIAMOND" and its logo are trademarks
belonging to Charter Communications, Inc.

PRINTED IN THE UNITED STATES OF AMERICA

10 9 8 7 6 5 4 3 2 1

Chapter One

June 7, 1816

MISS EMILY MERITON stared out the bow window onto the green stillness of Grosvenor Square. A solitary gentleman walked away from her door and across the square, the jaunty angle of his beaver top hat and the ebullient spring to his step indicating a state of extreme self-satisfaction.

Pleased, was he? Emily rather thought that it was she who had cause for self-congratulation, however. She had done it.

The sense of victory was short-lived. Almost immediately Emily castigated herself for thinking of her engagement in such terms. It made her feel uncomfortably like an adventuress luring a naive nobleman into a ruinous mésalliance, which was silly. Edward was far from naive, and the match was eminently suitable. Was it so very bad of her to make sure Edward realized just that? Surely not. Yet what other than guilt could so blot any feelings of joy from her heart?

And her countenance. The gray eyes reflected in the window were serious, even resigned. This was certainly not the proper expression to show the family.

"Well. Well. I think this calls for some celebration, hmmm, don't you think? Champagne?"

Emily turned from the window to face her brother. Even had

she not schooled her expression to reflect pleasure, John's warmth and eagerness would surely have called forth a smile. All the joy she wanted to feel shone from his bespectacled eyes. His broad smile showed up all the wrinkles around those eyes and his mouth—more than she remembered. He was much older than she, of course, old enough to be her father. Had he been worried for her, three seasons and still on the shelf?

Emily stopped her brother as he reached for the bellpull to call for a servant. "Let us wait until Letty returns. She should be back soon."

She could hardly tell John that she did not feel like celebrating. Clearly he was overjoyed with the match. Of course, he thought Edward loved her, as he loved his Letty.

The mere mention of his wife's name caused John's face to brighten even further, if possible. "Of course, she must be here, too."

He came to Emily's side to peer out the window. "Listen."

Emily looked at her brother fondly. As they leaned against the windowsill, he hardly appeared any taller than she. His eyes were closed, his head cocked attentively at an angle. "I don't hear anything," she said.

"No, nor I," he agreed. "Must be the first time since Napoleon was defeated that the streets are empty and quiet."

That was certainly true, Emily thought. The celebrations for the peace ending the long war with France had been anything but peaceful, and the arrival of the allied sovereigns had turned the town upside-down.

"The first time and the last as well, I fear," she said. "It looks like the madness is about to begin."

Within minutes a few carriages began to return to the square and with them came a sense of movement and life. To Emily there was even a sense of urgency in the *clip-clop* of the horses' hooves and the clatter of the wheels.

From the first of these carriages a vision in jonquil muslin disembarked in front of the Meriton house and quickly ran up the steps. Hardly had Emily and her brother turned around when the door burst open and Lady Meriton entered, already midsentence.

". . . staring out the window like a pair of country mice come to town for the first time. You put me to the blush, indeed you do."

Far from displaying annoyance, Lady Meriton saluted her husband with some energy. Such displays of affection were too common to make Emily blush any longer, but they did rouse a wave of envy.

"You could do that better if you removed your bonnet first, dear," John suggested to his wife. He had already removed his reading glasses.

"So I could. There." Lady Meriton obediently made another attempt, this time without her bonnet to get in the way or to obscure her golden tresses. "Was that better?" Without waiting for a response, she moved to greet Emily.

Somehow, after watching John and Letty together, Emily could not bear to talk about her own engagement. Not quite yet. Quickly she forestalled her brother.

"Well? Tell us, Letty, please. Is the tsar as handsome as they say?"

Letty sat down on the chaise longue with a flounce. "I couldn't say. The man never appeared."

Fortunately, Letty could always distract John. "Never appeared? Bad channel crossing?" he asked.

"Not a bit of it. He simply wished to avoid a public reception, so he traveled directly to his sister's apartments at the Pulteney."

"Wished to avoid . . . ?" John spluttered. "Knowing the prince would be there? I call that demmed insulting."

"So do I, or rather, I would if I were prone to such language. And, I expect, so would the prince, the Lord Chamberlain, all the officers of state, the two bands, and everyone who waited for him along the road and at the palace for three hours." Letty finally pulled off her gloves, tugging viciously in a way that did not bode well for the tsar.

"Strange," Emily commented, not willing for the focus of the conversation to move toward her yet. "All the accounts from Paris remarked how amiable and democratic he was."

"I know," Letty agreed. "On the other hand, his sister the grand duchess has done nothing but offend since she arrived. It hardly speaks well for the imperial family. Lud, you don't think they'll be at Palin's tonight? Certainly it would be a social coup for Edward to snag them, but if the grand duchess insists on stopping the dancing, I'm not sure it would be worth the trouble."

Well, that spelled the end of delay. The very mention of Edward's name had set John back on track, although Letty had not quite finished holding forth.

"You don't think Edward knew about the tsar's plans? He wasn't up at Shooter's Hill. It's not like Edward to miss an opportunity to put himself forward."

Emily lifted her head abruptly at the disparaging tone in Letty's voice. Suddenly she foresaw trouble.

John nudged her meaningfully. The announcement was hers to make and it could not be put off any longer.

"Letty, Edward was here this afternoon," she began hesitantly.

"Wanted to know if the Castlereaghs would come, I suppose." As if she realized how catty she sounded, Letty added, "And to claim a dance from you, of course."

Emily took a deep breath. "He asked John for my hand in marriage."

Her sister-in-law, stunned into silence, looked first to her husband and then to Emily for confirmation.

"John gave his blessing and I have accepted his offer. Edward and I are to be married."

"Is this true?"

"Really, Letty, such disbelief is hardly flattering." Emily's eyes twinkled as she spoke, but there was a warning note in her voice as well. "The announcement is to be made tonight at the ball to celebrate his majority."

For a moment more Letty remained silent, stunned. Before the moment stretched too long, however, her face relaxed into a congratulatory smile. It wasn't the smile Letty bestowed in the fullness of joy, but it was a smile nonetheless.

"Dearest Emily, I wish you all happiness. Think of it—my little sister to be marchioness of Palin. Oh, my, I'm speechless."

"By Jove, now that's saying something," John teased. "To have left my Letty at a loss for words."

"When I think of all that needs to be done—the parties, the trousseau, the invitations . . ."

"Look at her eyes light up," Emily remarked, carefully blocking her brother's view at the same time. "She loves it."

"But what could be more fun?" Letty evidently was willing to play along with her. "You know me so well, dear. Only promise me you have not entered into this betrothal merely for my benefit. I am not quite so selfish that I would push you toward the altar merely so I might have the fun of making all the arrangements."

There was a particular look in Letty's blue eyes that told Emily she was not jesting. Was that the reason for Letty's apparent dismay? Could Letty possibly think that she was in some way responsible for her decision?

"No, no, Letty." Emily reached out and gave her sister-in-law's hand a meaningful squeeze. "I promise you my decision to marry was made to please me, not you."

Evidently she was right about Letty's guilty thoughts, because her sister-in-law relaxed noticeably at her affirmation. Some concern still remained in Letty's eyes, however. Emily thought she knew what that might be due to as well, but if she were right, it was a charge to which she had no acceptable answer. She spoke quickly to cover up her embarrassment.

"Certainly I could not be sure you would enjoy having to arrange a wedding in so short a time. Edward wishes to be married by the end of July so that we may go to Paris first and then on to Vienna during the Congress for our wedding trip."

"What a charming idea."

Discreetly Emily gave Letty a little pinch. Even John would notice that acid tone.

"Does he not know what planning a wedding entails?" Letty added repentantly.

"I tried to warn him, dear," John said with an exaggerated sigh. Evidently he had noticed nothing amiss. John was not insensitive, but he tended to credit others with the same generous nature he possessed. It wouldn't occur to him, as it had to Letty, that Edward's wedding plans had more to do with his political aspirations than the urgency of his affections.

"You know how it is, dear," he said as he slipped an arm

around his wife's waist. "These young people in love—they simply won't listen to reason."

Young people in love. That was the problem, Emily realized as John drew his wife away, leaving her alone with her thoughts. They were not in love, she and Edward.

Without conscious decision, Emily made her way to the nursery on the third floor. The twins always cheered her. They would never make her feel guilty or cowardly for what she was doing. They might even help her ignore for a while those uncomfortable twinges of doubt that troubled her on occasion.

It was too late now for doubts, but now more than ever they disturbed her. Even an energetic game of peek-a-bo and a number of pick-a-back rides could not drive the worry from her mind. Why did she have to be afflicted with the only family in all fashionable society that believed in love matches? Any other family would have spent the last three seasons advising Emily to secure herself a comfortable future before it was too late. All the other girls Emily had come out with had been warned against pursuing romantic inclinations. They were told to be pragmatic, to be reasonable, and they had done so and found suitable husbands.

Emily could never believe her friends when they insisted, as they had been taught, that love matches never worked. How could she believe such nonsense when she had seen the devotion between her brother and Letty, between her godmama and Lord Castlereagh? No, to say love matches were dangerously unreliable was patently false. What Emily had had to face was that they were a miraculous and rare occurrence. Love like that did not come to everybody. It would not come to her.

She did not want to tell John that, however. Because John had been so fortunate as to marry Letty, he thought everyone capable of achieving the same felicity. Letty knew the ways of the world far better than he. She might not like it, but she would understand.

The sound of a footstep at the door hinted that Emily would soon learn precisely how understanding her sister-in-law was. "Mama! Mama!" the twins announced.

Without considering the possible effects to her fashionable

gown or the arrangement of her coiffure, Letty joined the trio on the nursery floor.

"I thought I should find you here," she said to Emily. "You need not look at me in that apprehensive way. I don't mean to tease."

Emily fetched one of Katy's toys for the seventh time and waited.

"I merely want your assurance that this decision of yours is not based on some misunderstood statement or action of mine. It has occurred to me that because I have pointed out a number of eligible gentlemen to you over the past year," Letty said with some difficulty, "you might suffer from the strange delusion that I wish to be rid of you."

"Letty!" Emily stared at her, open-mouthed with astonishment, ignoring even Connor's insistent demands for attention.

"Connor, stop pulling at your aunt," Letty said automatically. "I worry that somehow I have managed to make you feel unwelcome, as if John and I were not perfectly content to have you make your home with us forever. Or that you might fear becoming a sort of family drudge. It's true, we depend on you far too much."

"Family drudge? Don't be silly, Letty. You could not have made me feel more welcome. I know very well that it can hardly have been easy for you to start married life with a fifteen-year-old sister included into the bargain."

Letty made a face at her. The twins seemed to find this hilarious and spent some time begging for its repetition and then in trying to imitate it.

"I know why you've been pushing all those fellows at me, too," Emily said over the twins' noise. "But it's no use. If I could fall in love, I would certainly do so, but I cannot seem to manage it. And none of these fellows seem to regard me with any passionate fervor, either."

"Why, I know a dozen gentlemen who would rush to your side at the slightest hint of need."

Emily laughed as she disentangled herself from Connor's stranglehold. "True. But their affection for me is no more romantic than . . . than Connor's. I have some very good friends. What I do not have is suitors."

Letty looked uncomfortable at her inability to deny this assertion. "And if they do not see you as more than a kind of sister, whose fault is that?"

"Oh, mine, no doubt," Emily agreed cheerfully.

"No," Letty contradicted, her face very serious now. "I'm afraid that I am very much to blame for that. I was the one who kept warning you about your behavior. 'Don't let them see how intelligent you are,' I said. 'You'll make people uncomfortable.' And what was the result?"

Emily leaned forward to add emphasis to her answer. "The result is that people neither yawn in my face nor seek to escape the room when my name is announced. I have also achieved a number of wonderful friendships that I might otherwise not have done, friendships which I hope and confidently expect will last as long as I live. You are certainly nŏt to blame for showing me how best to go on in society."

"Blame Mama," said Connor, who was clearly hoping for another pick-a-back ride.

"No, don't blame Mama." Emily waited a moment while Letty prevented her daughter from trying to climb up to the window and then continued. "This was no impulsive decision, Letty. I thought long and hard about what I want for the future. And what I want is a home and family of my own."

Puffing a little from the exertion of holding a squirming child in her lap, Letty remarked, "I cannot think why." She pulled a ribbon from her hair and handed it to Katy. A moment of silence rewarded them. "But why now? Why Edward? Twenty-one is not exactly on the shelf. Surely this is a little early to give up hope of anything better. Wait a year—or longer."

Emily rose from the floor and began to pace. "Don't you see, Letty? That is how spinster aunts are made. You wait, and wait, and every day you say, 'Just one more day, maybe something will happen tomorrow.' Then suddenly you wake up one morning and find that it is too late for anything to happen, to change. You discover that your only place in life is making up the numbers at the dinner table and acting as chaperon to younger girls."

"Better that than wake to find yourself tied for life to a man you cannot care for."

"That is not fair!" Emily waited a moment to gain better control over her voice. "I do care for Edward. Indeed, I am very fond of him. And I respect him. He has intelligence and ambition. He doesn't drink to excess . . . or gamble . . . or associate with loose women."

"However did you learn about that?"

The corners of Emily's mouth began to twitch. "Edward is considerate, and responsible. He . . . he is kind to animals." She returned to her seat on the floor, laughing. "He does sound deadly, doesn't he?"

"Dull as ditchwater," Letty agreed. "You forgot to mention that he is extremely wealthy and titled."

"By all rights anyone with all those virtues—you forgot to mention his incredible good looks—should be dull. But he truly is not. He's charming."

Letty rose and brushed some dirt from her skirt. Her expression was not quite hidden from Emily, however.

"He never charmed you, though, did he, Letty?" Emily had just realized it. It was not simply her lack of passion for Edward that made Letty disapprove the match—it was Edward himself. This was a circumstance that had never occurred to her. "I cannot understand it. You have known Edward all his life. How could you not like him?"

Quickly Letty picked up one of the twins and began fussing with the child's hair. "I would not say that I do not like him," she denied. "And I have not known him all his life. Edward only came to Howe when he was twelve. His was a distant branch of the family. It was only when . . . when the heir died that the lawyers started searching for other relatives."

"Odd. I never realized Edward had no contact with the family when he was young. He never talks about a life outside of Howe."

"Doesn't care to remember it, most likely. I have an idea his father was a professional man, and not very successful at that. And after his death there would only have been Edward's mother's jointure to support them. No, I can quite see that the Marquess of Palin would not like to look back on those days."

It wasn't comfortable to think Edward had kept more than half of his life secret from her, but Emily would not let herself be distracted. "You have never been such a high stickler to look down on a man for that, Letty. That hardly explains your objection to Edward at all."

Letty sighed, no doubt realizing Emily would not let her avoid the question. "I suppose I never quite got over thinking of Edward as an interloper. Yes, I know that's foolish. But I had known the family for so long. I could not forget the boy who should have inherited."

"That was nine years ago, Letty. Why do you not like Edward now?"

"Very well, I think he is cold. He never does anything on impulse. And he has too good an eye for what will benefit him, and his career, in the long run. You cannot deny that marriage to Lady Castlereagh's goddaughter is like to help his political ambitions no end."

"No, I cannot deny that," Emily admitted. "But neither can you deny that it would be equally to his benefit to marry a woman with greater birth and fortune. The marquess of Palin could look a good deal higher for a bride than the daughter of a mere baronet, a girl who will bring no more than a competence with her as dowry."

The very way Letty clamped shut her lips told Emily that her sister-in-law was struggling to control her tongue and her temper. Stiffly, Letty changed the subject. "Come, Nurse is giving us one of her looks. If she is unable to make the twins take their afternoon nap, we shall have to face her displeasure. Yes, Nurse, we're going," she promised, bestowing a final embrace on the little ones.

By the time Aunt Emily had acceded to the twins' demands for hugs and managed to slip away, Letty had already disappeared, successfully eluding continuation of their conversation. Emily was left feeling unsatisfied and disappointed. She had anticipated that Letty might be a little difficult, but only a little. This unexpected antagonism toward Edward, who had always seemed such a friend to the family, troubled her. What was most distressing, however, was the realization that Emily had depended on her sister-in-law's understanding and approval. Emily knew herself for a strong-minded person. If she was convinced of the rightness of the match, why should she need

Letty, or anyone, to confirm her opinion? If she was convinced . . .

The rest of the day seemed to pass with abysmal slowness. Emily tried to pass the time with a book and then with some needlepoint, but she could not seem to concentrate. The company of her brother and sister-in-law only exacerbated her feeling of disquiet. Even a note from Lady Castlereagh regarding tomorrow's dinner at Carlton House failed to rouse her from her doldrums.

Emily tried to regain some enthusiasm as she prepared for the ball. It would not do for Edward to see her with a long face. Once the decision was made, she had thought she would feel more relaxed, relieved to finally have her future settled, but she did not.

It was at this inauspicious moment that Letty knocked and entered the room. Of all people, Letty must not be given the chance to encourage her foolish insecurities.

"I have come to apologize," Letty announced to Emily's surprise.

"Apol—Letty, there's no need. I know you meant well."

"Yes, well, it was not well done of me to insult your choice or your decision. I do understand why you chose to do this, dear, I really do. But oh, my dear Emily, I had hoped for better for you."

Emily took Letty's hands in hers and looked her in the eye. "I am going to marry a man I respect and admire, one with whom I share a number of interests and of whom I am very fond."

"A man you can manage," Letty accused, a little tearfully.

"A man who respects my opinions and wishes," Emily amended. "I hardly see how I could do much better than that."

She lied, and Letty undoubtedly knew it, but was too kind to tease her further. When they had both wiped away their tears, Letty offered her grudging support.

"I cannot say that I will not pray in my heart for you to experience some sort of revelation and call the whole thing off, or better still, for True Love to appear and carry you off before the wedding, but I'll say no more. No, not even to you. I may think you are acting the fool, but I will stand by you to the end. That being said, we must turn our minds to more important things, such as what you intend to wear this evening."

"Letty, you are incorrigible." Emily sat on the bed and watched her sister-in-law peruse and reject most of her wardrobe. "I thought we had decided on the rose sarcenet days ago."

Letty turned and looked at her as if she were a Bedlamite. "That was before this was to be the ball at which your engagement is announced. Every eye will be upon you. You cannot wear any old thing."

"The rose sarcenet is one of the gowns we bought for the victory celebrations. Hardly what one would call any old thing."

"It may have been good enough for Tsar Alexander and the king of Prussia, but it is certainly not good enough for the announcement of your engagement. The rose will do for Carlton House tomorrow," Letty agreed, carelessly delegating the prince regent's dinner to a subordinate role. "Tonight I think it must be the silver net."

"Yes, ma'am," Emily said meekly. Her spirits were beginning to rise with the promise of Letty's cooperation and support.

"Besides, I assume Edward plans to give you the Palin betrothal ring tonight, and it would look hideous against the rose. White gold and emeralds!"

"I have never seen it but it sounds lovely."

"Actually, it is immensely ugly. Oh, the stones are beautiful, but the setting is an antique monstrosity. You will probably have to rest your arm on something to prevent the ring from weighing you down on one side."

Emily smiled at the image, then wrinkled her brow. When had Letty ever seen the Palin betrothal ring . . . worn it? The late Lady Palin had been dead these twenty years or more, and the ring had been sitting in a strongbox at Howe all those years, a painful reminder to the late marquess and of no interest to the young Edward.

Still concentrating on the matter of dress, Letty did not seem to notice Emily's expression of surprise. Instead she continued to regard the silver net gown with an air of calculation.

"It needs something . . . some . . . Ah, I know. I have the very thing."

With the gown still in her arms, Letty ran from the room. Her steps could be heard echoing down the hall, and then, almost at once, returning. She re-entered the bedchamber with a curious expression on her face and a small casket in her hand. Letty carefully set down the evening gown. "Since you really do mean to have Palin . . ."

Emily fell back on the bed with an air of disgust. "Letty!"

"No, no more. Let this be my peace offering. I really would like you to have this, dear. It would be very . . . fitting."

With no little curiosity Emily rolled over and took the casket. She looked up, questioningly, at Letty once and then opened the box. Inside lay an opal and diamond pin of such extraordinary beauty that she sat up and had to catch her breath.

"I have never seen anything so lovely. Thank you, dear, dear, Letty." There were tears in her eyes as Emily embraced her sister-in-law. She knew Letty would come through in the end.

"Don't . . . don't. You will have me crying, too, and we must not show up at the ball with red eyes."

"But where have you been hiding this all these years? Was it your mother's?" Emily could scarcely credit it. Imagine owning something so lovely and never wearing it! She looked at Letty and found, to her surprise, that her sister-in-law, whose social aplomb was never shaken, was actually blushing.

"No. No, not mother's. This was . . ."

Emily watched in some amazement as Letty faltered in embarrassment. After a minute she joined Emily on the bed, her eyes fixed on the lovely ornament. "How strange that everything conspires to bring that time to mind." She fingered the pin and then finally met Emily's eyes. "I once had expectations of being the marchioness of Palin myself, you know."

"Letty, no. The old marquess was more than thirty years older than you."

"Not him, peagoose. His son, Lord Varrieur. Tony. It was he who gave me this brooch. It had belonged to his mother."

So that was why she had known of the betrothal ring, Emily

guessed. Not knowing how to respond, Emily took refuge in silence, and waited.

"I tried to give it back to Lord Palin when . . . But, poor man, he felt so guilty that he insisted I keep it."

Emily was confused. "Guilty?"

"For Tony's death. You see, Lord Palin had sent Tony off on the Grand Tour so that he might forget me. He had been very much against the match—thought we were too young— but he promised us that if Tony and I were still of the same mind after a year, then we might marry. The year was almost up when war was declared again. And Tony never came home."

Long ago, Emily remembered, Edward had told her the story of the cousin who had died in a French prison, leaving him heir to the title. The tale had seemed so distant then, merely another loss caused by the long war with France. It was not distant to Letty, though, even after the passage of eleven years. Young she may have been then, but clearly she had loved this boy, this Tony. John had courted long and patiently, Emily knew, before Letty accepted him.

"What was he like?" Emily asked quietly.

"Tony? I don't know. He was just . . . Tony. I had known him since . . . well, for as long as I can remember. How do you describe someone who has been almost a part of your very self?"

Somehow it seemed important to Emily that this unfortunate young man be given an identity. He could not have been dead more than ten years, and already it was as if he had never existed. It wasn't right, Emily's heart insisted, that in all the joy of victory, the young men who had lost their lives in the struggle should be ignored, forgotten.

Emily would not admit any other reason for her curiosity. Not even to herself would she confess the longing to understand what it was that made people fall in love.

"Well, what did he look like then?" she insisted. "He was Edward's cousin. Did he look like Edward?"

"Oh, no, not at all. Not that he was not handsome, he was, but in a very different way. Tony was a big fellow, not only tall but broad across the shoulders. If he had not been such a strapping lad, people would never have believed he was eighteen. Maybe it was his open expression. He had learned to guard his tongue, a little, but you could read his every thought on his face. He was dark, too, dark as a gypsy from spending so much time out of doors. His eyes were his best feature. And he had the longest lashes. I was always jealous of those long, dark lashes."

Emily knew better than to think that it was for his long dark lashes that Letty had loved him, however.

Letty shook her head as if to clear her thoughts. "You should not let me run on like that, Emily dear. It's time we both got ready." Letty rose from the bed and walked to the door. There she hesitated a moment before she turned to address Emily once more. "Don't ever think I regret what's past, Emily. The day I wed your brother was the luckiest day of my life. I love him far better than I ever could have loved Tony. But," she continued, echoing Emily's thoughts, "Tony deserves to be remembered, and with affection."

"Yes, of course," Emily agreed, but the thought was somehow disturbing. Perhaps it was because Emily suddenly realized how slim a chance had brought Letty into John's life and hers. Perhaps it made her uneasy to think someone so close to her should be able to keep such an important part of her life secret from her for so long. After all, if Letty were capable of keeping so much to herself, then . . .

"Letty? Does John know all about Lord Varrieur?"

"Certainly John knows"—Letty coughed and looked at her slippers—"that I was about to become engaged to Tony when he was detained in France."

Now, why should Letty look uncomfortable? Emily wondered.

"You know, Emily, I think you look rather pale. A discreet application from the rouge pot would not be amiss."

The abrupt change of conversation left Emily confused. Had she overstepped the bounds of friendship in encouraging Letty to talk? It was Letty, after all, who had chosen to confide in her.

Emily stole a quick peek in the mirror. Rouge pot, indeed.

It was only in comparison to Letty's flaming cheeks that Emily's looked pale.

Letty seemed to have recovered her equanimity by the time they left for the ball. True to her promise, she exhibited only enthusiasm for the evening's entertainment, praising Emily's appearance and prattling about the possibility of attendance by any of the royals. Emily noticed, however, that she directed the coachman to drive past Carlton House and Lord Castlereagh's home before heading toward Palin's house. Although her expressed desire was to view the illuminations, Emily could not help but think that Letty wished to delay the moment when the engagement would be announced in the hope that some miracle would take place to prevent it from happening.

The really dreadful thing was that Emily rather hoped for a miracle, too. It was all very well to know logically that one had done the right thing, but one's heart was not apt to be logical. One's heart was likely to wonder instead why Letty (dear though she was) should have known love twice in her life, and oneself should not know it at all. Was there something missing in her, Emily wondered, that she could not evoke that kind of feeling, that she could not feel it herself?

Emily tried to compose her features as the carriage finally pulled up before Palin's house. This was hardly the way to greet one's fiancé, she reminded herself. And he *was* her fiancé. Although it had yet to be announced, Emily had already given her pledge, and she was a woman of her word.

The sight of Edward waiting to receive them brought some ease to her troubled thoughts. Evening dress always made his tall slim figure look particularly elegant. His handsome face lit up with pleasure as they entered. Letty was a shrewd judge of character, but she was simply wrong this time. Edward was a better man than she knew.

At the moment he was full of affectionate concern. "Are the roads very bad? Lord and Lady Farnsworth had to come by the Pulteney and they said the crowds hoping for a glimpse of the tsar are simply immense. If they hadn't left the carriage and walked the rest of the way, they might be there still."

"We were very near doing the same," Emily said, not mentioning that if they had not gone out of their way to look at the illuminations it would not have been necessary. "It doesn't sound as if you will be short of company, however." She tilted her head in the direction of the ballroom. If the orchestra was playing, it could not be heard over the chattering voices of Palin's guests.

"Evidently not. Uncle and I had feared that with so much attention paid to the visiting monarchs, my poor party would be ignored but it seems we are to be spared that fate. I must say my interest in our foreign visitors is getting colder by the minute," Edward said with a twinkle in his eye. "If we gentlemen hear one more word about how handsome or how romantic these Russians are, we shall become violent. It was bad enough when we merely had Wellington's band of heroes as rivals. Now we must needs import competition for the attention of the fair sex."

"No, no, Palin," John contradicted. "Let the other fellows worry, not us. Others may let their heads be turned by so much gold braid, but not our ladies."

"Quite right, Sir John." Edward leaned forward confidentially. "I hope you don't mind. Ruthven plans to make rather a big to-do over the announcement, give a little speech after the birthday toast. When you see him making for the orchestra platform, you might try to get as close as you can."

Noise behind them signaled the arrival of more guests demanding Edward's attention.

"I hope we will have some chance to talk later." Edward's smile encompassed Letty and John. "Emily, of course, has promised me the first dance."

He squeezed her hand affectionately before he moved to greet the new arrivals. As they moved into the ballroom, Emily caught sight of a look of mild disgust on Letty's face. Before she could remonstrate, however, Letty recovered herself.

"It is fortunate that Palin's ballroom is so excellently well-proportioned, because his aunt has clearly done nothing to decorate the room or give it a festive air."

"Why, Letty, how can you say so?" Emily chided, trying to keep her expression serious. "When she has gone to the trouble of moving in at least six potted palms from the conservatory."

Letty reached over and held her husband's quizzing glass up to her eye. Sir John had long ago learned to wear it on a very long ribbon.

"Why, so she has. If they are any sign of Lady Ruthven's notions of entertaining, we had better avoid the lobster patties."

Despite Lady Ruthven's shortcomings as a hostess, the ballroom scintillated with excitement. No one could know, as Emily did, of the announcement to come, but she thought there was a sense of expectation in the air, a sense that something marvelous was about to happen. It might be due to no more than the hope that one of the royals would appear, but it added a peculiar quality to the evening's festivities.

Emily's composure began to fail, however, when she opened the ball with Edward. If Letty found Edward most calculating when in the pursuit of his political ambitions, Emily found him most boring and insensitive on the dance floor. It wasn't that he could not follow the steps. Her feet were in no danger. He always danced correctly, but without energy or much enjoyment. Indeed, Emily had begun to wonder if Edward were not a little tone deaf.

There was too little time after the dance, however, to recapture the warm feeling that had seized her when he greeted them as they entered this evening. Other friends claimed her attention and her dances. Mr. Templeton made her laugh with his description of ignominious failure on the hunting field. Lady Plunkett had filled her with enthusiasm for traveling on the Continent and had also provided some useful information for her wedding trip. Young Lord James had needed her sympathy.

Emily was only beginning to put aside her sense of uneasiness when she saw Lord Ruthven making his way to the platform where the musicians sat. Closing her eyes, she took a deep breath and tried to still her nervous qualms. For good or ill, the moment had come. Once the announcement was made there would be no turning back. A reputation as a jilt would as effectively bar Emily from making another match as would her engagement.

Emily's moment of inattention had cost her the opportunity to move closer to Lord Ruthven and Edward. All the guests who had been nibbling on the sparse refreshments or playing at silver loo in the cardroom had been gently encouraged to gather in the ballroom for the birthday toast. The room was, as a result, uncomfortably close and far too crowded to permit further movement. Even the footmen, endeavoring to distribute glasses of champagne, were having a difficult time doing so.

Edward gave her an understanding smile from where he stood near Lord Ruthven and gestured that they might as well wait where they were. Probably Lord Ruthven would like the fuss her extended passage through the crowd would occasion, Emily realized with some embarrassment. The old fellow liked to turn everything into a public ceremony.

"Ladies and gentlemen. Friends," Lord Ruthven began, rather pompously, after nearly tripping over one of the musician's stands. Emily covered up a giggle. Had he been reading *Julius Caesar* lately? "We have come here tonight to celebrate the coming-of-age of Edward, Lord Palin. I have had the good fortune over the last nine years to see this boy . . ."

The French doors had been opened to let a little air into the stuffy room. A surprisingly cool breeze ruffled Emily's curls and caused the crystal chandelier above to vibrate and send forth a jangling note. Ruthven's audience was getting restless. An occasional whisper punctuated his droning speech. Then louder voices and a determined tread could be heard approaching from the hall as the pontifical baron reached his peroration.

"To Lord Palin. Many happy returns of the day."

The audience obediently raised their glasses, but before anyone could take a single sip the silence was shattered by a vibrant voice.

"I thank you, cousin. But my birthday is in February."

An ominous shiver went down Emily's spine. If she was honest with herself, she would have to admit that a part of her had hoped for an interruption, something that would reverse the already irreversible. But this—this was not the True Love Letty had imagined for her, come to carry her off.

Emily had a dim sense of anger on Edward's part, sudden apprehension on Letty's, but she could not take her eyes away from the stranger who had interrupted the toast. There was raw energy here, coldly contained, that did not conform well to the formality and delicacy of the ballroom. She felt a sudden jolt when the dark eyes that scanned the room fixed first on Letty and then turned to examine her.

Lord Ruthven waved commandingly at one or two of the footmen, but none of them seemed willing to test their strength against the stranger's determination. There were murmurs from among the guests as well, but no action.

"You there . . . I say . . . who the dev—who do you think you are? Do you have an invitation to this ball?" Ruthven demanded.

"Do I need an invitation to come to a ball in my own house?"

He certainly acted as if he owned the place, Emily thought for a moment before the import of his words began to sink in.

"Come, cousin," the intruder continued. "Do you not know me? It has been a long time, I know, but now I have come home. To quite a welcome, I must say." His voice had become very soft and silky, and very frightening.

Emily found that she was shaking her head in denial. He couldn't possibly be . . .

"Ladies and gentlemen, since I have become your unwitting host for this evening, let me present myself. Anthony St. John Howe, earl of Varrieur, marquess of Palin."

"Tony."

Had she whispered the name or Letty? But it wasn't possible, her mind insisted. The boy had been dead these nine years. She recalled Letty's vivid description. Oh, this man was tall enough with dark hair and eyes, but thin, terribly thin, and so pale one would think he'd not seen the light of day in years. Could these cold eyes be the same ones Letty had found so beautiful? she wondered. Pain or trouble had etched lines on his face making him look older than the thirty years he claimed with the title. His nose had been broken at least once, and there was a small scar on his right temple. Handsome? No, but next to him, handsome faded into insignificance.

The dark eyes flickered over her again, shifted to gaze regretfully at someone behind her right shoulder, and then returned to the angry gentleman on the platform.

Only then did Emily realize that her sister-in-law had collapsed at her feet in a deep faint.

Chapter Two

THE NEXT MORNING Emily paced back and forth in the morning room, ten long and unladylike steps to the cold, unused fireplace and ten steps back to the door leading into the hall. At this time of day Emily and Letty usually reviewed the entertainment of the evening before and discussed plans for the coming day. Today, however, it did not seem that Letty wished to discuss anything.

Emily was halfway to the door when Edward was announced. Full of concern, she ran the rest of the way to meet him.

"Oh, Edward, your poor party!"

He kissed the hands she held out to him and kept them in his. "As if that mattered—except that it was supposed to be your party, too. How is Lady Meriton?"

Emily turned and walked over to the Hepplewhite sofa, hiding her face from him. It didn't seem right to start one's engagement keeping secrets from each other, but somehow it did not seem proper to reveal her worries about Letty, either. "Much better," she answered, aware that it was not entirely true. She proceeded with outright falsehood. "I think it was the heat of the room as much as the shock that made her faint. Once she was removed to a cooler area, she began to recover immediately. You know what a worrier John is, though. He insisted she come home and rest."

21

She waited until she knew she had her expression under control before she sat down and looked at Edward again. Guilt assailed her once more as she saw his troubled face. His finely drawn features looked pinched. The advent of this stranger was as much Edward's problem as anyone else's. If not to Edward, to whom could she confide her misgivings? There was something about Letty's behavior, however, and the memory of that private moment the night before when she had talked about her first love, that made Emily hesitate.

Edward joined her on the sofa. "I'm glad to hear it. I was sure she must recover quickly, if for no other reason but that she could not bear to miss this evening's festivities," he teased.

She tried to smile. "You're right, of course. John would have her rest longer, but Letty insists she is perfectly well and will go to Carlton House."

That Letty insisted on going to Carlton House was perfectly true, but Emily could not help but wonder if this insistence were not due to the fact that Letty's absence was sure to be remarked.

"I understand John's concern," Edward said. "The prince's rooms are always excessively warm and stuffy. We must hope that she won't be too uncomfortable." He gave Emily a wan smile. "At least we should be safe from the kind of scene that occurred last night."

Now Emily understood. Letty would go to Carlton House because it was the one place she would feel perfectly safe. The soi-disant Tony could not possibly have acquired an invitation.

"What happened, Edward? I felt wretched, leaving you like that, surrounded by chaos. But I couldn't desert Letty."

"Of course you could not. Better that you were spared such an ugly exhibition. The situation only degenerated further after you left. The fellow made some ridiculous accusations against my uncle. Can you imagine? Ruthven is the very soul of honesty. When the only response to that was laughter, he resorted to threats."

"Threats?" Somehow Emily associated threats with weaklings, and the man she had seen last night was not weak. He was a man to act, not utter meaningless threats.

Whatever the stranger had said had clearly troubled Edward, however. He rose and walked over to the fireplace. His face was turned away as he spoke, one arm resting on the mantel. "He says he is going to take me to court. In fact, he has already filed suit. I found out this morning from my lawyers."

Emily walked to his side and raised her arm as if to touch him. After a moment's hesitation her hand dropped to her side. "What will happen now?"

"If he continues this nonsense? There will have to be an investigation. He will have to produce witnesses to swear he is who he claims to be. I assume he can probably hire or bribe some poor souls to vouch for him. And there will probably be a panel—of family, friends, servants, that sort of thing—to question him."

Edward brought his fist sharply down on the mantel, making a Meissen shepherdess tremble and Emily step away. "There's not a chance he can get away with this," he continued. "Everybody knows my cousin died in France years ago." He stared into the cold fireplace a moment. Finally raising his head, he looked at her. "Uncle thinks the man wants to be bought off, but damned if I'll do it."

Lord Ruthven would think something that foolish. Honest he certainly was, Emily agreed, but not very bright, and perhaps not a very good judge of character.

"Try not to worry, Edward. It is a great nuisance, I know, but if the man is an impostor, I am sure it will be proven."

Emily knew immediately she had said the wrong thing.

"What can you mean? *If* the man is an impostor . . . Can there be any doubt?"

"I . . . I don't know, Edward. After all, you never met your cousin. And Lord Ruthven has said many times that until he became your guardian and trustee, he had not set foot at Howe half a dozen times. Neither of you would recognize Lord Varrieur."

"No. But I cannot imagine that any cousin of mine would go about the business of recovering his estate in this bizarre fashion. Given the impossible condition that my cousin were alive, wouldn't he come to me first? Or if not me, my uncle or the family solicitors? I am inclined to wonder from the fellow's

talent for dramatic entrances whether or not he might be an
actor."

"Not turning to the family first does sound odd, I admit."

Mollified, Edward confided, "The problem is in finding
someone who knew my cousin well enough to depress this fellow's pretensions immediately."

Indeed there was someone, but Emily did not wish her fiancé
to think of it. "Edward, was there not a clergyman?" she asked
quickly. "Some sort of bearleader who went on the Grand Tour
with him? I know I heard someone talking about him once, because he was able to return to England."

Edward answered stiffly. "He's dead now. He was an older
fellow. His health was ruined, so the French were so kind as
to let him come home to die. I'm afraid his wits were wandering
at the end."

The story came back to her now. The clergyman had managed to live another five years, despite poor health. He had insisted to the bitter end that the story of Lord Varrieur's death
was false. No wonder Edward was upset.

"I daresay we'll be able to round up some fellows who were
at Eton with my cousin," Edward said, hurrying to change the
subject. "Better yet, we should be able to contact some people
who were detained with him at Verdun. My uncle is already
checking into that and into the possibility of finding some servants or tenants at Howe who can trip him up."

Emily sat on the sofa's edge and stared at her clasped hands.
It was the emotional upset, she tried to assure herself, that
made Edward sound so ruthless. His next words disturbed her
even more.

"Actually, Ruthven suggested that Lady Meriton might be
able to help us. Her family have been neighbors to us at Howe
for generations. She must surely have known my cousin. They
were of an age."

Edward was trying to be discreet, she could tell. After
Letty's collapse last evening he would have to be a fool not to
conjecture about Letty's knowledge of the real Tony. And Edward was not a fool.

"Certainly, she knew him as a child," Emily admitted, entering further into deceit. "As you say, however, Varrieur had been away at school for many years."

If Emily, who was so close to Letty, had never heard of her earlier engagement in three years on the town, she doubted anyone knew outside the family. "Letty seems to think the gentleman we saw last night could not be Lord Varrieur," Emily compromised.

Actually, Letty insisted, again and again, it could not be her Tony. The more she insisted, however, the more Emily wondered. Yet Letty was clearly frightened. The lover she had described before could surely not occasion such fear, but then, neither could a man who was a stranger to her.

"That's wonderful!" Edward exclaimed. "We've made a start, then. I will let Uncle know we have one witness."

"Edward, I would not count too much on—"

"No, of course not. We will need far more than a single witness. Well, I begin to feel better already."

Emily felt worse. She did not think Edward fully comprehended her warning. Seeing his now cheerful smile, however, she did not have the heart to tell him that it was doubtful Letty could ever be persuaded to testify.

Her expression must have reflected some of her doubts, though, for Edward came to sit beside her on the sofa and took her hands in his. "Don't look so downcast, Emily. I feel sure everything will be resolved quickly. But in the meantime . . . oh, lud, this is embarrassing. I don't know how to tell you."

"You don't have to fish for words with me, Edward. Did you not tell me only yesterday that you felt you could talk to me about anything?"

"Yes. Yesterday." He gave her a sheepish glance. "Our announcement never got made, did it?"

"No, I am afraid your intruder very successfully put us in the shade," she laughingly agreed.

Edward took a deep breath. "Emily, I've come to ask you for some time before we announce our engagement. . . . To wait until all this is settled."

This time she could not read the emotions behind the blunt request. "Until all this is settled," she repeated in a blank tone. An unpleasant idea occurred to her. "Edward, you cannot think that the outcome of this claim makes any difference to me?"

"No, no," he assured her. "But think, dear. How can you announce that you are betrothed to the marquess of Palin at a time when that very title is called into question? What if, as you say, this fellow should actually be able to prove his claim? All I ask is that we wait until the courts decide by what name I should properly be addressed."

Reluctantly she had to agree. "I suppose it is only sensible. But surely there can be no harm in letting our closest friends know in confidence before we make a public announcement."

Thank heaven, Edward would never think that the pleading note in her voice was due to fear, fear of having time to regret her decision or fall victim to a hope that could only be false.

Patiently Edward tried to explain to her. "To tell our friends would be tantamount to a public announcement. You know that, Emily. And once it is known, the social demands on my . . . on our time will increase immensely. It's selfish, I know, but I haven't time for that while this lawsuit continues. My hope is that if I concentrate all my time and energies on this matter now, everything will be settled in time for us to enjoy our wedding trip in Paris and Vienna as we planned."

"Of course, Edward. I don't want to cause you any worry, especially when you have so much else on your mind."

Edward's words made Emily realize that if she were drawn into the social round of the newly affianced, she would have little time to concern herself with whatever was bothering Letty. And it was becoming increasingly clear that someone would have to get to the bottom of that problem very soon. After all, only Edward's title and fortune were at risk; Letty's very peace of mind had been overset.

Still, she felt guilty when she discovered that Edward had waited a few minutes after making his adieux to actually leave the house. Had he sensed her withdrawal? Had he hoped for more comfort from her? In any case, this challenge to his position obviously threatened him more than Emily would have expected. Whoever this claimant really was, he was going to find himself with quite a fight on his hands.

*   *   *

Tony entered the shabby apartment that had become his pied à terre with the air of a gentleman who returns home after a boring afternoon at the club. This ability to hide his feelings, he knew, was often annoying to Gus, but it had been a necessity to him for so long it had now become second nature. The first thing one learned in prison was not to let the jailers know they had succeeded in wounding you.

"Well, Tony, did you enjoy yourself last night?" August Sebastian Maria von Hottendorf greeted him. The fair-haired officer lounged at his ease along the only piece of furniture suitable for such behavior—the bed. He grinned good-naturedly. "It must have been spectacular. Your escapade is already the talk of the embassies. It provides a nice relief from gossip about the tsar."

"If it has served no other purpose but that, I have still accomplished a great deal. I am so glad you were amused."

Gus was getting a little better at reading him evidently. He raised a single eyebrow skeptically. His first attempt to respond to Tony's comment was interrupted by a racking cough, another reminder of Bitche. Although Gus now wore a particularly splendid uniform as an officer of the kingdom of Prussia, and he himself had acquired some fairly respectable clothes, they both still exhibited too many signs of recent incarceration. It certainly detracted from an elegant appearance.

"And have you had another productive day?" Gus asked, once his spasm had passed.

"She would not see me." Tony could not trust himself to say more.

Von Hottendorf thought about this for a moment. There was no question who "she" was.

"I assume you did not get past the servants?" After receiving a brief nod of assent from Tony, he continued. "It might not have been her order, you know. She has a husband now."

Tony pulled the room's only chair over and sat down. "I suppose it is possible. She might not have even known I called." He was only admitting the possibility, no more. "But if it is her husband, and not Letty, who has barred me from the door, how am I to get to her?"

"I think she will hear of your arrival in town," Gus assured him with a laugh. "She can hardly avoid it. Perhaps she will find a way to see you."

"Lady Meriton to come here?" With a gracious wave of his hand Tony indicated the accommodations. All in all, he had been fortunate to find anything remotely respectable, considering the influx of visitors for the victory celebrations. It was not, however, suitable for entertaining members of the opposite sex.

"I see what you mean," Gus conceded. "However, there are still other ways in which the lady might contact you."

"If she wishes to," he reminded Gus. "I would not care to risk my claim on it, however. She has proved unreliable before." His voice had grown very quiet. He was not willing to reveal yet that Letty had seen him already, had seen him and remained silent.

Tony could feel his friend watching him very intently. He responded to Gus's unspoken question with one of his own. "Did you manage to learn anything more about her through your embassy contacts?"

Gus hesitated a moment, then sighed and answered the question. "Oh, everybody knows her. She is one of the leaders of fashion. Everybody likes her, too, which is unusual. They say her tongue rivals Lady Jersey's for volubility, but not for malice."

"And?" Tony prompted when Gus seemed unwilling to continue.

"She is thought to be genuinely devoted to her husband. And their two children."

Tony pondered in silence this picture of domestic bliss, waiting until he could trust himself to speak.

"How long has she been married?" he asked, even though he knew the question itself was revealing.

"Five years."

There was a moment of silence before he resumed his questions. "What about the husband—Meriton?"

Gus shrugged. "His major claim to fame was having snagged Lady Meriton. Quiet, good-natured fellow. Belongs to Whites but is not often seen there. Not much else to say about him, except that he is considered to be equally devoted—actually, *besotted* was the word I heard used—to his wife and family."

A fellow that devoted—besotted—might very well wish to keep him away from his wife, Tony considered, whether he had much reason to do so or not. But Tony had no choice. Letty was the key. Somehow or other he had to reach her.

As if following his thoughts, Gus reminded him, "Do not be so single-minded. If your claim is to succeed, you will need a great deal of support. What do you think your rival is doing right now?"

Tony rose and walked over to the window. The window was the single thing he liked best about this room. It was a luxury he had been too long denied.

"Trying to gain Lady Meriton's support for himself," he answered. "I saw him going out the door. Just before it was shut in my face. I have not yet decided which is preferable—being refused entrance or being kicked out. Nobody seems to want my company anymore. I have been turned away from Lord Ruthven's and Lady Meriton's, and I have been kicked out of the solicitor's office and out of Palin House twice."

"Oh? I heard the footmen were too frightened to lay a hand on you last night."

"My presence was deemed an intrusion, nonetheless. But if you wish to be a stickler for detail, very well, once from Palin House. Don't you think even once was more than enough?"

"Ah, but I can't blame the boy for the first time." Gus grinned and coughed again for a moment. "Think, Tony. You looked not at all respectable, still dirty from travel and wearing clothes borrowed from some poor soldier. If you had come to me looking like that and telling such a story, I should take you for a madman. No wonder he threatened to call the watch."

"Such a story? I could hardly know I was supposed to be dead." He shook his head. "Don't waste your sympathy on that one, Gus. If he had taken me more seriously, he would have done more than merely threaten."

"You are correct." Gus suddenly dropped his cheerful facade. "Despite his treatment of you, he is accounted no fool. My friends at the embassy tell me he has political aspirations."

"Ah, I see. Many, many friends in high places."

"And the knowledge of how to use them."

"You need not remind me that I am conspicuously lacking

in influential connections. Meaning no disrespect to your honorable self."

Gus rose from the bed and executed an elegant bow. "I thank you, but agree that you will require more help than a junior officer attached to Prince Hardenburg's staff can provide. What I can do for you, I will. You know that. But what does that amount to in the end? Gathering a few scraps of gossip, running a few errands?"

"Acting as my banker," Tony reminded him. It was due to von Hottendorf's generosity that he was able to afford this small room and the few respectable garments in his possession.

"Pah, a mere nothing. You will not mention it again. I only wish I could do more, but as a foreigner . . . What you need is another Englishman, someone who is part of this society, to help you."

Or an Englishwoman. But he could not count on Letty. Who else was there? Of the crowd of people who had stared at him last evening, who would even be willing to listen to him?

"Gus—" He closed his eyes trying to picture the scene in his mind. "Do you know if Lady Meriton has any particular friends? A young lady," he clarified.

"Particular friends? No, not outside the family."

"Are you sure? Last night I saw her. As soon as I entered the room I found Letty. That golden hair stood out like candlelight in the dark. And next to her was a woman all in silver, eyes like silver, too, who looked me straight in the eye. She was the only one who did that, for all they were staring at me as if I were an exhibit at the Royal Academy." He opened his eyes to catch Gus staring at him, too. "I could have sworn she was with the Meritons."

"She made quite an impression on you."

"Yes, yes, she did. She was different." He tried to think of a way to explain, and failed. All he could say was, "She was the only one who kept her head. Letty actually fainted, and she was the one who saw that she was carried out of the room and taken care of."

Tony suspected that his friend was pondering more than simply the girl's identity, but Gus knew when to keep silent. After a moment's thought he said, "Meriton has a sister."

"With silver eyes?"

"I do not know."

"Well, what do you know?" Tony pressed.

"Her name is . . . her name is Emily. That is it—Emily. I remember now. Much younger than Sir John, young enough to be his daughter, in fact. Not married."

"Not?" Tony asked in surprise.

"Perhaps she has turned down many offers. She is certainly very much admired. If I am to believe report, Miss Meriton is extremely interested in fishing, hunting, all forms of sport, estate management, politics, fashion, art, literature, the theater, the difficulties of raising children . . ." Gus stopped to catch his breath. "Miss Meriton must be very adept at the art of flattery."

"No," Tony said with certainty. "I cannot believe that. Miss Meriton must be genuinely interested in people. And she must be a woman who has learned how to listen. What do you think, Gus? How would you like to see if Miss Emily Meriton will listen to me?"

Emily felt embarrassed to have to tell her brother and Letty that Edward had requested their engagement be kept quiet for a while. She might as well not have worried.

Considering Letty's stated feelings about Edward and the match, Emily expected some reaction, either hard words about Edward's behavior or hopes that the delay might make her reconsider. Instead Letty said nothing, not even in private. She had simply nodded her head when John had agreed to respect Edward's wishes.

John saw nothing odd in the request. In any case, he was too worried about Letty to concern himself with Edward's behavior.

Letty, of course, was known for her voluble tongue, but today she had outdone herself. When unable to avoid the company of her spouse and sister-in-law, she maintained a steady stream of talk, holding forth at length on any subject but the man who claimed to be Tony.

Only once was John able to pin her down, in the morning, when she must still have been perfecting her performance. She insisted then that the man who had interrupted the ball must be a fraud, that he could not have been her former fiancé. She insisted over and over again, pointing out ways in which he differed from the young boy she had known, but she was clearly grasping at straws. Letty might not be sure if the stranger was Tony, but she thought he might be.

Emily remembered every word of her conversation with Letty. She reviewed it in her mind time and again, trying to find a clue as to why her sister-in-law should be so overset, but in vain. Letty had obviously not told her everything.

Perhaps she had not told John everything, either.

Such thoughts did not leave Emily in a proper frame of mind for a ball, certainly not for an exclusive event hosted by one's sovereign.

It had already been arranged long ago that Edward would accompany them to Carlton House, a situation that only increased Emily's distress. Any attempt of Edward's to pressure Letty for assistance could only make things worse, and Edward could be remarkably single-minded when pursuing some goal.

Edward, instead, seemed reserved and distracted. His own worries kept him from noticing any peculiarities in Letty's conduct. With a twinge of guilt, Emily realized that the forthcoming gathering was likely to be as trying for him as for Letty. His eyes actually had a rather hunted look when she reached over and gave his hand a comforting squeeze.

She understood why almost as soon as they passed the colonnaded marble screen, illuminated by scarlet and topaz flares, at the prince's residence. The first murmurs of conversation overheard entering Carlton House mentioned the stranger. Once inside, almost the first person to address them was Lady Jersey, and she did not address Edward by title.

"Miss Meriton, isn't this a terrible squeeze? We shall all be suffocated by the end of the evening," she prophesied cheerfully. "I do hope your sister-in-law is recovered from her indisposition of last evening. I saw her a moment ago, but she seems to have disappeared."

Emily carefully controlled her smile. Perhaps Letty was feeling better. At least her instinct for self-preservation must be alert to have moved her so quickly out of "Silence's" range.

"Much better, thank you. I will be sure to convey your concern to her."

"I was a little surprised to see her here tonight." And Edward, too, her glance hinted.

Emily had to concentrate to maintain her smile now. "Lady Jersey, tell me, would you not do the same? We were all cheated of a glimpse of the tsar yesterday afternoon. No one could possibly miss the chance to see him tonight." There was small hope that Lady Jersey could be distracted from her real target, but Emily had to try. "It seemed hardly possible that he should live up to such favorable reports, but I confess, he seems very attractive from the short time I spoke to him. I like the attentive way he leans forward, as if your every word were important."

"That is not attentiveness, my dear. He's deaf in one ear. The old tsar used to force him to listen to the cannonades as the troops reviewed. You would think that might be a bond with Prinny—both of them with fathers who had passed the point of being deemed merely eccentric. Such, I'm afraid, does not appear to be the case. I suppose it would be too much to hope that you mean to provide us with some better entertainment." The question was directed at Edward, but once again she would not call him by name, a name that might not be his.

Edward handled it well, however, with his usual charm. "I cannot take the credit for last night's . . . diversion, Lady Jersey. I only wish I could find it as amusing as everyone else seems to do."

"Then he is pursuing the claim? Yes, I see he is. Well, well, this will make for an interesting summer. I only wish I had known Lord Varrieur before his trip to France. Of course, he was only a boy then."

Lady Jersey was so successful in annoying Edward that Emily was glad to go into dinner, even though she knew it would be excessive in terms of both food and duration. Edward's ill humor made it difficult to enjoy even the beauties of the house and the spectacular arrangements made for the evening. Double doors had been opened between vast apartments to create a single room three hundred and fifty feet long. There were gold moldings on the paneled walls and shields emblazoned with the quarterings of England. So immense was the crush of guests, however, that to Emily the most beautiful sight was the view at the west end of the house, where wide Gothic doors opened onto a green expanse of lawn, with weeping willows and the occasional peacock, gilded by the setting sun.

Emily was at least fortunate in the seating arrangements for dinner, which placed her far from Edward's scowling countenance. Her dinner partners included a military gentleman who was himself the father of two officers serving under Wellington, and Mr. Dominic Neale, a gentleman who worked at the Foreign Office whom she had previously met through Lord Castlereagh. Knowing her connection to that family, he entertained Emily with stories of the myriad details involved in preparing for the Congress in Vienna.

Emily's luck could not hold forever, and she knew it. Eventually the gossip spreading up and down the room regarding Edward's party was sure to reach her. Emily had thought that by now she would be prepared for it, but the strength of her neighbor's reaction surprised her.

"But that is utterly ridiculous!" Mr. Neale exclaimed dogmatically. "The man died in France more than ten years ago."

"Lord Palin will be glad to hear you say so," she responded. "However, Mr. Neale, that fact remains to be proved. None of us was in France at the time it happened."

"But I was," he said, to her great astonishment.

"You were there?"

Whereas Mr. Neale had always been a gentleman of a certain distinction, he now became an authority. Emily looked at him with a greater interest. Judging by the touch of gray at his temples, she guessed him to be of an age with her brother, old enough to have seen beyond the discomfort of his own situation in France. She doubted that his sharp eyes would miss much.

"Yes, I was one of the unfortunates to be caught still in Paris when Napoleon's decree was issued. Most of us were sent to Verdun, like Lord Varrieur. My financial situation did not permit that I travel in quite the same social circles as he did," he confessed. "But the number of *détenus* in the town was not so large that I could be unaware of him. He was rather well known for his habit of getting in trouble with the authorities, I'm afraid."

"What sort of trouble?"

Mr. Neale smiled. "Not the sort you are obviously thinking of, Miss Meriton. It took very little. One insult to the emperor and you could find yourself on the way to Bitche. Which is what happened to his lordship in the end. Bitche was the punishment prison," he explained.

Not any prison, but a punishment prison. Emily could not even begin to comprehend what that might entail.

"Is that where he is supposed to have died?" she asked, her voice hushed.

"That is where he certainly died. Fever was always rampant there. The clergyman that had been with Varrieur kicked-up such a fuss that the body was sent back to Verdun for burial. Poor fellow, he was never quite the same afterward. There was a very nice service for Varrieur. I daresay there are a number of people who attended it who are now in London."

She would have to tell Edward. He would be pleased to gain so many witnesses. There was something about the story that did not satisfy her, however. The clergyman had claimed Tony was still alive, presumably after seeing the body. On the other hand, there must have been other witnesses who saw the body as well who did believe it was Varrieur.

Emily pondered the question after dinner and during the endless round of presentations to the queen. Once again she had been deserted by Edward, who had urgent business to discuss with another of the guests. All the prince's rooms were warm, but in the crowded Throne Room, the temperature was nearly unbearable. A slight rend in the flounce of her gown gave Emily the chance to disappear for a few minutes to make the repair.

She was not anxious to reenter the stuffy room. The soldier standing just outside the room undoubtedly felt the same. The thin silk Emily wore was uncomfortable enough in this heat. How terrible those poor fellows in their stiff uniforms must feel! He caught her pitying look and smiled engagingly.

"If you tell no one that I have deserted my post, I will not tell on you," he promised.

Emily was not familiar with the uniform, but she judged by the accent that the young man must belong either to the Prussian or Austrian contingents. Of course, he ought not to have spoken to her without an introduction, but there was such a look of humor in his eyes that she could not give him a setdown. On the other hand, his presence and forwardness made it difficult for her to stay as she wished.

"Pray, do not go in on my account," he urged.

Emily tried to keep her tone and expression repressive. "My sister-in-law will be looking for me."

"Lady Meriton is deep in conversation with the Countess Lieven at the moment."

As far as she knew, Letty did not number any German or Austrian gentlemen among her acquaintance. "You know Lady Meriton?"

"I know of her. No," he added, moving slightly to block her path, "she will not be able to introduce us properly when you find her. However, we have a friend in common—Lord Palin."

She knew then who it was he meant, although she chose not to acknowledge it. "Lord Palin is within, talking to Sir James Whitby-Edwards."

"Mr. Edward Howe may very well be talking to Sir James inside there, but Lord Palin did not receive an invitation. A mistake on the part of the prince's social secretary, no doubt."

The cheerful expression and confidential tone had not changed at all. She really ought not to stay and listen to this, Emily thought, feeling guilty. It was improper, and it was highly disloyal to Edward as well. According to Mr. Neale's account, the claimant had to be a fraud. What did that make his friend?

While Emily's curiosity fought with her sense of propriety, the officer made his plea quickly. "He wants to talk to you."

Curiosity won. Her eyes widened in surprise. "What did you say?"

"He was right, your eyes are silver," the officer said obliquely. "I said Tony wants to talk with you."

"Why me?" She did not have the courage to question his first remark.

"Because you are close to Lady Meriton," he admitted. "Because you are known to be honest. Because you listen to people. Listen to him, that is all he asks."

"You and your friend make a great many assumptions about my character."

"Is he wrong?"

Emily ignored his challenge and answered with another question. "Why should I agree to do this?"

"For the truth, because you are curious. For Lady Meriton, because she is your friend as well as your sister-in-law."

The officer's voice was not threatening, but the words could be construed as such. Whether the man knew it or not, whether he was the man he claimed to be or not, the dark stranger was a source of worry to Letty. Emily had to know why, and for once it did not look as if Letty were going to tell her.

The officer had one card left, and he used it.

"Are you afraid? You think Tony is a fraud, a criminal?"

"I am not afraid," Emily denied. "But I have no reason to think your friend is telling the truth."

"Then let me give you one. Ask Lady Meriton if she remembers the occasion on which Tony gave her the opal brooch you wore to the ball last night."

Chapter Three

EMILY SAT IN the high-perch phaeton, nervously clasping her gloved hands and peeking out of the corner of her eye at the Prussian officer who was driving her so expertly through the crowded paths of Hyde Park. It was not the height of the fashionable carriage that made her feel apprehensive, but the possible depth of her own folly. What had ever possessed her to accept this foolish challenge?

The officer's name was Captain August von Hottendorf, or, at least, that was as much of the long string of names and titles he had rattled off she could remember. He was clever, she had no doubt of that. Once he had seen that her interest was caught, he had quickly found someone to formally introduce him, not only to Emily but to her family. Perhaps because he was aware of Emily's eyes on him, he made no attempt to discuss their "mutual friend" with Letty. However, he had carefully ingratiated himself with them all by introducing them to his superior, Prince Hardenburg, one of the more distinguished and respected members of the visiting royal parties.

The invitation to drive had been accomplished very publicly and very skillfully, phrased in such a way that Emily would look ungracious had she refused. She did not refuse. It was much too important to discover what the stranger calling himself Lord Palin wanted, especially what he wanted of Letty.

Nonetheless, Emily was concerned over the propriety of this

meeting. She was, after all, an engaged woman, even if no one outside the family knew it. It was true that no one, not even Edward, would think it odd if one of her old friends should act as her escort when Edward was unavailable. This captain was not, however, an old friend. Neither was the gentleman they were going to meet.

With luck Edward would never learn about the meeting that was soon to come, but he would certainly hear about this drive. The bright blue Hussar uniform, with its gold trim, plumed shako, and jacket worn negligently off the shoulder, was too romantic and picturesque to go unnoticed. The care Emily had taken with her own costume, a sprig muslin trimmed with periwinkle, would also be remarked. What would Edward think?

Brooding on the situation, Emily paid little attention to the lovely June sunshine, the brilliant foliage, or the elegant costumes of the people who crowded the park's drives and walkways.

The gentleman at her side recalled her attention. "I would appreciate it if you would smile occasionally, Miss Meriton. My reputation as both a whip and a gallant will suffer if you continue to look so uneasy."

"I am sorry," she apologized automatically. "It is just that I cannot help but feel guilty."

The captain, having won her consent, was disposed to be agreeable. "What is there to feel guilty about in taking the air on a lovely morning? Or in helping a person in need?"

Emily, however, was not in a mood to be mollified. "If there is nothing to feel guilty about, then why the air of secrecy? I am not in the habit of deceiving my family about my plans." She had deceived Edward, too, and not for the first time, she thought, remembering their last meeting.

Von Hottendorf's voice turned colder. "I also am sorry that deceit was necessary. It should not have been. But when my friend was turned away from your door in such a way . . ." He shrugged.

"Do you mean to claim that To—" She caught herself just in time. Thinking of this man as Tony was a trap she must avoid. "Your friend actually came to call?"

"Yes, of course. You did not know? He came the day after

seeing you both at the ball given by the young lad using Tony's title. The boy was leaving the house as Tony came down the street."

"But . . ." His story made no sense. From where Emily had been sitting in the morning room she would have known if any of the footmen had gone in search of Letty, or John, to announce anyone. The day had been unnaturally quiet after Edward's departure. Emily was inclined to think the man was lying—except that he was right about Edward leaving the house.

"To whom did he speak?" she asked. "Did he see my brother?" If he maligned her brother, Emily would know how to treat the rest of this fellow's claims.

"No, he saw no one but the butler." Noting her furrowed brow, von Hottendorf continued. "I assure you, he was there."

She could easily find out for herself. "You trust his word implicitly?" she asked.

Von Hottendorf stopped the carriage and turned to face her. "Yes, yes I do."

"And you believe that he truly is Lord Palin, then?"

"Of course." He smiled and clucked at the horses to start moving again. They were both silent for a time while the captain negotiated his way out of Hyde Park and discreetly wended his way toward Richmond, where they would meet the man who called himself Tony.

Emily watched the pale handsome face beside her. There was something very compelling in von Hottendorf's expression of faith in his friend. After the captain had engineered his introduction and invitation to her, Emily had done a little investigating into his background. What her careful questioning revealed was a reputation for loyalty, integrity, bravery—and intelligence. Fools did not achieve places on Prince Hardenburg's staff.

"How did you come to know him?" she eventually asked. She could not make herself give the stranger a name.

"We were at Bitche together," von Hottendorf told her in a very quiet voice, as if that said everything. And perhaps it did. Was there any other tie that could so strongly bind men together than having survived such misfortune together?

"That was a punishment prison." Emily remembered that was what Mr. Neale had called it.

"It was—" Clenching his jaw, the captain cut off his words, then forced himself to relax. "Unfortunately, there are no words fit to be used before a lady that can adequately describe Bitche. Yes, it was a punishment prison. I had been at one of the other forts and was caught trying to escape. I had not given my parole, I assure you," the captain hastened to explain. "But I had offended the governor a few times refusing to pay what he asked. So to Bitche I was sent."

Two sprigs of fashion recklessly jockeying for position as they raced their curricles against each other forced von Hottendorf to devote all his attention to his handling of the ribbons for a few minutes. When they had passed, he continued. "This was near the end of the war. I was fortunate not to have to stay there very long, although it was long enough to give me the gaol fever."

He spoke as if it were not an unusual occurrence. This was also as Mr. Neale had described. So far Emily found the story only gave credence to the belief in Lord Varrieur's death.

"When the allied armies started getting close, we were moved further inland. Varrieur planned to escape en route. I simply fell and was left for dead. He found me still breathing and got me to a safe place, got someone to take care of me."

"I understand why he has earned such loyalty from you." Better men than Captain von Hottendorf had been fooled before, however, she thought.

"But not why I believe him," he answered, as if he had read her mind. "I admit it. I cannot prove Tony's claim. I only wish I could. What I can swear to is that Tony had been left at Bitche longer than any other prisoner, longer than most could remember, and no one ever heard him call himself anything other than Anthony, Lord Varrieur. If my friend is making a fraudulent claim, he must have begun his playacting more than nine years ago. And he has never slipped up once in claiming his identity, not once in ten years."

Could a man be so tenacious, so determined either on profit or revenge, to hold tight to a false identity for so long, with no assurance that he would even live long enough to bring the plot into action? Emily pictured in her mind the gentleman who had made such a stir at Edward's ball and thought perhaps he might.

Once they turned the corner into Richmond Park, Emily no longer needed to depend on her memory to assess the stranger's character. He stood waiting for them under a large elm to which he had tied his roan mare. His expression was unreadable, although Emily thought him a little more relaxed than he had been when he made his famous entrance.

Emily had relaxed, too, comforted by the captain's excellent manners and amiable personality. Now she began to consider again not merely the impropriety of her situation, but its possible dangers. They had chosen Richmond Park because, although usually crowded with lovers of nature and lovers of other kinds, during the victory celebrations it had been deserted in favor of the London parks, where one had the chance of seeing a visiting monarch or a picturesque Cossack. This meant no one was likely to observe her assignation with the claimant. She now realized that no one was likely to come to her assistance should she need help.

It was too late to change her mind, however. The stranger stood at the side of the phaeton ready to help her down. He looked rather severe in his plain dark coat, especially compared with his friend's extravagant costume. With a smile, Captain von Hottendorf introduced them.

"Miss Meriton, may I present to you Anthony, Lord Palin. Lord Palin, Miss Emily Meriton. Now even such a stickler as you, Miss Meriton, cannot complain that you were not properly introduced." The captain took her hand in farewell and promised to return for her in half an hour. Quietly, so that his friend should not overhear, he assured her, "You have nothing to fear, Miss Meriton. Whether you believe Tony is marquess of Palin or not, I promise you he is a gentleman. On that I pledge my honor and my life."

Emily certainly hoped he was right, because for the next half hour she would be quite alone with this man. Her brother and sister-in-law were not terribly rigorous as chaperons. She had been alone with a gentleman before, but she had never been so aware of it, or of the man himself.

"I thought we might stroll through the grounds," he suggested. "That is, if you don't mind, Miss Meriton."

"No, I don't mind," Emily answered, unsure of herself. What was she to call him?

He was shrewd enough to see her difficulty. "I have a suggestion for you, Miss Meriton, one that I hope will not shock you. Until such time as you feel secure in calling me by my title, will you do me the honor of using my given name—Tony? I can understand that with your concern for propriety, you may find this a bit presumptuous. . . ."

Emily watched his expression carefully. Was he laughing at her with his reference to propriety? Proper misses were hardly wont to make assignations like this one.

"But," he continued, "such friendliness on your part will commit you to nothing. After all, the world is full of Tonys."

Not like you, she thought to herself. "Very well," she agreed. "Tony it is. And do you mean to explain to me why you requested this meeting, Tony?"

She tried to maintain a stiff, unbending attitude, but it was not easy to keep up while one was ambling through the park, leaning on the gentleman's arm where the ground was rough.

"Yes, I will." He stopped beside a bed of pink flowers with a long Latin name. "But there is one question I must ask you first."

"Yes?"

"How is Letty?"

Of all the things he might have asked, this was the question Emily would have least expected. And the one she least knew how to answer—now.

"Letty was very disturbed by your appearance the other evening," she confessed, picking her words carefully. "Of course, she believed her Tony dead for many years."

"And before that, has she been happy?"

Once again he had surprised her. She had expected him to immediately press for some indication of whether Letty believed in him or not. "Yes, she has been happy," she assured him. "Letty and my brother . . ."

How could she possibly convey the joy and affection she saw in their marriage? She began again. "Letty and my brother are most sincerely attached to each other. Only a few days ago I recall Letty said that the day she married my brother was the luckiest day of her life."

After she said it, Emily realized that if she were indeed talking to Letty's past love, he might not be particularly comforted to hear such things.

His face showed neither grief nor pleasure, although he said, "I am glad." Emily found herself examining him for some sign, some hint that tied him to the Tony that Letty had described. The biggest difference was in personality. Letty had drawn a picture of an open-hearted youth, quick to show emotion. But Tony wouldn't be a boy anymore, if he still lived.

"Did Letty tell you anything about me, about Tony?" he asked.

"A little," she conceded. She did not want to give this man any information he did not already have. However, it had been he, through his envoy, who had challenged her to ask about the brooch. "She told me that you gave her the opal pin and that it had been your mother's."

He looked at her as if he, too, were trying to decide how much to disclose. "Did she tell you we wished to be married?"

"Yes." Her voice was hushed. If he were not Tony, he would have to be someone very close to him. There cannot have been more than a few people who knew of his relationship with Letty.

"I cannot understand why she would refuse to see me," he protested, for once in a voice that failed to hide some pain. Immediately he strove to regain control. "I would have hoped that Letty would realize I have no wish to disturb her present happiness."

"You are assuming Letty has recognized you as Tony," Emily reminded him. "In private Letty has voiced considerable doubt regarding that." She would not tell him that she likewise had doubts about Letty's assertions.

This time there was no attempt at concealment—or else the man was an extraordinary actor. Such an idea seemed not to have occurred to him. He was astounded. "I know I have changed a great deal," he admitted. "But I thought Letty at least would know me."

"It has been a very long time," she reminded him. She meant her voice to sound noncommittal, but a note of sympathy crept in without volition in response to the pain she heard in his. Firmly she forced herself to return to the question of this alleged visit of his. "Captain von Hottendorf told me you came to call. I cannot believe either my brother or my sister-in-law would send you away like that."

"I cannot believe your butler would resort to such brusque behavior if he had not been under orders to do so," he countered.

"You may be sure I will look into that matter."

"Will you also intercede with your sister-in-law on my behalf?" he asked.

At last. Emily had known this question must arise and she had considered long how to handle it. "I would be happy to intercede with my sister-in-law on behalf of her former fiancé, but you already know, sir, I am not at all convinced you are that person."

"I could prove it to Letty immediately," he argued, "if she would only see me. It is not only that we were in love. We grew up together at Howe. She knows things about me no one but my nanny knew."

"That may be so, sir," she agreed. "However, I will need further proof before I will consent to disturb my sister-in-law's peace. If that is all you had to ask me, you must consider this meeting a wasted effort."

"No." He stopped her before she walked away. "It was not all I wished to ask of you."

Emily raised an eyebrow in inquiry. What else could she do for him?

"Miss Meriton, I will admit to you that beyond my own need to . . . to say a kind of good-bye to Letty, I need her as a witness on my behalf. Indeed, she is a pivotal witness, for without Letty's testimony to support me, all others become doubtful, lacking in authority. At the same time, Letty's testimony will not be enough, by itself, to reclaim my home and title. I need a great deal more."

"What you say is quite true, but what have I to do with all that?"

"I want you to help me find other witnesses who can support my claim."

If the man only knew! Emily laughed out loud. This man was actually asking her to prove that her own fiancé had no right to the title of marquess of Palin.

"My dear sir," she said, wiping a tear from her laughing eyes, "if I will not approach Letty while I am unsure of your claim, I am hardly like to approach anyone else with the same purpose. You do know that my family and the . . . the person presently recognized as Lord Palin are very close."

The crackling energy Emily had sensed in him in the ballroom had returned. "Oh, yes, I know that. Forgive me, I phrased my request improperly. I do not ask you to help me prove my claim."

"No?"

"No, I simply ask you to find out the truth."

Emily turned and stared at him. "You seem very sure of the results." She wondered what answer he would make to the story of his own funeral.

"I am."

His very assurance unsettled her. "But what could I possibly do?"

"What you do best, Miss Meriton. Listen."

"I don't understand."

He led Emily to a natural rock formation which formed a convenient resting place. After she had settled herself, he sat beside her to explain. The bright sunlight accented the extraordinary pallor of his features, and Emily found herself considering the effects of ten years in prison. The scars might be due to fights—with the guards, perhaps. Clearly he had lost none of his spirit in all that time.

"I have learned a few things about you, Miss Meriton," he said.

Emily blushed. Suddenly she remembered the captain's strange outburst. *He was right. You do have silver eyes.*

Emily was further embarrassed to think how her blushing reaction must confuse him. His statement hardly warranted such an extreme response. What must he be thinking of her now? "I cannot imagine anything concerning my life or character that would be considered worthy of remark."

"Nothing to your discredit, I assure you. In fact, I doubt whether there is another in London who can boast so many true and faithful friends."

But no suitors, Emily said to herself. His words recalled her conversation with Letty regarding her matrimonial prospects. She wondered if he would be frightened off, as others were, if he realized exactly how intelligent she was.

"You flatter me," she said.

"Not at all," he assured her, and she believed he meant it. "There's something about you . . ." He stared deep into her eyes as if he hoped to find some answer there. "I can't explain it, but I've felt it myself. People tell you things, things they might not say to any other person alive."

"And you expect me to betray my friends' confidences?" She made no attempt to hide the scorn in her voice. This time he had gone too far.

"No, of course not," he insisted. "Why do you persist in deliberately misunderstanding me? All I ask you to do is listen. If you hear of someone who knew me years ago, make note of it. If you come across someone who went to school with me, or was detained at Verdun, attend to what they have to say. I am well aware that not everything you hear will be to my advantage."

That was certainly true. Emily wondered again whether he would care to hear the story about his "own" funeral. She wondered, too, if he was right, if she had been deliberately misunderstanding him. She was so afraid of being taken in by a false claim that perhaps she was ignoring a true one. If he was telling the truth, if he really was Tony . . .

"What am I supposed to do with the information then?" The image of Edward's face rose before her for a moment. Even if this Tony was telling the truth, it would be a betrayal of Edward's interests to help him win his claim. Edward would never understand; he would be hurt and angry.

"What you will. I am willing to trust that your sense of justice will encourage you to share the information with me."

"My sense of justice is more likely to encourage me to share the information equally between you and your rival."

This proposal did not seem to dismay him at all. "If you wish. I should still benefit greatly. You must realize, Miss Meriton, that I enter this claim at a severe disadvantage. The burden of proof rests with me, and my proof depends on the word of people I have not seen in ten years. Quite beside the problem of whether the memories of these people, or indeed my own memory, will provide any helpful details, there yet remains the greater difficulty of simply finding these people. Here my rival holds an immense advantage. Not only has he the funds to send for witnesses, or hire others to find word of them, he has the contacts established over the last ten years to do so. I don't know where to begin."

His impervious facade had begun to crack. For all his energy and determination, he sounded lost and helpless. There was, after all, only so much one could accomplish by will alone. If he had hoped to engage her sympathies, he had certainly done so, but Emily would not let herself be swayed by emotion.

He was wise enough to let her think in silence as they walked back to the place where the captain was to meet them again. In fact, it was his very intelligence that in some ways made Emily distrust this Tony. He was quite clever enough to have figured out the ways most likely to manipulate her sympathies in his favor. The slight breaks in his self-control might be carefully staged.

On the other hand, it might all be true.

"I will give the matter my full consideration," was all she would concede. He did not look disappointed, however.

"Thank you, Miss Meriton." In an old-fashioned gesture, he took her hand and kissed it. "Until we meet again."

He sounded very sure that they would indeed meet again.

The first words to come out of Gus's mouth as he entered Tony's room were, "Well, will she do it?"

"Oh, yes, she will do it. She has not yet agreed to it, but she will do it."

Tony nudged a bottle of wine and a glass toward his friend before resuming his favorite place by the window.

"How can you be so sure?" Gus asked as he helped himself to the refreshment thus offered. "She was quiet the entire ride back. I could not get the least idea how she had reacted."

"It does not matter," said Tony. "Now that I have placed the problem before her, she will not be able to avoid the question. She will have to discover the truth, for herself if not for me."

Gus shook his head over such complicated reasoning and sat down, resting his feet on the military chest he had loaned his friend. "I hope you are right."

"I am surprised at you, Gus. How can you have spent so much time with Miss Meriton and not have appreciated her unusual quality? Those silver eyes and dark curls must have distracted you."

"It was you who noticed her eyes," Gus pointed out. "And obviously those lovely curls did not escape you, either."

"Oh, she has charm. I would be the last to deny that. It is the very quality that will make her useful to me." He chose his words deliberately to sound cold, unfeeling. The attraction of Miss Meriton's company had been only too manifest. He had revealed far more of himself than he had meant to do.

Perhaps he was not maintaining the proper attitude of impassivity at all. Gus did not seem at all fooled by his callous words.

"I liked her, too. You were right—she does not flatter."

Tony wondered for a moment if his friend might not become rather more than interested in Miss Meriton. The thought bothered him, but he was not sure why.

"So," Gus asked, "what is our next move?"

"The next move must be hers," Tony answered. "When she is ready she will contact us, or, rather, you. All we have to do is wait."

His friend grimaced. "Nothing a man of action likes more."

"Right now there is nothing more a man of action can do. Fortunately," Tony said with a wry smile, "I have become quite good at waiting."

Later that night Emily sat before her dressing table, slowly brushing her dark curls. She had come to the unhappy realization that she, to whom everyone turned with their tales of woe when they looked for sympathy or solutions, had no one to whom she could turn in her time of trouble. And she was troubled. Very.

First there was Letty. Letty should have been the first person to whom she could run with all her problems, but this time Letty was the problem. When Emily had returned from her drive she found that Letty had taken to her bed, refusing all callers and canceling all social obligations.

Emily knew the ball at Carlton House had been more of a strain than Letty had envisioned. Although she had been safe from Tony's appearance among the company, his presence was still strongly felt. The story was on everyone's lips and could not be avoided, except, it seemed, by retreating to one's chamber.

She might fool society, Emily had at last conceded. All the gossiping matrons were only too likely to suppose Letty to be increasing again, a not implausible guess. It was not one that would fool John, however.

John had expressed his own worries about Letty at length that evening. Another man might have reacted to the present situation with an understandable feeling of jealousy, but not John. Eventually he talked himself into accepting a false sense of guilt as the most likely reason for Letty's behavior. Letty, he said, would blame herself for not having remained true to her first love, even though he had been believed dead these many years. She would feel that she had let Tony down by accepting his demise and going on with her life. It wasn't reasonable, he agreed, but it was just like Letty to think that way.

Her brother's reasoning had set Emily's thoughts in another direction. When John described Letty's supposed reactions to the return of her lover, Emily imagined instead what the real Tony would feel. With anyone else Emily would say that it was not reasonable to expect any woman to wait ten years, or more, for a lover's return. Letty would have waited, however, if she had thought him still alive. Emily knew it.

It tore at her heart that she could not decide whether or not she believed in this man who claimed to be Tony. If he were indeed who he claimed to be, it was probably all to the good that Letty had not waited for him, Emily thought. The last ten

years had changed both of them too much. All of which would
prove poor comfort to a man who had waited ten years to see
the girl he loved.

Emily tried to imagine Edward in such a situation and failed
miserably. Edward was incapable of so much feeling. Even
when Tony tried to hide his feelings, Emily was never in doubt
that this was a man who felt deeply.

Oh, he had trapped her neatly. She would have to discover
whether he spoke the truth or not. The difficulty was in finding
a way to gain information from him without being cozened into
feeding him tidbits which he might then use to his own advantage. Like this afternoon. If she had admitted first that she
knew of Letty's engagement to Tony, she would never have
been sure afterward whether he really knew of it or whether
he had simply followed her lead and agreed with her.

Emily put down her hairbrush and blew out the candles. In
bed she stared up at the ceiling, still unable to stop thinking
of him. Was he doing the same? she wondered. Was he thinking
of their meeting and wondering if she believed him? Maybe he
was congratulating himself on a clever performance.

Maybe he was lying in bed, thinking of Letty, whom he had
loved for so long. Emily had always bemoaned the fact that
she had never been able to call up such strong feelings for any
man. Tony, if he was Tony, must be wishing he had never fallen
in love, to find the woman he loved in love with another man.
It would take quite a man to care first whether his lost love
was happy, before he considered his own future.

Emily finally fell asleep, and dreamed fitfully of a fair, slender gentleman with luminous dark eyes whose feelings were far
from tepid and were easily readable on his scarred face.

Chapter Four

"WITHERS," EMILY ADDRESSED the butler, "my brother has no doubt informed you that while Lady Meriton is indisposed, I will undertake to supervise the household in her place."

The picture of the perfect butler, with precisely the obligatory amount of paunch and baldness, indicated assent with a bow.

It had been hard for Emily to make herself wait until a reasonable hour of the morning for this interview. She sat, hands neatly folded on her lap, and wished she had thought to provide herself with some needlework to keep her fingers busy.

"Sir John has also assured me that I may count on you for assistance," Emily continued. "There is a matter of some concern to me that I would like to broach with you."

The butler's habitual air of melancholy seemed to dissipate. His straightened shoulders indicated a state of preparedness. "How may I serve you, miss?"

Emily hesitated, uncomfortable with her task. Asking questions of the servants made her feel as if she were spying on her family. It had to be done, however. It was three days now, and Letty still refused to respond. Emily stiffened her resolve.

"It would be foolish to pretend that the staff are not as *au courant* with society news as the family is," Emily stated as prelude. "I am sure, therefore, that you have heard of the arrival in town of a gentleman who claims to be the lost son of the late marquess of Palin."

She considered how best to phrase her question. Withers was exceedingly loyal; he felt very much a newcomer in the servants hall and was always trying to prove himself. Would he have taken it upon himself to rebuff Tony? she wondered. On the whole it would be much easier to discover that this Tony had been lying all along. Something told her, however, that the situation was not going to be that simple.

In his haste to reassure her, Withers obviated the need for circumspection. "I have indeed heard the story, miss," he interrupted. "And I want you to know that you have nothing to fear from that quarter. Lord Palin warned me the other day that the person might come snooping around here. I've already taken care of that," he announced in his rich, fruity voice. "That impostor won't bother us again."

At the mention of Edward's name Emily tensed. Whatever she had expected, or feared, to hear, it was not this. She had thought all along that Tony's story had the ring of truth, not simply because he knew Edward had been at the house but because Emily believed he had been honestly hurt by the implicit rejection and angered by the servant's rudeness. But that Edward could be involved . . .

"Lord Palin warned you . . . ?" No, it must be a mistake. She was stunned into silence for a long moment. At last, becoming aware of the butler's inquisitive gaze, she asked unwillingly, "What exactly did he say?"

Withers looked a little surprised, whether at her question or at her shocked, breathless tone she could not tell.

"Well, miss, he told me about the terrible scene the person had made at his own ball. To tell the truth, we had heard a bit about that already. And his lordship said he feared that the person might try to embarrass Lady Meriton as well. He said as how the person might even appear to be a gentleman, but that, of course, I would be able to see through him."

"Of course," Emily flattered. She made an effort to smile, to hide the hurt inside. This conversation with Edward must have happened right after he left her. "And?"

"Nothing more, miss. Only that I should keep a few strong

footmen nearby to keep the person from annoying Lady Meriton."

But there had been something more. His guilty look confirmed it. Perhaps a *douceur* to encourage the butler to help Edward out? Edward was always so generous with the servants.

"And did the person come to the house?" Emily knew the answer now, but still she had to hear the words, to be given proof.

"That he did, miss. His lordship was quite right—the person seemed quite sane otherwise. Of course, I could tell he was trouble, though. I sent him off with a flea in his ear. He won't come back again, you can be sure of that."

Withers maintained his self-congratulatory attitude for another minute before he began to realize that Emily was not regarding him with any degree of approbation.

"Did I do wrong, miss?"

Emily clasped her hands more tightly and controlled her impulse to tell Withers what a fool he was. Closing her eyes, she reminded herself that the man thought he was protecting the family. After a moment she sighed and opened her eyes.

"Withers, I cannot think it right of you to have taken instruction from Lord Palin. He is and has been a good friend to the family, but that does not give him the right to direct our affairs. I am right, am I not, in assuming you did not confirm with either Sir John or Lady Meriton that this person was not to be received?"

"No, I mean, yes, miss. I did not ascertain their wishes." The butler was now patently horrified. "I beg your pardon, miss. It was only that I understood from his lordship . . . I mean . . . it was my understanding that his lordship was not merely a . . . friend of the family . . . ?" His voice lifted in a questioning note.

Had Edward actually intimated to Withers they were to be married—after refusing to let Emily announce the news to any of her friends? Emily's hurt and disillusionment began to be replaced with a growing indignation. She had to admire Edward's cleverness, nonetheless. He had chosen well. Although in many ways a fool, Withers was probably the only servant in all of London who could be trusted to keep news like that secret.

And how was she to respond to Edward's hints—with lies that would offend her sense of honor or with the truth and offend Edward's sense of propriety?

Emily hoped her cheeks were not as warmly red as they felt. "Whenever Lord Palin's relationship to this household changes, you may be sure that it will be announced properly, and that the servants will be given the news by the master of this household, as is correct. But it is my brother who is and who will remain the master of this household, not Lord Palin. And it is to him you should turn for instruction, not Lord Palin."

"Yes, miss," Withers agreed, by now thoroughly demoralized.

"And if my brother is or chooses to be unavailable," Emily decided on the spot, "I will be at home to the gentleman if he should call again."

"Yes, miss." The butler acknowledged his dismissal and departed several inches smaller, bowed with shame.

Emily felt a little ashamed of herself as well. To receive a gentleman, especially one refused by her brother, would hardly be proper. The butler, if he had not been overcome by guilt, would no doubt have recognized the impropriety as well. When John had given her authority over the household while Letty was indisposed, this was not how he expected her to exercise her rights.

Her motive, Emily realized, would not hold up to much scrutiny, either. Certainly she wished to demonstrate to Edward that he could not blithely direct her life—not the most felicitous way to begin a betrothal. If she was honest, however, she would have to confess to a sense of indignation on Tony's behalf as well. Which was also not the most felicitous way to begin a betrothal—to another man.

Wise or no, the indignation aroused by Withers's account festered throughout the afternoon. Emily tried to contact Edward, more than once, hoping he might be able to shed a different light on the situation. Had he answered the first message, perhaps he might have been able to assuage her irritation. There was no response to the first message, however, nor to the next four messages. No response at all.

Indignation simmered and grew into anger, as well as a determination to pull some hard truths out of Edward. He might avoid Emily all day, but this evening she knew where to find him. Tonight the Castlereaghs were to play host to the allied sovereigns. Edward, with all his political aspirations, would not miss it for the world.

Nor would Emily.

Since Letty remained immured within her chamber, and John remained in attendance upon her, Emily might have run into difficulties. She could not help but wonder if Edward was aware of that, perhaps even counting on that, too. Fortunately, Lady Castlereagh had graciously offered to chaperon Emily for as long as Letty remained ill, despite her own involvement with the festivities for the visiting sovereigns, and she sent her carriage to fetch Emily.

Even the Castlereaghs' coach could make no better headway along the crowded route than the other vehicles, however. The long wait to approach the entrance left Emily in no mood to appreciate the handsome illuminations—an immense transparency of a dove holding an olive branch in its mouth. Only the welcoming smile of her godmother brought a return to her customary good humor.

"How lovely you look, Godmama," she complimented the plump matron. "I'm sorry to have put you to such trouble."

"It's no trouble at all," Lady Castlereagh responded to her expressions of gratitude as she greeted Emily in the receiving line. "To be truthful, I shall be glad of your support through the next week or so."

"And so will I," Lord Castlereagh concurred. He gazed fondly at his spouse. "It will be a great relief to me to know you are by my lady's side when I cannot be there."

"You're both very kind. I only hope I may be of some real service to you during this hectic period." Emily smiled with genuine pleasure. The furious momentum that had carried her so far dissipated a little further.

"*Hectic* is not the word," Lady Castlereagh announced with a heartfelt sigh. "But there are some very real pleasures to be found. Have you met the Austrian delegate, Prince Metternich

yet? No? Later in the evening Cas must introduce you to him—
a true gentleman. His manners are so polished and elegant."

As opposed to those of the tsar and his sister, Emily surmised. Evidently she was not the only person to experience
some irritation of nerves. Her godmama had never come so
close to sarcasm before. Smiling with amusement, Emily left
the receiving line eager to find Edward, only to be claimed by
a group of her friends in the ballroom.

"You gave me quite a shock," Georgianna Parkhurst accused as she gave Emily a peck on the cheek. "When I saw you
come flying through the doors, I thought it was the Queen of
the Night from that opera you forced me to sit through."

"I don't know that I care to be compared to a woman who
asks her daughter to kill her own father." Emily's tone was jesting, but she was genuinely taken aback. Had she looked so very
angry? she wondered.

"It must be your gown that reminded me of her," Georgianna improvised. "Especially with the tiara." She stepped
back and looked admiringly at Emily's attire, a diamanté evening gown of midnight blue. "Rather a daring color for you,
my dear, but I like it."

"At least only the color is daring. Really, Georgy, isn't that
a bit much?" Emily asked, gesturing toward the décolletage of
Miss Parkhurst's gown.

"Not nearly enough, I should say," a passing dowager mut-
tered in disapproval.

Unabashed, Georgy responded, "The tsar seemed to like it."

"I'm not surprised. Georgy, have you seen Lord Palin here
tonight? I was hoping to speak to him for a few minutes."

"Palin?" Georgy uttered the name as if it tasted badly. "Why
would you want to talk to that bore? All he cares about is politics. Now, if you want to ask me about that handsome Austrian
I saw you with the other day, I certainly noticed him. You *are*
going to tell me about him, aren't you?"

So her ride with the captain had not gone unobserved. "You
mean you don't know already? Really, Georgy, you're incorri-
gibly prying." Seeing her friend did not mean to give up, Emily
sighed and admitted, "His name is Captain August von Hotten-

dorf and he is one of Prince Hardenburg's aides-de-camp. Prussian, not Austrian."

"And?"

"And nothing. He seems to be a very nice gentleman." She shrugged her dismissal of the subject.

Georgy smiled a smile of pure disbelief, but dropped the subject. Emily did not mind. As long as Georgy didn't catch wind of Captain von Hottendorf's friend . . .

It was nice to be relaxed and have time to gossip with friends, but Emily was a little sorry to lose that hard edge of anger. Because when she stopped being angry, Emily began to be a little afraid.

If there had been no romantic love between her and Edward, there had at least been real affection and friendship, or so Emily had thought. She thought, too, that she knew Edward's weaknesses as well as his virtues. That he should scheme so behind her back, in effect to deceive her, was almost beyond comprehension.

She needed to talk to him.

In her circuit through the room Emily heard the name Palin often enough, but could not always be sure if people talked about Edward (present) or the claimant (absent). Finally she dared to simply ask her hostess if she had seen him.

"Palin? Oh, yes, he's here," said Lady Castlereagh. "I overheard him talking to Sir Charles Stewart. You would think that any conversation that does not revolve around the tsar would be an improvement, but I must say that I am finding this fuss over his title quite as boring already. Oh, excuse me, my dear, I had quite forgotten that young Palin was rather a friend of yours."

Rather a friend? Edward obviously need not fear that anyone would guess they were betrothed. Certainly not when he was avoiding her like this.

"Please, don't let that hinder your tongue," Emily said. "I am afraid Lord Palin does not seem to have reacted well to this recent challenge." She was surprised nonetheless. Had Edward been bending everyone's ears about his troubles?

"No, he hasn't responded well," Lady Castlereagh agreed. "I suppose I should not blame the boy. Who knows what I would do in the same position? The pity of it is that too many people will take the boy seriously."

The ladies joined their separate partners on the dance floor before Emily began to think seriously about what Edward's loudly expressed sense of grievance could mean.

She could still remember Tony's every word. "My rival holds an immense advantage," he had said. Edward had the money, the information, and the contacts. Tony had only referred to contacts as a way to further information, but Emily was not so naive as to ignore the fact that there were a number of other ways Edward might use those contacts, ways she was hardly likely to approve.

Suddenly Emily understood. Edward didn't want her to know what he was doing to resolve his claim. That was why he was eluding search. She had not wanted to admit he was doing so, but she could no longer avoid the conclusion.

If Edward had wanted to speak to her at all, he could have found her. She had been seen on the dance floor. She had chatted for some time with Lord Castlereagh and Prince Metternich. Since these two men attracted all eyes, both for the political power they wielded as well as for their extreme good looks, she could hardly escape notice while with them.

Avoiding her was easy, however. As long as Edward eschewed the dance floor, he could escape her eyes.

As Emily watched an elderly gentleman approach her, she realized Edward had forgotten one thing, though. He had forgotten to confide his intentions to his uncle, Lord Ruthven.

That kindly, pompous old gentleman was full of sympathy. To him the interruption of Edward's coming-of-age ball and the delay of the betrothal announcement were catastrophes of the first order. Since he considered alliance to the house of Palin to be the greatest bliss any woman might expect, he naturally assumed Emily would be crushed at having her happiness thus postponed. Far from avoiding her, he was taking the first opportunity to commiserate with her.

"Miss Meriton, I am so sorry that I have not had a chance to speak to you since the terrible events of the other evening." For once the older man's tones were muted. Indeed, his entire demeanor rather suggested the funereal. "Your sister-in-law, Lady Meriton—how does she?"

Emily wished he wouldn't talk of Letty as if he expected her imminent demise. "Still indisposed, unfortunately."

Ruthven raised an eyebrow and waited hopefully, but Emily refused to assuage his curiosity. Little though she sympathized with Letty's present behavior, she had no patience for those who insisted on twisting a momentary illness into something either embarrassing, scandalous, or deadly.

"We must hope that the Present Unfortunate Situation will resolve itself soon and that the promise of your coming good fortune will help restore her to health."

"Indeed," Emily answered noncommittally. If only her nerves were not so much on edge. . . . The temptation to let Lord Ruthven know exactly what Letty thought of Edward and the match was very strong. She reminded herself strongly that Edward's uncle, although often pontifical in manner, was truly a good man at heart.

Ruthven looked over his shoulder to make sure no one could overhear them. "This frightful mess has disturbed me no end, but I feel utterly disconsolate that it should have come at such an inauspicious moment for you and for Edward. To have such a thing happen at a time when you should be celebrating . . . ! Edward has convinced me that your announcement is better postponed, and I suppose I agree with him, but my heart breaks for you two."

He probably felt worse about it than did the two principals, Emily thought with a sense of guilt.

"I will confess to you, my lord, that I find the situation a little embarrassing, but it is, after all, only a small delay. The important thing now is to make sure the truth is discovered and revealed as soon as possible."

"Absolutely. That scoundrel must be exposed for what he is—a fraud."

This was not what Emily had said, and certainly not what she meant, but she doubted she could convince the old gentleman that the search for truth and the exposure of Tony as a fraud were not necessarily one and the same thing. Emily only wished she could be as sure that it was so.

"Lord Ruthven, do you have any idea how long this investigation will take?"

"Anxious to get on with the wedding preparations, are you?" Ruthven nudged her and winked meaningfully. "I can't blame you. I only wish I knew how long it will take to get this mess straightened out. This fellow is devilish determined, I'll say that for him. We made the mistake of underestimating him at first, and look where that got us. Well, we won't make that mistake again, I can tell you. But it does mean we have to go more slowly and more carefully."

"I don't understand, my lord. What do you mean—you underestimated him at first?" Foolish Lord Ruthven might be, but Emily could not believe him so dense as not to realize that the gentleman who appeared at Tony's party was a man to be reckoned with.

Ruthven looked a little flustered. "Edward didn't want me to mention it. Embarrassed, no doubt, especially after that incident at the ball." He leaned forward to whisper to Emily. "The fellow had shown up at the house before, you see. Looked quite the ruffian, I'm told, unshaven and dressed in a ragged infantry uniform. Well, what was Edward to think but that it was some poor soldier trying to scare up a few pounds?"

Emily's head was swimming. *If the fellow's claim were valid, he would have gone to the family first,* Edward had said, as if Tony's not having done so proved a point against him.

"This was before the ball?" In disbelief, Emily tried to prove to herself that Edward had not, by implication, lied to her.

"Yes. To give Edward his due, I am sure he thought the matter finished. He let the fellow know that if he tried playing his games any further, he would find himself in the lockup." Ruthven shook his head as if he, too, could hardly believe the situation. "I didn't find out until after the ball that the fellow had been to my house as well and to the solicitors."

So Tony had done all the things the real Lord Palin, returned from captivity in France, would have been expected to do. And Edward had lied to her about it.

However much Edward had let her down already, Emily was not ready for this. She bit her lip to keep herself from speaking. Or crying.

Over Lord Ruthven's shoulder she could see Edward approaching the group now, a concerned expression on his face. No wonder, Emily thought with a new cynicism. He must know only too well that his uncle was likely to reveal too much.

Other than the slight frown that creased his forehead, he looked the same as usual. His fair hair was carefully brushed in the Brutus cut, his eyes were the same clear blue. Perhaps there had been a momentary pinching of his mouth, but now his lips framed the same welcoming smile he had always reserved for Emily. Nothing in Edward had changed—except the way she looked at him.

"At last," he announced with a sigh. "In this crush I was afraid I would never find you. How are you, my dear?"

"Quite well, thank you." One good lie deserved another, she supposed. She could see clearly now how impossible it was that Edward could miss seeing her on the dance floor, or that he could have failed to notice her tête-à-tête with two such powerful men as Castlereagh and Metternich. Definitely he had been trying to avoid her.

"How very beautiful you look tonight. That shade of blue certainly makes you look very . . . very impressive."

The Queen of the Night had returned, evidently. Good. She wanted him to know she was angry. "I'm sure you must be tired of being asked, Edward, so I have let your uncle fill me in on how your case is proceeding."

"Have you indeed?" He looked from her to his uncle, who had the grace to look a little ashamed. "Then you must realize that we are in hopes of a speedy resolution."

"Oh? Lord Ruthven was just saying that you would have to proceed slowly and carefully." Emily wasn't in a mood to let Edward get away with anything.

Edward looked from Emily to his uncle and then back again. "I have a feeling Lord Ruthven has said a great deal. Would you excuse us, Uncle? I think Miss Meriton and I need a moment's private conversation."

There Emily agreed with Edward completely, but privacy was not a commodity much encountered in crowded ballrooms. It seemed likely to her that Edward had no intention of prolonging this conversation beyond this evening or this room.

"I think you need a glass of orgeat to cool you down," Edward suggested, leading her toward the refreshments. "Now, what did that old fogy say to overset you so?"

This was Edward at his best, as she most often thought of him, kind and considerate. But was this Edward truthful as well?

"Lord Ruthven said that T—the claimant had come to your house, and to his, after all. When we talked last, you implied at least that he had done no such thing." Emily was glad that her voice no longer carried that tone of accusation, only one of confusion. She *was* confused. It was if she suddenly found herself promised in marriage to a stranger. If Lord Ruthven had not confirmed his knowledge of the betrothal only moments ago, she might even have wondered if that was only her imagination as well.

"And you thought I . . ." Edward threw up his hands in a gesture of helplessness. "Well, I don't know which is worse— to have you think me a liar or a fool. Believe me, Emily, I had no idea it was the same fellow for some time. You saw what he looked like when he interrupted the ball. The man who came to the house was the veriest ruffian. I actually pitied him, he looked so down on his luck. I even offered him a fiver, and he threw it back in my face!"

Emily accepted the glass of orgeat and took a sip. "And you didn't make the connection when he showed up later?"

"Of course I made the connection, but I thought it was no more than that some story about my cousin was making the rounds due to all the returning *détenus* and soldiers. This fellow must have known my cousin in that French prison, don't you think?"

That idea had occurred to Emily before. She had assumed, however, from Letty's attitude, that whoever Tony was he must be someone from Letty's past. Letty's behavior, she realized, could just as likely be caused by the mere idea of her old lover's return. John could be right about her oversensitive heart being plagued by guilt.

"Yes, he must have been in that prison," Emily said, her voice low. No one who had heard Tony's voice when he mentioned Bitche could doubt that. It would be interesting to see how Edward would react to the fact that in nine years Tony had never, to anyone's knowledge, used any name but Varrieur. That telling circumstance would certainly carry weight at the hearing. But she would not see that reaction until then, because she would not give Edward the information.

"You're not to worry, Emily. I can take care of this."

"By telling our butler to turn the man away from our doors?" She looked him directly in the eye, challenging him.

"You are angry with me." Edward sounded as if he were surprised, but Emily was sure he was not. After a sigh and a quick check for observers, he motioned Emily to a quiet corner. "I asked if your brother had already warned the staff, and found that he had not," he explained in a reasonable tone. "Considering he had hardly moved from Lady Meriton's side, that was not too surprising. So I took it upon myself to do what I thought Sir John would certainly do if his thoughts had not been elsewhere. I suppose it was presumptuous of me, but I only did it to protect you, my dear."

"Did you?" One of the things Emily had always liked about Edward was that he never treated her as incapable or fragile. She thought he respected her too much for that. "I'm sorry, Edward, but it seems to me that your conduct regarding this challenge to your estate has been particularly ruthless."

"I should hope so. Do you think I can hold on to what is my own by sitting back and assuming that right will triumph? If I relied blindly on British justice, I should likely find myself back in my grandmother's cottage in Tunbridge Wells. This man is tough and he's clever. If I'm to beat him, I have to be tougher than he is and a lot more clever."

Edward's posture of calm reason had begun to fray. Now he was speaking the truth, with more passion than Emily had ever thought him capable.

She was distressed by his attitude, and a little distracted by Edward's reference to his grandmother. The only family he had ever talked about was his uncle, Lord Ruthven.

"I've always seen you as such a kind person, Edward. I don't like to see you behave like this."

"You'd like Tunbridge Wells a great deal less, I assure you, my dear. Now, stop worrying. And trust me."

But she couldn't trust Edward now, Emily realized as she watched him walk away. Perhaps she never had. Maybe that was the one element that had been missing, the one thing that had kept friendship from developing into something warmer.

She pleaded a need for fresh air when her next dance partner, an old friend of her brother's, appeared. Once she had turned the conversation to the prodigies of his numerous offspring, Emily knew she need not fear investigation into her troubled state.

Not everyone was so blind, however.

Emily thought her emotions and countenance well under control when she returned from the terrace, but discovered herself mistaken when she encountered the young Prussian officer some time later.

Captain von Hottendorf was charming as usual, but also astute. He approached Emily a little hesitantly, as if he were unsure of his reception.

"Miss Meriton, why are you sitting here with the chaperons when you should be on the dance floor? I cannot believe your dance card is not full. It would be too much to expect the good fortune of a dance."

There was an unspoken question in his glance that referred to more than a dance.

"What you may expect is to have your feet stepped on," Emily told him with returning good nature, cheered by the genuine concern in his eyes. "I have not yet learned this new dance that you have brought with you from the Continent."

"You are not such a high stickler to find it so very shocking, surely?"

Emily watched the dancing couples with envy. They looked as if they hadn't a care in the world.

"I think it looks delightful. See how gracefully the tsar whisks Lady Jersey about the room? With such a noble example, I doubt the high sticklers will be able to hold out for long. The waltz looks to be the new rage."

The envy in her eyes must have been more obvious than she realized.

"Then certainly you must learn it, and with all speed," Captain von Hottendorf encouraged. "May I say, with all modesty, that I am no mean practitioner of the waltz myself and that I would be more than happy to instruct you." He looked at her hopefully.

"Thank you, Captain. I will remember that." If Letty had been herself, she would have seen to it that they both learned the waltz the moment the tsar first demonstrated its charms. Perdition take Letty. Emily was ready to shake her. Her world was becoming twisted all awry, and she needed desperately to set it right again. She needed to see that her judgment was as clear as it had ever been. She needed . . .

Emily looked around at the guests surrounding them. One gentleman was shouting himself hoarse trying to talk to the deaf Prince Hardenburg. Hetman Platov stood in solitary isolation since he spoke only Russian and looked far from approachable.

"Captain, would it be possible to meet with your friend again?"

"Yes, of course," he responded immediately, without question. He obviously realized, however, that her request had not been premeditated. "No, don't be embarrassed," he told her. "And don't think you need to explain anything."

That was a good thing. Emily didn't think she could define her reasons, even to herself, but she told the captain, "I think you don't need explanations because you are remarkably sure of yourself, sure that you have succeeded in persuading me to your friend's side."

"Not at all."

Emily raised a single expressive eyebrow.

"However, Tony said we might be sure of your sense of justice, that you would not be content with less than the truth."

"If you think I will know the truth when I see it, you know more than I do." She had thought that she knew Edward, too.

"You are troubled. I saw you enter this evening. You looked like a Valkyrie, a female warrior from the old legends. Now all the lightning has left your eyes. Why? Is it Tony and I who have done this to you?"

"No, no," she assured him, grateful for his kind attentions. "It is not your fault." It wasn't his fault that Letty was acting like a coward and a fool and Edward was becoming manipulative and dishonest. For all that Captain von Hottendorf had pressed for her assistance, he did seem to care.

"And you are quite right," Emily admitted. "I do have to discover the truth."

The next morning Emily received an informal invitation from Georgianna Parkhurst to join her and a few friends for a lesson in the finer points of the waltz. Georgy was a good-hearted girl, but there was no denying she was a bit rackety. She had enough innate good sense to stay on the safe side of scandal, but it sometimes alarmed Emily how close she came to that border.

Arranging a rendezvous with Emily for someone who claimed to be greatly taken by her charms obviously appealed to Georgy's sense of adventure. Emily could only hope that Georgy continued to assume that the Prussian officer who snared and delivered the invitation was her suitor, and not the other gentleman she hoped to meet.

The seal on the note was broken. "Please come," Tony had added, as if he guessed that she was already having second thoughts about the meeting. He had signed himself as Mr. Howe, presumably to forewarn her that it would be in that identity that he would attend Georgy's gathering. It was courteous of him to respond so quickly to her request, and kind of the captain, too, to remember that she expressed a desire to learn the new dance.

It was fortunate, too, that Tony should be free to meet with her so soon. Emily felt a little guilty making such claims upon his time. Sternly she reminded herself that it was he who had asked for her help. All the same, he must have a hundred other things he needed to be doing to advance his case. Edward certainly had been too busy to respond to her messages. Yet when she asked for Tony, he came.

As she left for her engagement, she made an attempt to lure Letty away from her sickbed by dangling the invitation in front of her. What she would have done about Tony's presence had Letty accepted, she had no idea. Letty didn't, of course. For one moment, however, there had been an eager gleam in Letty's eye that said she wanted to go. Four days in bed were rather more than the energetic Letty could easily endure, even paralyzed with fear. Emily felt distinctly hopeful as she joined her friends and set off for the Parkhurst home.

In the entranceway there was a flurry of greetings and removal of wraps. This gave Emily a chance to observe Tony for a moment before he noticed her.

He looked very handsome, leaning negligently against the piano in the Parkhursts' ballroom. There was a sense of power and energy there that all the uniforms in the world could not achieve. His eyes were cast down for the moment as he looked over some sheet music, and Emily could see that his lashes were indeed long and silky. Exactly as Letty had said.

Fortunately, the captain came forward to greet her before Tony could notice her staring at him. She must learn to control her reactions better, Emily told herself. If Georgy, or any of the other young ladies and gentlemen in the room, were to conjecture about Emily's interests, she did not want them describing "Mr. Howe." It would not take Edward very long to realize who Mr. Howe was, and despite her fiancé's disturbing behavior, Emily did not want to hurt him.

It was soon clear that she need not worry. There were enough gentlemen present for any interest to be camouflaged. When Georgy said she was organizing a gathering of "a few of her friends," she was really describing an afternoon rout party.

A large military contingent was present, as well as a number of diplomatic representatives. Emily wondered whether her friend was in fact acquainted with the half of them. That Georgy likely was not, however, was to Emily's benefit, since it was only thus that "Mr. Howe" was able to attend.

Monsieur LeBlanc had been engaged to provide instruction, Georgy explained, but everyone could see that his true function was merely to provide the music for the dancers to teach themselves. Some of the girls had already learned the steps and lacked only the opportunity to practice with a member of the opposite sex. Most of the soldiers and diplomats had already acquired a notable proficiency which they were eager to share.

Emily found herself dancing first with one of the tsar's Cossack troops, a young boy with fierce mustaches and innocent eyes. He spoke no English, but he knew how to use those eyes effectively.

Even as she focused on her feet and the music, Emily was aware of a great deal of giggling and flirting going on, so much so that she began to wonder if she was the only person to use this gathering as a cover for an assignation. To her relief, Georgy showed some sense of responsibility, however. She kept all the dancers changing partners, so that it was late in the afternoon before Emily found herself opposite Tony.

Emily had thought by then that she had become accustomed to the unusual closeness and contact between the dance partners, but now she saw that she was wrong. It must be because she was no longer concentrating so hard on the steps, she decided, that she was now so intensely aware of Tony's firm hand at the small of her back, guiding her.

"Gus—Captain von Hottendorf said you wanted to see me," he said.

There was both a question and an affirmation implicit in that simple sentence. The question was obvious. Why had she asked him to come? Emily was still trying to understand herself why it had seemed so important to see him again. How could she explain, even to herself, her sudden conviction that somehow if she saw and talked with him again, everything would become perfectly clear in her mind?

If her reasons were complex and confusing, however, his response was comforting. She had called for him and he was there. It was as simple as that, his attitude seemed to say.

As if he sensed a certain hesitancy in her, Tony continued, "You can tell me later. Gus and I will see you home. That will be all right, won't it? Everyone will be so busy admiring the epaulets on Gus's uniform, no one will notice me."

Emily doubted that. Tony was not the sort of man who ever went unnoticed. She did wonder, though, if society had really begun to recognize Tony easily yet. Strange as it seemed, he had only appeared in public once—at Edward's ball. Somehow Emily felt sure that if anyone else had met him, she would have heard of it.

"That will be fine," she told him. She blushed with shame. This was the kind of behavior she often warned Georgy would lead her astray. "I told the coachman that one of my friends would see me home."

"Are you embarrassed at having asked to meet with me again?" Tony asked, evidently misreading the cause of her chagrin. "Please, don't be. I assure you I think no ill of you for it." His voice took on a lighthearted, teasing tone. "I shan't make the mistake of confusing you with a bold piece like your friend Miss Parkhurst."

Emily lifted her gaze momentarily from his striped waistcoat. With some difficulty she assumed a prim expression. "You might remember, however, that Miss Parkhurst is my friend. And that it is due to her boldness as well as her kindness that you dare come here today."

Tony grinned. At once he looked much younger. Emily realized then she had never seen him smile before, not with genuine amusement. It was hard to believe that it was only days since Tony had first appeared in London, only the day before yesterday that she had last seen him.

"Oh, don't mistake me," he responded to her admonition. "I like her very well, but she's a minx nonetheless. She lets her sense of adventure lead her into doing outrageous things. Now, you . . ." Tony looked at her with a measuring eye. "Whatever unusual things you may be drawn into, it won't be for that reason."

Emily sighed and lowered her gaze again. "No, no one will ever mistake me for the adventurous kind." She would rather have liked to be thought adventurous, anything other than quiet and sensible. Why was it that virtue always appeared so amazingly dull?

"Yet you have it in you to be far more shocking than your friend."

"I?" In surprise, Emily looked him at last fully in the eyes, the eyes that reminded her more and more of Letty's description. Of Letty's lost love.

"Without doubt. Miss Parkhurst would risk a good deal for the fun of setting the ton on its ears. If one day she misjudges and goes too far, she will be very sorry. For the right person, the right . . . friend, I think you would risk everything, and not count the cost."

Emily felt for a moment as if she were *en déshabillé,* too open and vulnerable to the world's eyes. It took her a moment before she realized that the music had stopped and that the other couples were applauding M. LeBlanc's efforts.

Tony had made his pronouncement as if that facet of her character were quite obvious, as if it had taken no great perception on his part to discern such feelings in her. Emily knew better, however. No one else in this room would ever believe her capable of behaving in any way out of the ordinary. Some of them were even surprised that she maintained a friendship with one so carefully balanced on the edge of propriety as Georgy. But not Tony.

Emily felt bereft for a moment, as Tony was obliged to give her up to the partner who immediately claimed her next dance. She was disappointed to have their conversation broken off so abruptly. It was such a strange, and somehow intimate, discussion to take place in the middle of a dance.

In a moment, however, Emily began to feel grateful for being spared the necessity of further comment. She remembered, too, that Tony would expect to talk about something else in a short time.

Now all she had to think about was how to explain why she felt she needed to see him.

Chapter Five

EMILY'S HOPES FOR an inconspicuous exit after bidding Georgy a fond, temporary adieu in the ballroom were dashed as her friend chased after her in a flurry of silk and perfume. Clearly Georgy had noticed that Emily had two male escorts now, not just one.

"Emily, dear, you've forgotten your fan," Georgy lied fluently, catching up with her at the top of the stairs.

"No, I have mine. See." Behind the opened fan, Emily mouthed, "What are you up to?" to her friend.

"Oh? I thought surely this was yours." Georgy lowered her voice to a whisper and pulled her, none too gently, into a window alcove. "Don't be miffed, Em. I only wanted to help. It seems a pity you should not have a chance to be alone with the captain after all. Do you want me to take care of Mr. Howe for you?"

The two men were waiting for Emily below, watching this interchange with no little curiosity. How had Georgy discovered Tony's inclusion in the party? The girl's ear for gossip was incredible.

By the way Georgy was looking over her erstwhile guest, Emily could see that her friend would count it no sacrifice to deal with Tony. This was a danger she should have foreseen. It would not do for Georgy to become too curious about Mr. Howe.

"That won't be necessary."

"No need to get sarcastic, dear," Georgy replied with a twinkle in her eye. "Can't you make up your mind? He has got a certain . . . élan, I must admit. I noticed the two of you while you were dancing together. You made quite the couple."

Fortunately, another departing couple called for their hostess's attention, and Emily was spared the necessity of responding to Georgy's hints. For the time being.

"I'll see you later tonight at the opera, I suppose," Georgy promised as she left, clearly disappointed at having to wait so long before she could pin Emily down. "You can tell me all about him then. And you can tell me what he said to you at the end of the dance. You looked like you had been struck by lightning. Did he make an improper suggestion?"

"We leave the improper suggestions to you. May I remind you, Georgy," Emily said sternly, "that the gentleman is your guest. Do you mean to tell me that you invited him without knowing anything about his background?" Her attempt at sounding shocked was foiled by the hint of laughter in her voice.

"One can't afford to turn down extra gentlemen," Georgy explained, as if stating the obvious. "Until tonight, then. Perhaps then you can tell me if you've made a decision." She gave a long final look at both Tony and the captain, making it clear exactly what decision she meant.

Emily's cheeks were pink as she left the Parkhurst home and climbed into the captain's perch phaeton.

"I'm afraid even to ask what our hostess might have said to cause that lovely blush," Tony hinted as he followed her into the carriage. He tried to allot Emily as much room as possible, but the close confines of the phaeton did not permit much movement.

"She was quizzing me about you," Emily admitted, conscious of turning a deeper shade of rose. *Lovely,* he had said. "She is becoming rather curious about Mr. Howe."

"It's your cursed charm, Tony," the captain teased.

"My charm? I was probably conspicuous by my gauche behavior. Miss Meriton is the first lady I've spoken to in ten years. I felt like a boy at my first grown-up party all over again."

He made light of the experience, but Emily realized with surprise that despite his arrogant appearance at Edward's ball, Tony did feel uneasy about his reentry into society. Of course, the real Tony had gone to the Continent as a mere boy of eighteen with no town polish yet. His experience of the world would be limited to a year of the Grand Tour under the tutelage of an elderly cleric and another year or so in the dubious elegance of Verdun's Upper Town.

Tony interrupted her train of thought. "Is Miss Parkhurst likely to discover anything? Will her questions cause trouble for you?"

"Yes and no. Georgy is quite likely to keep at it until she finds something out, but, believe it or not, she can be very discreet. She likes to tease, but she won't let her questions lead to my being talked about. If she does realize who you are, she won't let anyone else know we're acquainted." To be unmercifully quizzed by Georgy was the least of Emily's worries.

Emily gave a furtive glance, looking for observers. It was a foolish act. She could barely see around her two companions—how could she be seen? The not uncomfortable press of Tony's shoulder against hers reminded her that there were even greater perils than being discovered. What Emily herself discovered during this inquiry was like to change her life. Somehow she felt sure that whatever step she took now, nothing would ever be the same.

On Emily's other side the captain gave a disdainful snort. "I daresay Miss Parkhurst will not care to admit publicly that she entertained Tony while unaware of his identity in any case."

Was there some bitterness, as well as derision, in his tone? Emily supposed that given the captain's belief in his friend, he must hate to see Tony reduced to skulking about incognito. Her own refusal to openly recognize him yet probably seemed rather insulting.

"None of us care to be fooled," she reminded the captain. "I suppose that's one reason people are so afraid of appearing to take sides. If you choose wrong, you look such a fool. And right or wrong you are sure to offend someone. Edward, I mean the . . . er . . . incumbent Lord Palin, has been a close friend of the family for many years. It would hurt him a great deal to think I had even considered doubting the validity of his position."

Both Tony and Captain von Hottendorf turned to observe closely her embarrassment. Had she revealed too much? she wondered. Was she being too sensitive about the feelings of a gentleman who was supposed to be no more than a family friend?

"Of course, it would not," Tony responded calmly, although he continued to watch her in a calculating fashion. "The young fellow may not have made it easy for me to like him, but I have to admit he's in a very awkward position—through no fault of his own. I'm sure he really believes I'm an impostor. Naturally he would feel betrayed and abandoned by any of his acquaintance who seem to disagree with him."

"Naturally." Emily sighed with relief that her explanation was so quickly accepted, but the thought of Edward's recent behavior still caused some pain. No, nothing would ever be the same again. "I suppose it is natural, too, that Edward's whole concentration should be on maintaining his position."

She didn't really believe that, though. There were other affairs that had an equal call on Edward's attention, like the small matter of his betrothal. Tony, in the same situation, had also made extraordinary demands on her, but he had also shown great concern for her feelings and for her reputation.

Emily turned unhappily toward him. "For all I know, you may be no more concerned with the truth than he is, but you deserve an equal chance. You were quite right. The truth of this has to be sorted out. More than that, it has to be proved beyond doubt."

"You did not invite us here today merely to tell us that," Captain von Hottendorf prompted.

"No, you already knew I would have to search for the truth, didn't you?" she said in a slightly acidic tone of voice. "I'm afraid, however, that you rather flattered my abilities to find anything out given the amount of information I have."

"I don't understand. What do you mean?" Tony asked.

"I mean that I don't know where to look for information. I can listen from morning until night, I can even subtly lead every conversation I enter toward that one subject, but if the people I talk to have never come in contact with you or any of your friends, it won't do any good. Oh, I may be able to learn something in time, but I suspect time is one thing you do not have."

"No, I don't," Tony admitted. "Your family friend is pressing for an early hearing. I want the matter settled as soon as possible. As you said, however, it will take me longer to get my witnesses together. Are you saying you can't do anything after all?"

His face became devoid of expression. All the warmth and concern disappeared from his voice as well. He was not cold. Cold was too positive a word for his behavior. He was just . . . opaque.

She shook her head in denial, suddenly anxious to reach past this barrier. "Not at all. What I'm saying is that I need guidance. I don't know where to look, or rather to whom I should be listening." She looked down at her hands. In the close confines of the phaeton it was hard to avoid looking at her companion. Tony's hands were only inches away from hers. He was not, after all, utterly expressionless. She could see his fist slowly relax.

"I don't want you to feel you have to present your case to me," she told him, "or that you have to prove anything to me. I'm not your judge. But if I'm to discover anything, whether it is to your benefit or not, I need help. I need some names, at least to start with."

"Yes, certainly," Tony agreed. "You must think me obtuse, but I'd assumed that you must know about me, about my life."

The reminder that Tony's life had been virtually obliterated from present memory pained Emily, but his voice sounded more cheerful. He became more enthusiastic as another thought occurred to him.

"Yes, yes, of course. In fact, what we really need is to set up a regular meeting time and place so I could give you names as I think of them. And to let you know what we've been able to do. Yes, a meeting. We cannot always count on Captain von Hottendorf to act as go-between."

"I don't mind," the captain hastily interposed.

He was ignored. "What if you needed an answer right away?" Tony asked Emily. "Or if you had information on how to find someone that needed to be acted upon immediately? It's not simply a matter of getting word to me," he said, giving his friend a forbidding look. "We would then have to think of a way to meet inconspicuously. Now, if we set up a time and place in advance, we could save a great deal of time."

"You mean, I would only have to send word that I needed to see you. The circumstances of the meeting would already be set."

"I was thinking more of setting up a daily meeting," Tony explained, warming to his subject. "Or at least of setting up a time and place where you know you can contact me. If you are not free at that time, or if you have nothing new to impart, you need not come. On the other hand, if you did need to see me, you would know exactly when and where to find me."

"I see." Emily was careful to sound noncommittal. Did she dare agree to such a plan? It was risky. The more often she met with Tony the more likely it was that someone would spot them together and mention it to Edward.

What troubled her most, however, was that she wanted it. She wanted it very much.

"I think I understand what you need," Tony continued. "I really ought to write some names down for you. I can't expect you to remember them all. And, as I said, if I think of more later, I can pass them on to you."

"Perhaps Miss Meriton and I could arrange a regular engagement to go riding," the captain suggested in a strangely pointed fashion.

"Oh, that shouldn't be necessary," Tony insisted, rather hastily it seemed to Emily. "I hate to put you out. You do have some duties as aide-de-camp after all."

"Not so very many. I would like to help."

There was a teasing note in the captain's voice Emily did not understand. She had the feeling that the two friends were arguing about more than the proposed meeting arrangement, but she could not think what it might be.

"Miss Meriton might not care to have people speculate on her relationship with you any more than she wishes to have people talk about her meeting with me," Tony reminded his friend.

"Would anyone present care for Miss Meriton's opinion?" Emily interrupted. She was beginning to feel like a shuttlecock tossed back and forth.

"Of course," said Tony.

"Yes, Miss Meriton," the captain agreed simultaneously. "Tell this oaf how difficult it would be to do as he asks."

"Actually," she admitted hesitantly, "I think I know how it may be done." Finally she had their attention.

Now she had let herself in for it. In her annoyance at being talked over, like a prize mare, she had gone too far. Nothing to do now but brazen it out.

"You know I have a niece and nephew? Nanny is quite a zealot about outdoor exercise. For the children, of course. She won't take a single unnecessary step herself. I often accompany the nursemaid when she takes the twins out early in the morning for some fresh air. At eight in the morning there really isn't anyone in the square. Only a few nursemaids and footmen walking the family dog." She gave Tony a mischievous smile. "Lady Connaught's young footman is walking with our Nancy. And the children love her ladyship's poodle."

The captain's face fell noticeably. Clearly he was not interested in any plan that involved getting up before eight in the morning. Tony, on the other hand, was delighted.

"Perfect. I shall be walking in the square, then, at eight in the morning. I will wait for you to recognize me before I approach you. That way if someone else is up and walking about at that ungodly hour, you may simply walk on."

A shiver of apprehension assailed Emily. Was she really sure she knew what she was getting into? Setting up assignations with a gentleman whose very identity was held in question, keeping secrets from her family and her fiancé—where would it end?

"With luck that won't be necessary," she responded with a firmness she was far from feeling. "I will meet you in the square tomorrow morning."

*   *   *

Like many another gentleman at the Italian Opera House that evening, Tony trained his opera glasses not on the stage, but on the box tier.

"Who is that woman?" he asked, noticing the cause of a veritable hurricane of huzzas and applause. He had become accustomed to the enthusiastic response that greeted the appearance of any of the visiting royals, but the party that had entered their box at the Haymarket included no one he recognized from the Prussian, Russian, or Austrian delegations.

Gus laughed. "That, my friend, is your Princess of Wales."

"That?" Tony, aghast, took a second look at the blowsy, raddled woman, tastelessly bedecked in diamonds and a black wig, presently accepting the accolades of the audience from her box. "I have been away for too long." He shook his head. Even then Princess Caroline had been persona non grata at court, but she had not been quite such a figure of fun.

"You should pay more attention to gossip. The more she annoys your prince, the more the mob loves her. Look at the tsar," Gus uttered in disgust as he watched the Russian emperor recognize the princess. "They say Lieven was forced to threaten to resign in order to prevent Alexander from visiting her. How childish! Alexander may think poorly of your regent, but he could learn much from the prince's graciousness. Yes, he handled that quite well," he added as the prince regent also rose to bow—to the audience, accepting the applause as his own.

Tony, however, had ceased to regard his sovereign's dismissed wife and had trained his opera glasses on a box somewhat to the right of the princess.

After another pause Gus asked, "Is she here?"

"Yes, with the Castlereaghs," Tony answered.

"Really?" Gus said in surprise. "So she has finally come out of hiding."

"Letty? No, I'm sorry. I misunderstood you. Not Lady Meriton, but Miss Meriton." How odd! Why had he not thought of Letty immediately? It must be because his mind was so much taken with thoughts of tomorrow's meeting and what he might tell Emily. "She looks . . . distressed."

"Do you think so?" Gus looked for himself and shrugged.

"I do not see it. It's true, Lord Castlereagh made it quite clear to everyone that the princess is not to be recognized. That's Castlereagh behind her."

"I don't think Miss Meriton cares that much about the tsar's behavior. No, I think something else has troubled her." Tony took another look through his opera glasses. Yes, she was smiling now at something one of the party had whispered to her, but clearly her mind was elsewhere.

"Second thoughts about meeting you again, perhaps."

Could that be it? Somehow Tony doubted it. Miss Meriton had not seemed so very reluctant earlier in the day—unless someone had told her something to make her doubt him further.

"Perhaps." Tony shrugged and tried to keep his voice casual. It had become too important to keep Miss Meriton's support. "I suppose I will find out tomorrow."

The enthusiastic response to the princess's appearance finally died down and the second act began, but Tony was unable to pay much attention to the tenor's sentimental outburst. There had been one phrase from the conversation earlier that day that he had been unable to erase from his mind.

"Gus, when you were asking questions about Miss Meriton, did anyone mention her relationship with my cousin?"

"No, why should they? I believe he is a close friend of her family. You know that he is neighbor to the Brownlees." Gus looked at him, perplexed, then his features relaxed in comprehension. "Oh, you are thinking she spoke of him rather intimately, but she could hardly refer to the lad as Lord Palin in front of you. A charming sense of delicacy, I thought."

Tony shook his head. He would have liked to believe that, but he could not. "No, she said it too easily, too fluently. As if she were accustomed to calling him by his first name."

"I don't think it means anything. She has many friends and she is not, after all, so formal a person." Gus wrinkled his brow. "The boy is around here somewhere. Have you seen them together?"

"No, and that's odd, too. Why has he not greeted his old family friend?"

"You place too much significance on trifles, Tony. First you would invent a romance between the two, and then you would assume the boy is avoiding her. Think for a moment. If Miss Meriton cared so much for this Edward, would she listen to you?"

"She would always be fair."

"Then why should you be concerned?" Gus asked reasonably. "As long as she helps you prove your case, what does it matter?"

"Not at all. You're right, of course," Tony answered.

But somehow it did matter.

Not a soul could be seen in the square as Emily joined the nursemaid and the twins for their morning excursion. The night before she had suddenly become worried over the possibility of rain, and thus the loss of her pretext, but the weather continued lovely. Now Emily worried that the nursemaid might become suspicious of her behavior—a foolish worry since that was inevitable. Today's meeting might appear a chance encounter, but even Nancy would be bound to get suspicious if the meetings continued. The girl would say nothing, Emily was sure, but she would know all the same.

The fact that Nancy might be a willing conspirator in these assignations did not make Emily feel any better. It was depressing to think that the servants felt her love life needed all the help it could get.

The twins, however, never allowed their aunt to fall prey to introspection for very long. Katie decided to chase a squirrel and had to be chased in turn. By the time Lady Connaught's footman and poodle had joined the group, Emily was exhausted and had very nearly forgotten the original purpose of her outing.

"Gen'man," Connor announced as Tony appeared.

He doffed his hat respectfully and knelt to give the fat poodle a pat on the head. To any observers he would appear merely a nice gentleman who took a kind interest in dogs and children. A careful look toward Nancy assured him that the nursemaid's attention was fully occupied by the handsome footman resplendant in green livery.

"Good morning. I hope you are not too tired after your late night."

Emily raised an eyebrow in question.

"I saw you at the opera last night."

"Quite an evening, was it not? I can only be thankful the opera was not one in which I had any real interest, because I doubt whether I could have heard a note with all that was going on."

"It was difficult to concentrate on the stage," Tony agreed, but somehow Emily had the idea he was not thinking of the appearance of the Princess of Wales.

Now that he was here he looked as if he knew no better than she how to begin. He looked at his feet and watched the twins staring at their own reflections in the highly polished sheen of his boots.

"This is your niece and nephew, I take it. What are their names?" he asked politely. "How old are they?"

"This is Connor, and this young lady putting fingermarks all over your boots is Katy. They are a year and a half."

"They don't look like Letty at all," he said.

Emily watched Tony's face but could see little sign of reaction. Strange, she thought, but it was in some way his very failure to make an open exhibition of his emotions that made her believe in him. A false Tony would surely try to gain every ounce of sympathy possible from the situation, wouldn't he?

"No, they don't favor her at all," she agreed. "I think poor Katy looks rather like me, but Connor doesn't resemble any one person."

If he were Letty's Tony, what must he feel now, looking down at the children of the woman he had loved, perhaps still loved? More than anything else these children represented all that Tony had lost during his years in prison. If his claim were just, Tony would recover his identity and his inheritance; he could never recover his lost dreams.

"I keep trying to picture Letty as a sedate matron," he told her with a smile, "but I cannot. All I can remember is how she looked at fifteen when she broke her arm trying to race her father's prize gelding. And how she looked when we said good-bye."

Now that Emily was getting to know him better, she could see a touch of regret, of sadness, about his eyes. She wanted to comfort him, but if he still loved Letty, there was no real comfort that could be given.

"Letty may be a matron, but I do not think one could call her sedate," Emily admitted. "I do not think she has changed much in all the years I have known her."

"No? I suppose seeing her every day you would not be aware of the changes. When I saw her at the ball . . . She was different. I would have known her anywhere, but she was different."

The change appeared to disconcert him—a strange reaction when Emily considered how much the intervening years had changed him. The same thought evidently occurred to him a moment later.

He laughed. "I know. I myself have changed past recognition. Past recognition," he repeated quietly. "But, you see, in prison it was as if time stood still. My life came to a complete halt, not to move forward until I was free again."

To find that the world had left him behind, Emily thought, sensing the pain he strove to hide. That, she realized, was what the blank expression he so often affected really meant. Pain, above all else, was to be hidden.

"But the change in you goes far beyond mere appearance. You neither think, feel, nor act like a boy of eighteen," Emily argued.

"Sometimes I still feel like that boy of eighteen. Like yesterday at your friend's impromptu party."

And when he thought of Letty?

They fell once more into an embarrassed silence. The twins had found a number of interesting sticks and pebbles and were now using the sticks to dig some holes to plant the pebbles. Nancy had evidently decided to use Emily's conversation with Tony as an excuse to walk a little ways with her footman friend, so they had only Katy and Connor to overhear their conversation.

"Are you sorry you agreed to meet me?" Tony asked after a long silence. "Have you had second thoughts about the whole thing? I thought last night that you looked troubled."

Emily hid her surprise that he had noticed so much. She had

indeed been troubled, but not by thoughts of him. Only two boxes away she had seen Edward chatting with some of his political friends and paying respectful attention to their daughters. Any hopes she had entertained regarding conversation with him were soon dashed. Edward refused even to look her way.

News of Edward did filter back to her, however, and it was not pleasant. When Tony had asked for her help, she had never even considered relaying any information she had gained privately from Edward. It wouldn't have seemed ethical. Now . . .

Now it seemed that Edward had left ethics behind altogether. How could she not warn Tony?

"I did find out one thing last night which disturbed me," she finally admitted. "You know your rival claimant is very active in Tory politics. He has evidently been reminding a number of very powerful gentlemen that while his views are known and his support secure, you are very much an unknown quantity."

"In other words, don't lose the vote you've got. Clever."

Was it her imagination or did Tony watch her more carefully whenever she spoke of Edward? She must be oversensitive about the situation. Tony would naturally be extremely interested in anything that had to do with his cousin.

"You said before that Edward had an unfair advantage. Were you expecting something like this?" she asked.

"Not specifically like this, but I expected him to use all the means at his disposal. He would be a fool an he did not."

"You're not offended by his behavior?"

"No, I can't really blame him. It's not as if he ever knew me. Considering the way his branch of the family was treated before my supposed demise, he can hardly realize I would be willing to help him out now. My only concern is that his attitude may make any reconciliation more difficult once this is settled. Stepping down will be painful enough for him, I imagine."

Could this be true? Could Tony possibly be so generous? Emily considered his years in prison and thought perhaps he might. When little of your family remains, she knew, you cherished what you had all the more. Regardless of slights or injuries, evidently.

The twins, having given up digging for the nonce, were playing at peek-a-bo behind one of the trees. In running around the tree Connor fell, and having been alerted by Tony's countenance that this was an occasion that might be milked to advantage, interrupted their conversation with a demand for immediate consolation.

"You must remember," Tony continued as Emily murmured over the hurt child, "how much my cousin stands to lose. He came from nowhere to become a wealthy peer and a leader in society. To go back to being a nonentity in . . . wherever it is he comes from . . ."

"Tunbridge Wells," she said automatically as she released the now squirming twin. "Yes, I see. He said much the same himself, but I didn't realize then what it meant."

"But you are disappointed in him nonetheless."

"Yes." Disappointed did not express the half. She felt betrayed. She might not have loved Edward, but she had believed in him, in his character.

"Then I feel more pity for him than ever. I would hate to earn your friendship and then disappoint you."

Tony took her hand. Before he could speak further, however, the twins pushed them apart and ran back toward their nursemaid. The moment was spoiled and Emily would be left to wonder later what more he would have said, had there been time. Now she could see that Tony had at last gained the notice of the nursemaid, Nancy. Lady Connaught's footman and poodle had left the park when she was not looking, and it was very nearly time for the twins to be brought back in.

Reluctantly she nodded toward her home. "It's time for me to return, and we haven't even begun to discuss your situation."

"It seems as if we just arrived," Tony agreed with a regretful note in his voice. "Don't worry, though. Last night I couldn't sleep, so I stayed up late to write you this list." He pulled a folded sheet of paper from his vest pocket and spoke more quickly. "This first group of names includes people who were at Eton with me. They will probably be the easiest for you to find. These others . . ." He sighed for a moment and then squared his shoulders. "I didn't take part in the social life at

Verdun, but I did have some contact with the other *détenus*. I'm hoping some of them may remember something helpful."

He did not sound very hopeful at all.

"Why didn't you?" Emily asked. "I'm sorry, I don't mean to be rude or intrusive, but it seems strange that you should hold yourself aloof from your fellow captives." It did not sound at all like something the young, open-hearted Tony who had been described to her would do.

"I didn't intend to." He paused and stole a look at the nursemaid. Emily, following his look, saw that Nancy was doing her best to be helpful and had no intention of returning to the house until Emily was ready to go.

"You see, I could not forgive the French for what they had done to me," he explained. "All the civilians resented being held, of course, but all I could think of was that they were keeping me away from Letty. Most of the *détenus* were concerned with trying to live as normal a life as possible."

"That's understandable."

"Yes, but the only way that could be done was by paying all the bribes the French demanded—and they demanded a bribe for everything. If you wanted to avoid the *appels,* the daily muster, you paid a bribe. The clubs had to pay bribes in order to exist. If you held a ball you not only had to make sure the governor, General Wirion, and his wife, were invited, but you had to ensure that he won at the gaming tables. It was the same story for the races."

"And you weren't willing to pay the bribes?"

"Oh, some even I couldn't avoid. My tutor was ill and elderly. In order for him to be cared for properly I had to pay for private accommodations and pay for his exemption from the *appels.* One of Wirion's favorite tricks was also to send one's servants to another of the depots so that you would have to ransom them back. I had to do that a few times. But I would not do more. It wasn't moral indignation at the thought of paying bribes. I don't want you to think me a martyr to my conscience."

His attitude was one of self-deprecation, but Emily was impressed nonetheless. It would take a lot of courage to stand up to the French prison authorities, especially for a boy of eighteen who had only been refused one thing in his entire life.

"Why refuse to pay, then?" Emily pressed him.

"It was the knowledge that this was good English money going into French hands. Oh, originally it all went straight into Wirion's pockets, but from there it would spread out. Every English penny spent in Verdun ultimately had to help Napoleon's cause. And that I would not do."

"So you did not go to the balls . . ."

"Or the clubs or the races. I attended the *appels* religiously, but the only *détenus* to be found there were the ones who could not afford the fees. As a result I was much better acquainted with the sailors in the fort than with the civilian prisoners. So the names you will see here are mostly naval men, plus the names of a few clergymen who used to come visit my tutor regularly."

The tutor who had insisted Tony still lived. It was possible that those connections might be the most helpful.

The nursemaid was starting to look very impatient, and too interested. Emily was definitely going to have to make some kind of explanation. There was one last thing, however, that she realized she must tell Tony.

"Very well. This should prove very helpful. In fact, I have met one gentleman already who was one of the civilian prisoners at Verdun."

"Really? Did he know me? What was his name?" Tony was so eager for the information that question followed question without any pause for response.

"His name was Mr. Dominic Neale. He did not claim to have met you personally, but said he had seen Lord Varrieur around the town." She hesitated. "He said he had been to your funeral."

Chapter Six

HE HAD NOT known.

After the words left her lips, Emily realized how it must have sounded to him. Like being forced to face one's own grave. His face had gone completely blank, as if a curtain had fallen over his eyes. He must have assumed his long incarceration had given rise to rumors of his death, not realizing people had valid reason to believe it a fact. And she could not stay to explain, to somehow ease the shock and pain, but must rush away without further conversation in order to bring the twins back to the nursery.

From inside the door she looked back, once, to see him still standing beneath the great oak tree. Even as she looked at him, he recovered, bowed, and moved away. His step, however, did not seem as firm as usual, lacking its usual energy.

"A very handsome gentleman, miss," Nancy commented in a prim voice, keeping her eyes carefully lowered as they followed the twins making their slow progress up the stairs. "Though for meself I like a fair-haired fellow, one as doesn't look like a gypsy that might cut your throat as soon as look at you."

Emily prevented Katy from going down the stairs again and silently weighed her chances of trying to persuade the nurserymaid that her meetings with Tony were only to conduct business. On the whole she would guess they were pretty low.

Something in Nancy's words struck a familiar chord, however.

"Yes, I suppose he does look dangerous," Emily agreed tentatively. "And perhaps a little rough. Certainly not as refined a gentleman as, oh, Lord Palin, for example."

Nancy seemed to relax a bit. "Ah, well, miss, there's few as measures up to Lord Palin, if you'll forgive my saying so. Quite the gentleman he is, and so very fine looking."

If only his ethical standards were nearly as refined, Emily thought. Clearly Nancy had a good idea of what his relationship with her was. More hints from Edward? Or a result of normal gossip? No matter. The girl certainly seemed to be an ardent supporter of Edward. Perhaps it was time, Emily decided, to put their secret engagement to good purpose.

As the twins scurried ahead into the nursery and into the waiting arms of Nanny, Emily pulled Nancy aside for a moment.

"Nancy, I know I can trust you," she said, praying it was true. "You know Lord Palin is placed in the uncomfortable position of having to prove his right to the title?"

"Aye, miss. We've all heard about the fellow that says he's the old lord's son." The nursery maid's eyes were wide with curiosity. She had not made any connection between that fellow and Tony.

Why should she? Emily suddenly realized with relief. The butler had probably described Tony to the other servants as some sort of madman, practically foaming at the mouth. Maybe, she thought as she took her measure of Nancy's avid gaze, just maybe this would work.

"Edward is so terribly distressed by all this he can hardly think of anything else," Emily explained.

Like his fiancée.

"And no wonder. It's a downright shame, miss, that's what I say. Poor man, hasn't had a chance to stop by here for days and days," Nancy commiserated.

"It is indeed a shameful situation," Emily agreed. She took a breath and then forged ahead. "So I decided to do something about it. I decided to look into the matter myself. But . . . I found I needed more information, so I arranged for someone to help me."

It sounded a little lame to Emily as she said it, but perhaps her own reputation would lend credibility. Everyone knew Emily had a multitude of loyal friends, some of them decidedly odd by society's standards.

"Oh, miss, that was ever so brave of you." Nancy clasped her hands to her breast in excitement.

"Hush, not so loud," Emily warned, although encouraged by the girl's response. "I thought it only right. It would be a horrible thing if the real Lord Palin were to lose his title and his fortune merely because there wasn't enough proof. But . . ." She bit her bottom lip in a nervous gesture. "I'm afraid Edward might not like the idea of me doing this." Sincerity made her voice wobble effectively on the last word. "He is so very proud, you know."

"Ahhh." Nancy nodded wisely in agreement. "Men never do like to admit that they need the help of a woman. Don't you worrit yourself, miss. None'll hear about it of me." The point Emily was trying to make finally sank in. "And is that the fellow as is helping you with his lordship's trouble, that fellow you was talking with this morning?"

At last. "He is indeed trying to prove Lord Palin's identity," Emily affirmed, sternly quelling a sense of guilt. The fact that she had not uttered a single outright lie to the girl did not in any way make the deception less real. "He is to meet me each morning," she continued, "to exchange information and receive instructions."

The nurserymaid stood up straight, after glancing furtively to see whether she were missed yet in the nursery. "You can count on me, miss. Me lips is sealed. And if I hear of anything that'll help his lordship, I promise to tell you straight off."

"Thank you, Nancy. I shall not forget your kindness."

The girl rushed off in answer to Nanny's imperious summons, leaving an unhappy Emily alone with her thoughts.

Seeing Tony again had at last made all things clear to her. Sometime in their stolen moments in the park she had come to an inescapable conclusion. Tony was telling the truth.

Looking back Emily could almost pinpoint the moment.

Something had happened to her when Tony said he felt sorry for any friend who disappointed her. Although he had never claimed friendship of her, only assistance, somehow she knew in her heart, then, Tony would never let her down. Knew that failing to stand by one's words and one's friends was a terrible crime to him.

Emily tried to persuade herself that she was imagining things, that she had fallen for a clever performance designed to win her sympathies. Her faith in her judgment had been greatly shaken by Edward's recent behavior. Yet for all their friendship, she had never expected Edward to understand her or her deepest feelings. This man did seem to understand her, what was important to her, in a way that both pleased and frightened her. Was it so very strange that she believed she understood him in return?

Strange or not, she did believe it was true.

And since it was true that Tony was not capable of abusing his friendship with her or with Gus, then his claim must also be true.

The implications of this fact were almost too painful to bear. To imagine that Letty could behave in such a way to her old friend and sweetheart. To think that Edward could coldly seek a title and fortune that were not his by right. Worst of all, to recognize what Tony had been through all these years and how he had been treated on his return.

These melancholy thoughts were still much on Emily's mind when she was joined at the breakfast table by her brother, John.

"What's this?" he asked. "It's not like you to be blue-deviled of a morning, Em. I don't know whether I can have both my ladies in the megrims," he teased, but with real concern in his voice.

"I'm sorry, John." She conjured up a smile, albeit somewhat faint. "How is Letty this morning?"

"Blessed if I know. She still says she's not well enough to receive visitors. As if I didn't know she was running up to the nursery every hour!" He shook his head despairingly. "She's bored to flinders, but she won't budge. I don't understand it. I've never seen her like this before."

"Once," Emily reminded him. "It was the only time I ever

saw you angry with her. You remember. Letty'd gone out alone
and unaccompanied—"

"And on foot no less! Yes, I remember. Scared me half to
death."

"Now that I think of it, that was also the only time I ever
saw you lose your temper."

Emily remembered it well. A frantic message from an ailing
friend had sent Letty rushing to the woman's aid, leaving only
the barest explanation behind. The fact that there had recently
been a rash of attacks by footpads in London had not occurred
to Letty at all, but it did to John. In his exacerbated state, after
fearful hours of waiting for her return, he had given Letty the
most blistering lecture on propriety Emily had ever heard.

Letty never could endure having the people she loved truly
angry with her. Could it be that, more than simply feeling
guilty, she was afraid Tony would make a scene, accusing her
of infidelity? Was that what she was hiding from?

"I know what it is," John said with a sigh. "When Letty hid
herself in her room, she was acting on the spur of the moment.
Now she can't think of a way to get out of it gracefully, not
without making some explanation."

"And the longer she waits, the greater the need for explanation." Emily nodded her head in comprehension.

"The harder it becomes to make one," John continued. "So
she lies in bed and worries all day. At this rate she'll work herself into such a state that she really will be ill."

"Can't you make her come out, John?" Emily hated to see
her brother look so glum. It was not like him to worry so.

"I could," he admitted. "But what would be the use? I don't
want to have to force Letty's confidence. No, this is something
Letty has to resolve for herself."

That was all very well, but Emily was not so sure they could
afford the luxury of allowing Letty time to come to her senses.
As John had said, each day it would become harder for Letty
to admit her foolishness. Too many others were being hurt by
Letty's behavior—John, Emily herself, and Tony.

Her disappointment must have shown.

"Well, I may not be able to do much about Letty right now,
but maybe I can do something to take that unhappy look from

your eyes," John said as he addressed the kippers. "What is it, puss?"

Emily sighed, but hardly knew how she could present her troubles to her brother.

"Not the ideal way to begin a betrothal, is it?" John guessed.

There was a great deal of truth in that, even though Edward's behavior was only a part of all that troubled her. "No, it is not," she agreed heartily.

"I thought that might be it." John nodded, satisfied with his powers of deduction. "I must say I think Edward should be able to find some time for you. We haven't seen him since the day after he made his offer."

"I did see him at the Castlereagh's ball, but he could hardly think of anything but his case." No need to tell John that she had had to hunt Edward down in order to gain those few moments of conversation.

"It won't be much longer now, Em," John offered as consolation. Poor consolation. Even John couldn't really find an excuse for Edward's ignoring her.

"Are you sure? What if the evidence is inconclusive? What if it drags on longer?"

John could see where she was heading. "No." His mild countenance suddenly took on an awesome authority. "I will not let you pester your sister-in-law. Let that be understood."

Emily bowed her head. John rarely uttered commands, but when he did, they were to be obeyed.

"John," she said hesitantly. "What if he really is Lord Palin?"

"The genuine article? I don't believe it." He shook his head. "Think of it, Em. What are the chances Varrieur would reappear after being thought dead all those years? In any case, I cannot believe that my Letty would fail to step forward if he were in truth her old friend. You cannot distrust Letty's integrity, can you?"

"No, of course not! But . . . she had only the merest glimpse of him at the ball. How can she be sure?"

"Why should she think him other than an impostor? Have you heard of anyone else, any of Varrieur's old friends, come forward to support his claim?"

It was true. As of now, no one had publicly accepted Tony as Lord Palin. Until that happened, others would be very slow to endorse him.

"I tell you this, puss," John continued. "If I thought there was the slightest justice in this fellow's claim, I would not permit Letty to hide upstairs. You may be sure that if this fellow's claim is just, Letty will support it."

It would hardly comfort Tony, however, to know his former love had to be forced to speak out on his behalf. Tony had not asked Emily a second time to intercede with Letty. How must he feel, she wondered, about Letty's continued silence toward him? To be disappointed by a friend was painful enough; to be denied and ignored by someone you loved was nothing less than agony. It was the very worst sort of betrayal.

"Em, you're not worried about what will happen if Edward loses the case, are you? I didn't think you were the kind of girl who placed much importance on being called marchioness."

"I don't," she protested, dropping her fork noisily. The clatter irritated her nerves even more. How could she tell John her greatest fear was that justice might fail and Edward might keep the title? "That's not why I agreed to marry him at all. I couldn't care less if we lived in a cottage in Tunbridge Wells, if only . . ."

"If only . . . ?" John prompted, clearly startled by her unexpected display of emotion. When she didn't respond at once, he demanded again, "What?"

If only Edward were still the friend she had agreed to marry, the boy she had always known and liked. Emily looked into her brother's concerned face. He was trying so hard to understand.

"I'm a little worried by Edward's behavior since this trouble began," she confessed, carefully keeping her voice even this time. "No," she forestalled her brother, "it's not simply because he's neglected me a little. I hope you know I am not the sort to expect a fiancé to hang about my neck all day. But I keep hearing things . . . about the way he's conducting himself. I told you, John, that I would not care if Edward lost his fortune, but I fear he cares. Too much. This challenge seems to have changed him, made him more ruthless. He's becoming a stranger."

There. She'd said it. Typically, she'd mentioned her terrible fear as if it were of no greater moment than this morning's burnt toast, but this time she hoped John would be able to see through that ruse. Emily held her breath and waited for her brother's response.

"Well . . . well, puss, are you sure Edward realizes you truly don't care about the money and the title? A man has his pride, you know. He likes to know he can offer the woman he loves all the extravagances she might ever want. Edward might not care about a cottage in the country for himself, but might desperately want better for you." John seemed pleased with this solution. "What you need to do is drag him aside, by force if necessary, and make him understand that it's him you love, not luxury," he advised cheerfully, as usual judging Edward by his own kind nature. "Yes, that's the ticket, Em. A good talking to is what's needed. And a few kisses, eh?"

Happy he had dealt with Emily's little problem, John saluted her on the brow and went about his business. Emily, however, was far from comforted by his analysis of Edward's behavior.

She knew Edward realized she cared nothing for his wealth, for being a marchioness. If her deeper thoughts and feelings were unknown to him, her standards certainly were not. She had even reminded him of that fact the day after she had accepted his offer. The day after Tony had appeared.

Disgusted with her train of thought, Emily pushed aside her breakfast and tried to immerse herself in domestic responsibilities. She reviewed menus with Cook and set aside some linen to be darned, but activity did not chase these thoughts from her mind.

Even an old and favored remedy—playing the loudest pieces she knew on the pianoforte—helped not at all. After a few minutes Emily realized she was playing the piece she and Edward had danced to at his ball. Not a good choice.

She tried to call up the warmth and happiness she had felt when Edward had first greeted her that night, but instead she remembered clearly the discomfort of the dance. Were those other feelings gone forever? she worried.

Even if Edward had been proved indisputably the rightful Lord Palin, Emily was not sure she could forget his lies, her hurt. If Edward somehow won his case now, how could she marry him, knowing how badly he had behaved and knowing he was not the rightful lord? How could she ever respect him?

And if he lost, as surely he must do, what then?

Perhaps he would surprise her, Emily thought as she searched for another piece of music. It was still possible he might find his lost humor and honor, and face his reduced circumstances bravely. He was probably imagining the worse sort of penury. His situation as a private gentleman would mean a great change, true, but it would not be nearly as impoverished as he believed. Tony seemed to bear him no grudge. Indeed, he seemed to sympathize more than she did. If only Edward allowed him, Tony would be generous. Of that she was sure.

Why did she have to remember now Letty's disapproval of her match with Edward? Emily banged determinedly at a sonata she had never quite been able to conquer. Still she continued to ask herself the same questions. Why couldn't she remember Edward in happier days? Somehow, instead of picturing herself and Edward riding through the fields near Howe, it was Tony she imagined as an eager youth chasing after Letty.

Emily winced as she hit a false note.

How could she marry Edward now?

Yet she had given him her word. She had a responsibility to their long friendship, too. If she turned her back on him now, when he needed her most, she would be a traitor to all she believed in.

How could she not marry him?

Emily soon realized her pounding on the piano had not gone unnoticed. In order to raise her obviously flagging spirits, John offered to escort her to the ball that evening at Lady Salisbury's, a gathering she knew he expected to be excessively boring, especially without the benefit of his wife's sparkling company.

In this John was mistaken. The regent came to Lady Salisbury's from his own dinner, obviously drunk. He did not stay long, but his brief appearance was sufficient to enliven an eve-

ning already made more interesting by the presence of the foreign visitors.

Emily was surprised to find she needed no such entertainment to lift her spirits. Although the thought of a ball or party
rarely excited her, tonight she found her heart beating faster
in anticipation. Tonight she was not merely the girl society
thought it knew as a kind person and a good friend. She was
a woman with a purpose, a woman determined to further the
cause of justice, the cause of the rightful Lord Palin.

A lead might come from almost anyone, Emily thought with
a sense of adventure as she looked around the ballroom. The
energetic officer whose dancing left her exhausted, the boring
matron who poured out her troubles while Emily helped repair
a torn flounce, the shy debutante she found hiding behind a
swag of decorative bunting, any of them might suddenly reveal
hidden sources of knowledge.

There were more private sources of delight, too, friends to
greet and welcome. The gallant Prussian captain seemed to be
kept busy at Prince Hardenburg's side for most of the evening,
but he managed to find time to dance with her and make her
laugh. When Emily found some time to relax with friends while
the orchestra took a break, she was pleased to find Mr. Scrope
Davies, for once outside the gaming room.

Although she had long suspected that Mr. Davies earned
most of his income at the card tables, rather than from his
Cambridge fellowship, Emily had always found the gentleman
kind as well as witty. It was a combination of virtues that was
very rare, and therefore all the more appreciated by her. Smiling, she patted a place next to her on the settee.

He joined the group just in time to hear one of the gentlemen
comment that Emily had not been seen in Hyde Park that afternoon. Mr. Davies complimented her on her good sense.

"But what a glorious spectacle!" the other gentleman protested. "Eight thousand cavaliers following the sovereigns as
they passed through the gates of Kensington Gardens!"

"Yes," Mr. Davies said, leaning back comfortably, "but the
spectacle that followed as they rode toward the Serpentine was
even greater. Ladies screaming, boots pulled off! I must confess
I did enjoy the sight of the Master of the Horse thrown onto

the grass. And the fearless General Blucher, poor man, finally routed by his admirers, backed up against a tree."

The picture he presented made Emily laugh. "But still protecting his flank against attack, it seems," she pointed out. "Ever the soldier, even in Hyde Park."

"He is indeed," Mr. Davies agreed. "And he at least is deserving of all the admiration our nation can give."

Emily turned in greeting as Georgy joined the group in a flurry of silks and feathered fan. "No, you don't even have to tell me," she interrupted before anyone could bring her up to date. "I can tell you what you have been discussing. First, Prinny's disgusting behavior this evening. Second, the debacle at the park this afternoon. Third, the mysterious claimant to the Palin title. I've heard it all three times already." As Mr. Davies relinquished his place to her, Georgy favored him with a dazzling smile. "Do you know, I begin to think that the greatest benefit of the visit of the foreign royals is that any English peccadilloes have been forgotten in the general excitement."

Georgy's statement was greeted by a chorus of protests and cries to know what Georgy had done recently that no one knew about. Without even thinking, Emily turned the conversation toward her own goal.

"Now, Georgy, you must admit the quarrel over Palin's title is an English scandal," Emily pointed out.

"But it's not a scandal! That's my complaint," Georgy answered.

"I don't see why not," Mr. Davies answered, echoing Emily's thoughts. "All the elements for scandal are there—character assassination, possible fraud, a man's name and fortune held in the balance. You are too severe, Miss Parkhurst."

"She's jealous," another gentleman responded. "Poor Miss Parkhurst hates to admit she is one of the few people who missed her chance to gawk at the claimant."

If only they knew, Emily thought. Georgy had had a better look at Tony than any of them. This then explained why she had not had a hint of his identity. "You weren't at the party Lord Ruthven threw for Palin?" she asked her friend. In the crush and excitement of that evening, she had never noticed Georgy's absence.

"No," Georgy wailed. Then, angling her body away from the others, she hissed in Emily's ears, "Not invited. It seems I am not sufficiently respectable for Lord Ruthven."

A spurt of anger distracted Emily for a moment. Edward knew Georgy was a good friend of hers, and he had had as much control over the guest list as Lord Ruthven. Here was one more betrayal to trouble her.

"I can't even find anyone who can give me a good description of the fellow," Georgy continued, addressing the group.

"You were close to the door, Emily," one person remembered. "Didn't you get a good look at him?"

The last thing Emily wanted was to tell Georgy what Tony looked like. She shrugged. "I'm sorry. My sister-in-law became ill, and I'm afraid she took all my attention."

"Come," Georgy demanded. "Someone must have observed his appearance."

"I saw him," a young debutante offered shyly. Emily could have strangled her. "I thought him very impressive. Very, very tall and slender. He had pale skin and dark hair, and commanding dark eyes. To be honest, I'm a little surprised he made so little impression on Miss Meriton."

Little cat. No, Emily admitted to herself, the girl was only telling the truth. No one who had seen Tony's entrance could have forgotten him.

"This begins to be more intriguing," Georgy confessed, to Emily's dismay.

"Not if you're forced to listen to Palin talk about it," one of the gentlemen complained.

Emily stepped in quickly. "What's boring is that no one has anything to add. After one has talked about the fellow's spectacular entrance, what more is there to say? Does anyone know him? Did anyone know Lord Varrieur before his . . . supposed demise?" she asked from habit. From the people she knew well, Emily expected no surprises.

"As a matter of fact, I did," Mr. Davies announced, to her delighted astonishment. "I was at Eton with him."

He wasn't on Tony's list, but then Tony could hardly list every boy at the school. The others were clamoring for more information, without any further urging from Emily.

"He was a big fellow, I do remember that," Tony's former schoolmate said. "I can't tell you much more. I didn't know him well. He was two years younger than I, and oppidans beside."

Emily knew that her friend Mr. Davies had had to endure the rigors of life in college. Oppidans, she remembered from John's schooldays, referred to those boys whose families were wealthy enough to board them with dames of the town.

"The only reason I knew him at all was because he was a cricketer—a good one, too. Now, there's something Palin might ask at his hearing. Have the fellow describe the Eton-Westminster match of ninety-nine." Mr. Davies scanned his audience as if seeking praise for his suggestion.

He did not get it, although Emily thought the idea worth considering.

"That's no good, Davies," another gentleman denied, shaking his head and quashing Emily's hope. "I can describe the match of ninety-nine and I wasn't even there."

"You couldn't bowl like he could, either," Davies countered. "I never saw anyone who could. After all these years, I wouldn't know Varrieur's face in a crowd, but I would recognize the way he bowled." He asked them all ingenuously, "Do you think that would be admitted as evidence?"

While Mr. Davies encouraged the general hilarity at the thought that a man might be recognized by his cricket game, he confessed more quietly to Emily, as everyone rose to resume the dancing, that Tony's case was more than a jest to him.

"You didn't know my friend Matthews," he told her. "He died four years ago. Drowned. He was Varrieur's age and oppidans, too. I remember that he talked about him once, long ago, talked about his kindness. A fellow that big has a lot of opportunity in school to become a bully, you know, but Varrieur was different."

Oh, yes, Tony was certainly different. Judging from his list of names, Tony had not even remembered the unfortunate Matthews. When kindness is such an ingrained part of your being, you do not count the individual acts of kindness, evidently. After ten years in prison that compassion still survived, Emily thought, remembering his tolerance of Edward's behavior.

Deliberately Mr. Davies threw off his pensive mood, but he added, "I'd like to think Varrieur could survive. If this fellow is he, I wish him well."

Emily merely smiled, but she was inclined to take Mr. Davies's good wishes seriously. Although she had been comforted by her brother's assertion that Letty would support a valid claim, she knew Tony would need every bit of help he could find. What John had also made clear was that Tony needed at least one old friend to recognize his claim soon, so that others might then feel braver about coming forward. Mr. Davies might not be the one, but Emily became more hopeful that she would find someone who was. Clearly Tony had underestimated his effect on the lives of others. He was a man not easily forgotten.

There were some hopeful leads gained while Emily waltzed and chatted with friends. Deliberately she spent a few dances sitting with the chaperons when she might have been on the dance floor. She knew well that it was the dowagers and the marriage-minded mothers who knew everybody's family tree. They could tell you who was related to whom, where they lived, what fortune they could claim, and what scandals they had caused for the last half-century.

Not only had Emily been able to discover the whereabouts of a number of Tony's Eton cronies this way, she had also gathered hopeful leads on one or two sailors, impecunious younger sons, who had been in Verdun. If only she could be more sure how helpful these men would be! She would have to content herself, however, with the knowledge that Tony would at least know where to look for them now.

Nevertheless, there was one person to whom she wanted very much to speak. Her parting from Tony this morning still occupied her mind. Emily did not think she could face him again, without being able to tell him more about that false funeral.

She knew Mr. Neale was here. Earlier in the evening she had seen him conferring with Lord Castlereagh. At the moment he was nowhere in sight. The greater problem was not finding him, but approaching him in an inconspicuous fashion. Emily had never been very good at luring men to her side. In any case, a distinguished gentleman like Mr. Neale would no doubt be nonplussed to find himself the object of inexpert flirtation.

In the meantime she was obliged to concentrate on other matters. At the end of a dance in which she found her greatest concern to be protecting her gown and toes, she was returned by her energetic partner to John, who had been joined by the Castlereaghs.

"Are you quite all right?" her godmama asked. Obviously Emily's performance on the dance floor had been noticed.

"I think so, if a little out of breath. Do you see any tears in my gown?" Emily asked, twirling around in a circle before them.

"No, you're fine," her brother assured her, laughing. "Let me fetch you a glass of punch to cool you down."

Lord Castlereagh shook his head mournfully, then excused himself to follow a member of his staff across the room.

At Emily's unspoken question, her godmama told her, "Cas is very unhappy about this waltz craze. If it continues, he can see no escape but to learn it. It looks to be a diplomatic necessity."

"I cannot imagine his lordship failing at anything he set his mind to."

"As you have discovered, dear, the feet do not always obey the mind's commands. The truth is"—Lady Castlereagh lowered her voice to a whisper—"one of this country's greatest statesmen simply cannot dance."

They both laughed, and Lady Castlereagh continued. "I was glad to see your brother here tonight, although he looks lonely without your sister-in-law. Is she improving?"

The question brought to mind all the unhappy thoughts Emily had been trying to push aside throughout the evening.

"John seems to think she is becoming restless, which I believe is usually an indication of recovery," she answered calmly.

"That's true," Lady Castlereagh agreed, then turned her attention to more immediate concerns. "You will be coming with us tomorrow, will you not? I believe the plan is to visit the pensioners' hospitals. Not perhaps the most cheerful of outings, but probably the only one to do any actual good."

"Certainly I mean to come with you." Emily had great hopes

of tomorrow's excursion. What better place to find navy men than at a naval hospital?

"My lady?" Both women turned at the sound of the gentleman's voice. Emily's luck was in. It was Mr. Neale.

Emily greeted him with so genuine a delight, the man looked slightly startled. Nodding briefly to her, he turned to Lady Castlereagh.

"His lordship asks if you might join him briefly in the cardroom, my lady."

"Oh, I suppose I'd better go," Emily's godmama said. "I don't like to leave you like this, however."

Emily smiled. "I think my brother must have lost his way returning from the refreshment table." Silently she prayed for a few more minutes' delay.

"Sir John?" Mr. Neale inquired politely. "I saw him not two minutes since talking with Lord Palin. May I escort you to him, Miss Meriton?"

"Thank you, Mr. Neale," Emily said, with no little gratitude. "That would be very kind of you." She took his arm and followed him around the ballroom, deliberately slowing her step. She didn't want to reach John—or Edward—too soon. There would be time later to wonder what her brother was up to. "Speaking of Lord Palin, Mr. Neale, did you ever present your story to him?"

"I did, Miss Meriton," he confirmed, "and his lordship was most gratified to hear it. I only hope I may have been of service, although there can be little doubt as to the validity of his claim. I am only surprised that people seem to take this impostor so seriously."

Emily could only think Mr. Neale had not seen Tony yet. His story, however, did trouble her. There had to be an explanation.

"Perhaps you are not aware, Mr. Neale, but the gentleman who traveled with Lord Varrieur continued to aver, long after his release, that the story of his lordship's death was false."

"Amazing how such delusions persist, is it not?" Mr. Neale responded, unfazed by her claim. "Some people may be influenced by it as well, I suppose. I do indeed remember the old parson. Who could forget him? It was because of his protests that the body was returned to Verdun for burial."

"He was able to assure himself of the identity of the deceased?" she asked, phrasing her words carefully. It did not seem proper to talk about corpses at a ball, even Lady Salisbury's.

"Well . . ." There was a note in her escort's voice that told her he was unwilling to say more.

"Please, Mr. Neale, do continue." When he did not, she urged, "One cannot help but be fascinated by the subject, by so romantic a possibility. Yet, as you have said, how can anyone take such a claim seriously if Lord Varrieur was absolutely identified as dead?"

"There was some delay before returning the body." Mr. Neale hesitated. He, too, was searching for the most delicate way to put the matter. "It was impossible that anyone should recognize it, but by the clothes and personal effects."

He did not like to have to admit that a possibility of confusion existed, either, Emily realized. Bringing her fan into use to cover the swiftness of her reasoning, she responded ingenuously, "Oh, you mean like a family ring, or something of that sort."

"I believe there was some jewelry, although I cannot remember whether it was a ring or a stickpin. May I ask why you are so interested, Miss Meriton?"

His sudden stiffness bewildered her. Surely she had not seemed more than normally curious, at worst a trifle morbid? She was sensitive to how her inquiries might appear, but she had seen clear evidence that curiosity about Tony was the order of the day.

"Lord Palin is a close friend of my family and I am concerned for his well being," she responded, looking up at him with wide-eyed innocence. "Like you, I am rather surprised this claim is being considered so carefully. Surely, the claimant must have some proof or knowledge to place the matter in doubt."

"True. I wonder what it might be." Although his words expressed interest, Mr. Neale's tone was dismissive.

On her mettle, Emily decided a little more flattery was in

order, although she had rarely found that necessary as a conversational tactic.

"I also admit, after our talk the other evening, I have become very interested in the vivid portrait you painted of the life of the *détenus*. It is a part of the late war that is very little discussed. Our heroes in uniform are encouraged to discuss the trials they endured, but you civilians are ignored."

"Thank you for your understanding, Miss Meriton," he answered civilly enough, but without warmth. "It's true we don't get much sympathy, and we civilians were the innocent victims. The soldiers entered into the war knowing what they would have to face."

Mr. Neale seemed unwilling to elaborate on Verdun life, however. This was a shock to Emily, who was used to being sought out as a confidante, willing or not. It was also a grave disappointment. Quite apart from her desire to discover people who might be helpful to Tony's cause, Emily wanted to understand what his life had been like during his long banishment. Verdun formed only the beginning of Tony's sojourn in France, but it was still an important part.

"Here's your brother now," Mr. Neale announced as they finally found him near the card tables. Was that a sigh of relief Emily heard in his voice? What could she have said or done to provoke such a reaction? she wondered.

John was still holding Emily's glass of punch. Beneath his spectacles Emily could see a faint and unaccustomed air of concern. Edward had managed to make his escape before she arrived, but Lord Ruthven still remained. He, too, looked ruffled.

"Thank you, Mr. Neale," she said, dismissing her escort. There was no point in holding him back if he was to remain silent and uncooperative. He left with unbecoming alacrity, she noticed, too. "And thank you for the punch, John," Emily added pointedly as she turned to her brother.

"Hmmm? Oh, yes. Here it is. Rather warm now, I'm afraid."

"So it is," she answered and turned to his companion, wondering if he, too, would now run from her. "Good evening, Lord Ruthven."

"Good evening, my dear." Although Lord Ruthven was still looking daggers at John, he managed a smile for Emily. "Yes,

Edward was just telling us how lovely you looked in . . . er . . . purple."

"Did he indeed?" Her dress was a pale lavender, a color that could hardly be referred to as purple. Either Edward was in need of spectacles or, more likely, he had said nothing of the kind. Obviously, if he had noticed her presence at all, it was so he could avoid it. "I'm sorry to have missed seeing him."

"Oh, well, you know how busy he is these last few days. So much to do." The pompous baron gave another sideways glance at John. "Poor Edward. I know how terrible he feels about not seeing more of you. I will certainly give him your regards, though. M'lady and I are ready to leave now, so I don't have time to stop, but I promise you we'll have a nice long chat soon."

Although Ruthven was clearly trying to get away from her brother, he seemed to be tendering a genuine invitation to Emily to talk. Perhaps she could learn from him what plans Edward had for the hearing. In hopes of this, she gave him her warmest smile as he slipped away.

"What have you been doing, John?" she asked. "It looked as if you and Lord Ruthven were about to descend to fisticuffs. Hasn't the prince regent displayed a sufficient lack of manners for the evening?" Almost as the teasing words left her lips, however, Emily realized what he had been up to. "You were scolding Edward, weren't you, dear?"

"What makes you think I would do a thing like that?" Embarrassed, John turned away and stopped to rub his spectacles on the tail of his coat.

"Because you are the dearest of all brothers," she said fondly. Didn't he realize that, like Letty, Edward had to find his own way?

"Ah, well. Hmmmph. I might have said something to the lad." He put his spectacles back on. "The boy still foolishly thinks if he pays you marked attention, people will guess you're betrothed. What I say is—if he doesn't come by to visit us soon, people will think he's giving us the cut direct. Sorry, puss, all I seem to have done is get his hackles up."

"That's all right, dear," Emily told him, and realized as she said it that it was true. She no longer cared if she had an opportunity to see and talk to Edward. If anything, she was a little afraid that she would meet him and discover that all the things she feared to see in him, the ruthlessness and deceit, were no illusion.

Emily also realized that for this entire evening she had hardly given Edward, as her fiancé, a single thought. Her thoughts had been of Tony. Only of Tony.

Tony sat by the window looking out at the night sky and tried to shake off a strange mood of disquiet. Usually looking at the stars soothed him. Only someone who had been denied that simple pleasure for nine years could understand what it meant to him. Yet tonight that comfort failed.

He'd been cooped up here too long, that was it. Oh, he was free now to go where he pleased, but where he pleased was not open to him, would not be open to him until he had reclaimed his name. Tonight he should have been at Lady Salisbury's waltzing with Miss Meriton, but instead that pup usurping his name attended.

Gus's news of the ball had bothered him; that must be why he could not relax. The thought that his rightful place in society had been denied him robbed him of peace. What else could it be?

The fact that Miss Parkhurst was beginning to ask questions was troublesome. She had been persistent enough to drive Gus away from the ball early. Although Miss Meriton had seemed to trust her friend, he was not so sure that even such an excellent reputation as Miss Meriton's would survive careless talk. His meetings with her had been innocent enough, in all faith, but would hardly appear so to the scandal-mongering gossips.

If he thought meeting her really could endanger her good name, he would stop it at once, no matter the cost to himself. And it would cost him a great deal to stop seeing her, he knew.

On the other hand, he persuaded himself, a person would have to be a fool to believe malicious gossip about Miss Meriton. Gus had said in the very beginning that her friends were legion, and very, very loyal. He was not surprised.

Was Gus himself developing a tendre for her? He spoke of her to Tony in the most teasing fashion, but Tony knew better than anyone what it was to hide one's deepest feelings under a mask of playful banter. Gus was a good man, but somehow Tony could not imagine his friend with Miss Meriton. He certainly could not imagine Miss Meriton ruling the roost at Gus's ancient schloss on the Rhine, although she was no doubt capable of managing anything. Here was her natural domain, however. She belonged in an English countryside. Someplace like Howe, for example.

He might not have been the only one to consider that, he realized uncomfortably. He'd been suspicious before of Miss Meriton's relations with the young Edward. Edward. The very way she spoke the name clearly indicated more intimacy than neighborly friendship. And tonight, Gus told him, her brother had had an interesting and acrimonious exchange with the young cub and with Lord Ruthven. Gus had surmised that Sir John was telling the boy in no uncertain terms to stop pestering Letty for support, but Tony knew that since the ball at Carlton House young Edward had not been near the Meritons.

The very fact that Miss Meriton had been so distressed by the boy's behavior meant they had been close. Perhaps they had been close enough to give her the right to remonstrate with Edward about his conduct. Close enough for Edward to have raised expectations.

Tony had been willing to overlook the boy's behavior toward him, but if what he suspected was true, Edward's treatment of Emily could not be forgiven. The hurt look on her face as she spoke of the boy this morning stuck in his mind.

If that boy had broken her heart by ignoring her, Tony would . . . Would what? Tony laughed at himself. What would he do? He had no place in Miss Meriton's life. He was only a man who had once been in love with her sister-in-law.

Once. Long ago.

Chapter Seven

WHEN TONY CAME to the rendezvous the next morning, Emily was embarrassed to be found playing "swingies" with the twins. This energetic activity, which involved lifting a twin high above her head and swinging around in a circle until they were both dizzy, had left her flushed and disheveled. As a result of earlier pick-a-back rides, Emily's curls were dangling loose down her back. It was not a dignified appearance to present to a gentleman. Emily did not want exactly to seem dignified with this particular gentleman, but neither did she wish to look a hoyden.

Although the twins were inclined to demand further attention, Nancy was quick to step in and lure them away as soon as she noticed Tony's approach. Once freed, Emily rushed to unburden herself of the guilt she had carried since yesterday's meeting.

"Tony, I am sorry I left you like that yesterday, with such terrible news. I should not have broken it to you like that." In her concern Emily had almost forgotten her self-consciousness. Tony's intent look brought it all back to her, however, and she struggled to quickly straighten her gown and pin back the escaping strands of hair.

"That's all right," Tony responded, watching her. With his fascinated gaze on her, Emily felt all thumbs, and she was sure she was blushing. "I'm glad that you told me. Everything

111

makes sense now. And I don't see how you could have made the news any easier to bear."

He laughed, evidently amused by her efforts to restore her coiffure. The more she tried to hurry, the more she made a mess of it. "Please, don't bother with that on my account," he said with a gently teasing note in his voice. "The twins will only pull it down again in a few minutes. There's no one else to see."

No, no one else would see. Only Tony.

He was right about the twins, but it was depressing to think that her appearance was of so little account to him. Until the twins had wrought havoc with her toilette, Emily had felt quite pretty this morning. Of course, Letty's golden curls and blue eyes always put hers in the shade. She had always known she had neither the looks nor the personality to drive men wild with desire. Or even pique some romantic interest.

All the same, one didn't like to feel invisible.

The blasted thing wouldn't stay up anyway. Emily abandoned the task in disgust. Trying to act as if it didn't matter, she asked Tony, "What do you mean 'everything makes sense now'?"

"I could never understand why everyone was so quick to believe me dead," he explained. A touch of anger appeared in his voice when he remembered. Evidently he heard it, too, and shrugged it off. "Perhaps that was naive of me. Now that I look back, I remember that the few acquaintances I met at Bitche would always say they had heard I was dead, but I always assumed that was because I had been away so long."

"I did manage to discover a few more details last night," Emily told him eagerly. Perhaps between them they could make some sense of what had happened. She could see that it was very important to Tony to be able to understand it all.

A look of hope flashed momentarily across his pale face before his usual poise returned. It was a feeling Emily knew only too well, the fear of hoping too much, and her heart went out to him.

Covering his lapse, Tony offered Emily his arm and escorted her to a shaded bench. Reminding herself the twins were well occupied, she joined him.

"The clergyman who was with you in Verdun—"

"Tavvy," he interrupted.

"Yes. Well, evidently he gave the authorities no peace. When the news came that you had died, of fever I think, he refused to believe it. Eventually they sent the body back, ostensibly for burial but really to calm down the old man."

"And it worked," he pointed out.

"No, and that should work in your favor. By that time the body could only be identified by personal effects. The *détenu* community gave you a big funeral, but Tavvy continued to insist it wasn't you. He never believed you died in prison."

"That's wonderful!" Joy shone from his eyes, only to be replaced a moment later by unease. His attentive ears had obviously caught the nuance of her wording. "You said 'believed.' Past tense. He didn't make it, did he?"

Emily hated to have to give him such painful news. "I'm sorry. He died about five years ago."

Tony accepted the news in silence. He got up abruptly and walked away for a moment.

Sadly Emily watched him, wishing there were a way to comfort him, wishing she had the right to offer comfort. All these events that had happened so long ago were new to him. The pain was still fresh.

By the time he returned to her, however, Tony's emotions were well under control. "He was a good sort," he said of his old companion. "He had to be, to endure my moods. I was not the best of companions that first year."

Emily noted that Tony did not bewail the setback to his case, only the loss of his friend. As evidence of his character, it impressed her greatly.

"Damn!" He struck the bench, momentarily succumbing again to grief. "I hate to think of him dying alone in Verdun, probably locked up in the Citadel for lack of bribe money."

"No, he was released," Emily said, leaning forward, glad to be able to offer that small solace. "About a year after your supposed demise, for health reasons."

"You jest." Tony stood stiffly, clearly too proud to accept false comfort.

Emily tried to look convincing, surprised that she should

need to do so. "No, it's the truth. He spent the last years of his life at Howe."

"They released him for reasons of health?" Skepticism was written on his face. "The French didn't release the English unless bribed with money and political interest to do so. Lord Yarmouth was released. The Viscount Duncannon was released. And Lord Elgin. People like Tavvy didn't get released." The bitterness he so rarely showed appeared now in his voice and the stiff way he held himself.

"Maybe he was causing too much trouble?" she suggested weakly. Part of her was beginning to agree with him. It did not make sense.

"Trouble sent you to the Citadel or to Bitche. It did not send you home." He still sounded a little angry, but he seemed to believe her now. "I shouldn't complain, though. I'm glad he was able to spend his last days in comfort."

"At least this should cast considerable doubt on the story of your death," Emily reminded him, well aware what poor comfort it was for the loss of a friend. "I suppose one of the other prisoners stole your belongings, and that's why he was identified as you."

Tony shook his head. "My belongings were stolen by the guards. I don't understand any of this. Even if it had been another prisoner who had taken my things, you can't make me believe that those few trinkets of mine would have remained in place during the trip back to Verdun."

It was strange, all of it was strange, and no explanation quite seemed to fit the entire story of Tony's supposed death and funeral. How did his belongings get from the guards who stole them to the body of an unknown man? From what Tony had told her, Emily had to agree it was extremely unlikely that either the guards or the governor of the prison should be so honest to return his things. Nor did it seem probable that the body would arrive without having been stripped of valuables.

There was no time now to ponder the matter in any case. While she had been talking to Tony, Nancy had been trying her mightiest to amuse the twins. Nancy's friend, the countess's footman, and the little poodle had also done their part, but the twins clearly were intrigued by the stranger who was spending

so much time with their aunt. They finally broke loose from
the nursery maid and ran back to the bench, throwing themselves enthusiastically upon Emily.

The nurserymaid came running after them, but Emily good-
naturedly shooed her away. If Nancy were to be a fellow conspirator, albeit an unwitting one, she deserved some reward.
Emily was glad of the distraction as well. Neither her thoughts
about Tony's past nor her awareness of Tony very much in the
present were very comfortable.

"That's all right, Nancy," she said. "I don't want to spoil
your conversation with James. We can talk and watch the twins
at the same time."

Nancy looked dubious at this announcement, but was glad
of the chance to whisper confidences with Lady Connaught's
footman.

"I hope I was not overconfident of our abilities," Emily had
to admit, after immediately giving chase to Connor and pulling
him away from an interesting mess on the ground. "No, Connor, don't touch that."

Tony laughed, but then became more serious again. "I'm
sorry for rattling on like that. Every time I meet you it seems
I spend more time simply talking with you, and not exactly to
the purpose. I know you haven't much time, and I don't mean
to waste it."

"You don't waste my time," she protested. "I like to hear
you talk."

"Do you? I can't imagine why, but I must admit I am glad
to have been able to talk with you. I've wondered, though . . ."
He hesitated a moment, as if he feared to be thought forward.
"Everyone comes to you with their troubles. Where do you go
with yours?"

He had surprised her again with his perception. His words
called up painful thoughts, however. The sad truth was that
the secrets of her heart remained her secret. Oh, she had explained logically enough to Letty her reasons for accepting Edward's offer. She had confessed to John that she was worried
about Edward's behavior. There had never been any mention,
however, of all the times she had cried herself to sleep.

Tony's beautiful dark eyes were watching her, waiting. He

really wanted to know, she realized with a sense of shock. The question had not been posed out of mere politeness or even curiosity on his part. It deserved an honest answer.

"The fault is, perhaps, mine. I do not like to burden my friends with such trivial problems." Or such eccentric ones, she thought to herself. Even her dear friend Georgy put little stock in love matches. How could Emily tell her she longed for such a love? Letty would understand that, but had no idea what it was to feel unattractive and unwanted. It was interesting that Tony had not mentioned Letty as a possible confidante.

Evidently her answer was not good enough for him. "How could anything you think or feel be trivial?" he asked. "Especially to a friend?" Perhaps he doubted his right to that title, because he stopped his quizzing abruptly.

"Forgive me. I don't mean to pry," he continued in a moment.

His shy smile reminded Emily of his statement the other day about feeling gauche in company. With his impressive tall figure and usual energy it was easy to forget that he, too, had doubts.

"And now I've let you lure me into further conversation, again," he confessed. "One more apology, however. Last night I meant to try to think of some more names that might be helpful to you, but . . . somehow I couldn't concentrate. I will try harder tonight. Where do you go this evening?"

"This evening?" Shutting her eyes in concentration, Emily reviewed her plans, glad to turn the conversation to less personal concerns. "To the theater and to Lady Cholmondeley's. This afternoon we are going to Chelsea and Greenwich."

"I hope all this activity is not on my account," Tony said with solicitude. "I wouldn't want you to exhaust yourself for me."

He was looking so concerned that Emily began to worry if already there were bags under her eyes. "Don't worry," she said brightly, as if she did not care that he thought she looked like a hag. "I should probably do the same, even if you had not appeared. The royals leave for Oxford tomorrow, so we will have a day of rest then, at least."

"That's good." He seemed a little taken aback by her response. Some of her irritation must have come through after all.

"Aren't you going to ask me if I've discovered anything else?" Emily reminded him.

"Did you really? So soon?"

He sounded so enthusiastic and hopeful that Emily was sorry she had so little to present. "I've made a start at least. Here, I wrote some of it down for you."

She offered him the sheet of paper. His hand brushed against hers as he took it. Earlier he had taken off his gloves when helping Katy retrieve a trinket from the dirt. Now Emily was extremely conscious of his bare skin on hers. She stepped back hastily and held her arms close, to cover her goosebumps.

"I think I've traced a number of your old Eton friends. Do you think with this much information your solicitor will be able to contact these men?" Her question came out all in a rush.

"Yes, this is a great help."

He did not sound disappointed to see how few she had been able to glean news of. "I even found one fellow who wasn't on your list," she pointed out.

Tony followed her finger down the page. "Scrope Davies of all fellows! I remember, he was one of the dandy set, a colleger."

"He is also quite the sportsman. He remembers you best for your performance on the cricket field and claims he would recognize your bowling style anywhere."

Emily was rewarded with a laugh. "Oh, lord, I haven't handled a ball in twelve years."

"Ball? Ball?" Connor asked, suddenly alert.

"No, sweetheart, we haven't got a ball." Emily tried to prove she wasn't hiding one, but the twin still looked suspicious. "I think I'd better bring these two back in now," she told Tony reluctantly.

"Of course. I'll be here tomorrow, but I don't want you to feel obliged to come if you are tired."

That was only courtesy speaking. The look in his eyes told her he wanted her to be there. That was not really surprising, Emily told herself. With only the captain and Emily willing to listen to him, he must be desperate for companionship, for simple conversation. What was surprising was how much Emily wanted to see him again.

"Miss Meriton," Tony began only to be contradicted by little Katy.

"No, no. Emmy. Emmy." She poked at her aunt to show what she was talking about.

Emily picked her up and explained. "This is Miss Meriton, you see. I," she said regretfully, pointing to herself, "am only Aunt Emily."

"You could never be only an aunt," he denied. The warmth in his eyes told her he meant it. Emily only wished that she could believe it were true. Yet Tony had shown that he saw more in her than even her family and cherished friends.

Of course, even if Tony had been perceptive enough to see that there was as much passion as common sense in her, that did not mean that he or any man would want that of her. She caught herself up at once. As if it mattered whether Tony thought her desirable or not! She was betrothed to Edward.

"What I wish to say," Tony continued in a teasing note, while keeping a watchful eye on the younger Miss Meriton, *"Emmy,* was that I appreciate all you're doing. I know, I know," he said, holding up his hands to ward off her protests. "This is not for me but only to satisfy your own sense of justice, but all the same I am grateful."

Now was the time for Emily to admit that she had come to believe in Tony, that what she did she did for him and not for an abstract sense of justice, but somehow she could not find the words. Her moment of hesitation cost her the opportunity. It was too late now, even for regret.

"Your nursery maid is returning." Tony spoke hurriedly, even a little embarrassed, she thought, by his show of emotion. Like her, Tony seemed to find it difficult to talk about himself. The open-hearted boy Letty had described was gone. "I'd better go. Adieu for now."

He slipped away before Emily could say another word, even farewell. Before he disappeared from sight, he turned and waved good-bye to her. The twins joined her in returning his salute.

Emily faced the nurserymaid with slight trepidation. Had

her conduct with Tony today cost her the maid's cooperation?
She should have been more careful. Their behavior today could
hardly have seemed like a business meeting.

Yet Nancy said nothing until they had delivered the twins
back into the welcoming arms of Nanny.

"You know, miss," she began, raising alarm in Emily's
breast. "You know, miss, for a fellow who looks like a thieving
gypsy, he's awful good with the babies."

It was only after Tony had scanned the glittering box tier
of the Theatre Royal Covent Garden for the tenth time that
it finally occurred to him that perhaps he had come to the theater tonight with more on his mind than mere escape from the
increasingly irksome confines of his chambers. It was certainly
not the program that drew him out. He had hardly spared a
glance for the allegorical festival in honor of the foreign visitors. Winter's overture to *Richard, Coeur de Lion* had likewise
been ignored, and the piece itself with music by Grétry looked
to gain no more attention from him.

He had come to see Emily.

The realization came as rather a shock to him. But one week
ago he had believed himself still in love with Letty, had blamed
Letty for not waiting for him. For the last ten years it was the
thought of Letty that had kept him going; now he could
scarcely call her image to mind.

It would be humiliating to think his father had been right
all those years ago. He was embarrassed now to remember how,
at eighteen, he had shouted his father knew nothing about love,
a foolish accusation. When his mother was still alive, he recalled, there had been laughter in the house all the time and
such open displays of affection as to make the young Tony
blush.

Now perhaps he could admit he had realized long ago that
he and Letty had been too young then to marry, a fact he dared
not face when he still considered himself promised to Letty.
No matter what anyone said about waiting and seeing, he had
told Letty he would marry her when he returned. Given the
circumstances, he could not break his word.

His word no longer mattered, however. Circumstances since

had saved them both from their youthful folly. Letty was happy with her husband and children, Emily said. His old friend would surely wish him the same happiness.

He was old enough now to know what he wanted, what he needed. The dream that had kept him alive in Bitche was not gone, only now it wore its true colors. The dream was a woman who would love and stand by him. It did not matter if she had blond tresses and blue eyes—or dark curls and silver eyes.

Yet he did not feel ready to face the emotions churning within him. They had come too fast, too soon. He felt overwhelmed. And frightened. If he allowed himself to care for Emily, there would be no getting over her as he had recovered from the loss of Letty.

He had no reason to think she would look on him with any favor, either. If his fool of a cousin had not angered and disappointed her, she might never have come to help him so eagerly. It was her sense of justice to which he had appealed, not her heart.

In spite of himself, Tony continued to look for her as if compelled. His opera glasses found at last the object of his search. She was seated again with the Castlereaghs. Dressed in white, she looked very elegant, very lovely, this evening. Something was missing, however. This morning when he had seen her with the children she had been glorious, so vibrant and alive with her shining hair falling about her ears, that it had been all he could do to keep his hands at his side and not reach out to touch those tangled curls, her flushed cheeks.

Her cheeks were a little pale now, he thought, still wishing he could brush his fingers across them—a foolish wish. Emily had obviously thought him terribly forward when he had managed to touch her fingertips.

Someone else dared to touch her, however, he noticed. A gentleman behind her leaned forward to whisper in her ear. To get her attention he first placed his fingers on her shoulder, above the low collar of her gown. And she did not even look surprised or remonstrate with the boor!

The fact that her answering smile was no more than polite consoled Tony not at all. Another look told him who the pushy fellow was.

Tony felt suddenly cold. All along he had felt there was something between young Edward and Emily, something more than the long friendship between his family and Letty's. Let Gus laugh if he would.

Yet Gus was correct in this much. He did not think she loved the boy, not as she was capable of loving someone. Although clearly she must care enough to be hurt by him.

Tony forced himself to look away. What if Emily caught him staring at her like a— He cut off the thought before he could complete it.

It was all very well to play games with semantics, Tony realized. He could deny the word, refuse to say it, even to himself. How long, however, could he deny the feeling that drew him here, to Emily?

Emily left the theater disappointed with the results of her day. She had had high hopes of the pensioners' hospitals. Surely among the retired and injured soldiers and sailors she thought she would find someone who had known Tony in France.

She should have realized that the pensioners would not be gentlemen recently returned from the Continent. If there were any such, she certainly did not see them. No, instead there were men who had seen service in the Americas, against the French and then against the colonials themselves, and even a few who talked about the forty-five as if it were yesterday. At another time she would have been fascinated by their stories, the beauties of the palaces and their history. Now all that mattered was there was no one here to talk about Tony.

The day had still been young then, and she hoped for better opportunities later. At the theater, however, Edward had stopped by to chat. Evidently John's lecture had had some effect. Typically Edward had chosen to interrupt the Act III ballet, to which Emily had been looking forward, for his appearance. If he had hoped to appease her this way, he failed miserably. It did not go unnoticed by Emily that Edward chose to approach her at a time when they could not possibly enjoy any private conversation. He had nothing to say after all; he merely wished to be seen.

Now they were off to Lady Cholmondeley's ball, and Emily's

spirits began to rise again. Even if she were unable to find any-one with memories of Tony, Emily told herself, she might at least gain more insight into his background.

Good fortune seemed to be smiling on her at last when she was able to catch a few moments with Lord Yarmouth. The tsar had snubbed his mother, Lady Hertford, again, so His Lordship was in a mood to talk and to complain. His com-plaints could hardly be taken seriously, though, when Emily realized that after two years he had been given leave to reside near Paris and after another year was released to go home. She understood better now what Tony had turned his back on in Verdun and how difficult it must have been for an active boy of eighteen to forswear races, balls, and clubs.

One more thing Emily learned. Lord Yarmouth had agreed to speak before the panel that would sit to decide if Tony was speaking the truth, and Lord Yarmouth did not believe Tony. By his reasoning, Tony could easily have obtained terms for release even as he had. The fact that Lady Yarmouth's relation-ship with Minister Junot, whispers of which had reached Lon-don, might have influenced the ease of his departure evidently did not occur to him. He would never understand the choices Tony had made.

It was to be hoped that others would understand, or Tony's case might indeed be desperate. Luckily, Emily was encouraged by meeting some of the men who had seen another side of cap-tivity, another side of the war. Captain von Hottendorf intro-duced her to them—British navy men, Austrian soldiers, men who had shared unimaginable conditions and survived. Some of them were little older than Emily herself. They must have been mere babes when they were captured, she realized with horror.

Tony's friend obviously wanted her to understand. That was why he had arranged for her to hear this. She was glad of it, but she wondered if there was more to be understood here than what had turned Tony into the man she knew. And if the cap-tain wondered about it as well.

The more Emily heard, the less sense she could see in the way the French had treated Tony. Wouldn't an English noble-man be more likely to be moved up to better quarters? Yet Tony had been left in conditions worse than those endured by common sailors. The governor at Verdun might have carried a grudge against Tony, but he had no power at Bitche. That she could not understand. She had to learn more.

The two boys had not really wanted to sully her ears with a description of conditions in the prison, but Emily's interest and sympathy worked their usual charm. Between them and the captain, she was able to put together a fairly clear picture, and it was not nice. The ugly thoughts kept her awake later that night, when she was at last able to seek her bed. She kept remembering what they had said. What they had not said.

According to the fair-haired gentleman, Bitche was not the worst punishment prison, but Emily failed to see how. A governor who hated the English beyond reason, aided by a treasonous prisoner, did not improve conditions already bleak.

In none of their information, however, could Emily find a reason for what had happened to Tony. It was all out of character, even for men as evil as his French gaolers appeared to be. They had not even tried to get money out of him once he was sent to the punishment prison, according to Tony.

There had to be an explanation.

Yet Tony, when she met him again the next morning, seemed as unwilling to consider her questions as he was to indulge in any self-pity.

When he first saw her and the twins, he had looked particularly pleased. There was a chill breeze today rustling through the treetops, although it was sunny enough, and Emily wondered if he had feared, as she had, that the twins would be kept inside. Soon, however, he became stiff and self-conscious, holding himself aloof, and using the twins as a sort of protective shield. From what? she wondered. Were her questions so intrusive? Only when the captain's experiences were under discussion, rather than his, did he appear willing to talk.

"We were the lucky ones," Tony insisted, kneeling on the ground to see what Connor was pointing out to him. "The English were treated far better than the other prisoners of war. We may have been given army discards for blankets, but at least we had them. The Prussians were stripped of everything and then treated like slaves, made to work in labor gangs. Gus doesn't talk about it much," he said, "but he had a rough time of it."

There was that strange intent look again. Every once in a while Tony would look at her as if she were a specimen for analysis, Emily thought. As if he were trying to gauge her reaction and measure it against some unknown internal standard.

Annoyed, she stared back at him. This seemed to disconcert him, and he returned his attention to Connor.

Suddenly it occurred to Emily. Did he think she was interested in the captain? Good heavens, what could have given him such a bizarre idea? Surely not the captain himself. He liked to tease, Emily thought, but he was too kind to pick such a tender subject for the object of his mirth.

"Captain von Hottendorf was a military man and knew what risks he ran," Emily reminded him. "You were a civilian and you were imprisoned far longer than he."

Tony stood up. The barking of Lady Connaught's dog had caught the attention of his little companion. "I've been deserted," he complained as Connor ran off to join Nancy and his twin sister.

Yes, and now he had no one to hide behind.

"You cannot expect your charms to compete with Sheamus," Emily teased, but then tried to return to the subject. "Tony, I've been thinking about your imprisonment, and it seems to me—"

"No." He held up his hand to stop her. "Please, no. I don't want to talk about France anymore."

He seemed to realize how brusquely he had spoken, and apologized. "Forgive me, but I don't see what is to be gained by going over old ground again. I am not looking for any pity."

Emily opened her mouth to deny his allegation, but he cut her off.

"You told me once that I did not need to prove my case to you. Was that a lie?" he asked. The question was blunt, but the look in his dark eyes told her it was important.

Is that what he thought? That her questions were designed to prove to herself whether or not he was telling the truth? A moment's pause told her that he had reason for his doubt. She had never found the courage to tell him before, but she had to say it now.

"I do not pity you, Tony," she said, quietly but firmly. "I would not insult you with such condescending reaction. If it seemed that I did not trust you, with all my heart, I beg your pardon. I do not need your evidence or anyone else's to prove to me who or what you are."

He turned to face her, his expression half hopeful, half fearful.

She meant exactly what she said. What she put her faith in was not merely Tony's identity as marquess of Palin but his identity as an honorable man. She hoped he would realize that.

"Thank you," he said in a low voice while reaching for her hand. It seemed he, too, was having difficulty finding the right word. Where words failed, however, his eyes and the pressure of his hand were eloquent. After a moment he added quietly, "That means a great deal to me."

The giggling of the twins and the flirting nursemaid seemed very far away right now. Was it her imagination, Emily wondered, or did the wind suddenly still? Emily was intensely aware, as she had been before at Richmond, of being alone with this man. He was standing very close. In the bright early morning sunlight she could see clearly the small lines around his beautiful eyes. The look he gave her, full of warmth and gratitude, and something else she could not name, made her a little ill at ease.

She took a step backward. "I suppose I ought to call you Lord Palin now." That would be difficult for her, not only because Palin had always meant Edward in the past, but because she had always, from the first moment Letty told her about him, thought of him as Tony.

"It does not sound very friendly to change from Tony to Lord Palin," he pointed out. "I would feel as if I had offended you every time you spoke it."

Emily knew what he meant. Whenever her nanny had scolded her, she had always used her full complement of names. To continue to address him so informally, however, no longer seemed so proper. Something in their relationship had shifted in the last few minutes, although Emily could not have said what or how.

Tony still had not released her hand. Now he tucked her arm in his and led her gently through the park.

"Of course," he continued, "it does sound odd if you call me Tony and I address you formally." He looked at her out of the corner of his eye as if to gauge her reaction. The hint of a smile played about his mouth. "Especially as it is so confusing with two Miss Meritons present." He nodded toward Katy, who stood some distance away, entranced by the poodle's antics. "The younger Miss Meriton insists upon exclusive right to the title, you know."

"I know," Emily said, fighting the desire to laugh. Oddly enough, she felt a little reluctant in granting Tony the freedom of her name. It was not that she was truly concerned about the proprieties. She had never been the type of person who insisted on proper address or all the rights and dignities of her position. Yet somehow she could not help but feel that in dropping that one little barrier, she would leave herself too vulnerable.

Tony was waiting for her answer. His dark eyes looked a little apprehensive. "Friends?" he asked.

Somehow Emily was sure that was not at all what he had meant to say. By chance or shrewdness, however, he had hit upon the one plea she could not deny.

After all, there could be but one answer. "My friends call me Emily," she said.

It did not seem to Emily that her daily routine was very different than usual in the days that followed. Her evenings, and sometimes her days, were spent at the various festivities held in honor of the Allied Sovereigns—balls and dinners at Lady Jersey's, Lord Liverpool's, and Lord Hertford's; military reviews; and visits to the great sights of London. Her mornings were spent with the twins, and, of course, with Tony.

The major difference was that Letty still remained incommunicado in her room. The truth, however, was that Emily did not have time to miss her. Only when she was with Tony did Emily find her annoyance with her sister-in-law flared up. At those times she was indeed reminded what Letty's behavior meant to Tony, to his case, and to his heart.

Yet she could sense a difference, if not in her routine, then in the way she approached it. The social round became easier for her. She laughed more often. She even sang.

It was not that she completely forgot her own problems. That would be impossible while Edward continued to claim a single duty dance at every event they attended (opposition entertainments excepted, of course).

Most of the time, however, she was simply too busy to worry about Edward. Or Letty. She was finally beginning to feel a sense of accomplishment in her efforts to help Tony.

A pious chaperon had helped Emily find the clergyman who ran the relief fund at Verdun. In expressing appreciation to the musicians at one ball, she had discovered word of a young pianist who had been imprisoned with Tony. Through the servants' grapevine, as transmitted by Nancy, she had discovered further leads to former friends and acquaintances.

Surely this encouraging news was why she felt so happy. Considering her problems with Edward and Letty, she was surprised to realize she was happy. Others seemed to notice a difference, too. Never had she received so many compliments on her looks. Even John, who had been particularly abstracted lately, said she glowed.

Georgy said it, too, but Georgy seemed to find this cause for suspicion. She came to visit Emily and poked about the contents of her room as if she expected to find love letters tucked carelessly not quite out of sight.

"Oh, this is nice." Georgy picked up a bottle of scent and dabbed a little behind her ears. "What is it called?"

"I don't remember. It was a present from Letty for my last birthday. What are you doing, Georgy?" Emily watched her friend pick her way through her small assortment of lotions and cosmetic aids.

"Nothing," Georgy insisted innocently. "I saw your friend the captain last night." She had moved toward the secretary, but clearly didn't dare go so far as to snoop within.

"Yes, I know. I was with you, if you remember," Emily told her with elaborate patience.

"Oh, yes, so you were. He seems a very nice gentleman. I quite like him."

Obviously her friend was hinting her way toward something, but what? "I like him, too," Emily admitted. "If you are asking if I have some previous claim that would preclude your setting your cap for him, however, I would simply offer you my best wishes for success."

"That's what I thought." Georgy joined her on the chaise lounge, plopping herself down with a determined flounce. "Who is it, then?"

"Who is what? I don't understand."

"My dear, you may be able to fool your amiable brother, but you can't fool me. There's only one reason I can think of that would make you look like an illumination for the victory celebrations." She looked Emily in the eye. "And that's a man."

Only Georgy could come up with such a ridiculous notion. Emily opened her mouth to deny the charge, but Georgy held up her hand. She wasn't finished.

"Now, I've watched you dance and talk to half of London this last week, and I'll swear that it's none of them. I had high hopes of the captain. There's a twinkle in his eye that I knew you would appreciate, but he's not the one, either. Since I know perfectly well how you spend your evenings, this leaves me with the unpleasant conclusion that you, Miss Emily Meriton, have been meeting some man on the sly."

This, on the other hand, was far too close to the truth. Emily would not have minded so much confiding in Georgy about Tony, but if her friend were to fall into the idiocy of thinking her friendship with Tony was more than . . . well, than friendship, then there would simply be no bearing it.

"Really, Georgy, can you picture *me* doing anything so shocking? You have windmills in your head, my dear." Emily was afraid her voice sounded less than convincing. Her friend's suggestion troubled her more than it should.

"You can't deceive me, Emily Meriton. And you can't put me off, either. I, of all your friends, should know that you are not so easily shocked."

"I wouldn't have thought you could be so easily shocked,

either. If I were conducting a clandestine relationship, I would expect you to cheer me on."

"No, Emily, no," Georgy said, completely serious. "You don't know how to do it, and so you can only get hurt. That sort of thing is only for those who know how to play the game, and you don't play at all. You're the sort of idealistic fool who believes in things like True Love, and that makes you easy prey. You're too serious, and the fellows who ask for that kind of meeting aren't serious at all, unless it's about money."

"Which I haven't got. Truly, Georgy, you have got this all wrong." Silly as Georgy's supposition was, the girl was honestly concerned. Emily longed to be able to banish those worries, but how? Now that Georgy had this foolish idea in her head, she would never understand about Tony. Perhaps she should tell her about Edward? No, she was not ready to do that.

She was not ready to do it, because then she would be reminded that the engagement was a *fait accompli.* She didn't want to admit to herself that she no longer wanted to marry Edward. And she certainly didn't want to examine her reasons for no longer wanting it.

Besides, Georgy would know perfectly well Emily could never love Edward in that joyous, open-hearted fashion. Betrothal to Edward would be all the more reason to seek some sort of escape, in Georgy's mind.

Emily sighed and spoke earnestly to her friend. "Georgy, will you believe me if I promise you on my word of honor that I have not entered into a romantic intrigue? Credit me at least with a little sense."

"As if sense had anything to do with such a foolish emotion as love."

Emily endured her friend's piercing examination and hoped her sincerity would work some influence, but Georgy only shook her head.

"My poor Emily. You really believe it." Georgy looked at her with pitying eyes.

Annoyed now, Emily answered with unaccustomed sharpness. "Clearly there is nothing I can say that will make you believe me. Did it ever occur to you, Georgy, that your suspicions are based on your own standards of conduct rather than mine?"

To compound her offense, Georgy now began to laugh helplessly. Conversation deteriorated from that point, and the friends parted with an unusual lack of mutual sympathy. Emily didn't even escort her to the door.

She regretted it almost immediately. It wasn't like her to be so sensitive, certainly not like her to be so rude. Georgy's notion was simply laughable.

Why had she not been able to laugh?

There was nothing romantic about her daily meetings with Tony. Oh, to be sure, Tony must seem a romantic figure, tall, handsome, and with a touch of danger. The setting itself was lovely, too. This last week the weather had been especially beautiful, making the little park blossom. It was the perfect place for young lovers to meet.

There was nothing romantic, however, about meeting a man who was in love with another woman.

This thought brought a terrible ache to her heart. Georgy probably would have made something of that, too, but it was only that she couldn't bear to think of Tony hurt like that.

She had been feeling so happy before, and now she was almost blue-deviled. What she needed was to spend some time with the twins in the nursery. That would cheer her up again.

Before she reached her chamber door, however, Emily realized that some terrible commotion was taking place outside in the hall. For a moment she almost thought she heard Georgy's voice in the melee, although she knew very well her friend had left quite half an hour ago. By the time she stuck her head out the door, there was a flurry of steps running down the stairs and a footman ran past her muttering to himself.

Emily followed the noise down the hall and realized suddenly not only where the noise was coming from, but why.

Letty was up and moving.

Chapter Eight

ODDLY ENOUGH, EMILY felt a little reluctant to face her sister-in-law, after waiting so eagerly and impatiently for her to emerge from self-imposed isolation. Curiosity overwhelmed reluctance, however, and she gingerly approached the center of the maelstrom.

This then was the result of leaving Letty to fuss and worry all by herself. She had evidently worked herself up into a fine state of hysteria. But what could have set her off? Emily had thought she was sneaking another visit to the nursery.

The first whiff of danger hit her as she reached Letty's bedroom door.

Nancy was there, apologizing incoherently to Letty, but Letty would hear none of it. She drew herself up in a dignified pose, somewhat spoiled by the effects of uninhibited emotional display, and pointed to the door.

Despite the girl's tears, Emily felt reasonably sure that she had not been given her walking papers. No matter how angry or annoyed Letty got, she never had been able to fire any of the servants. Emily was concerned for Nancy, however. She would hate to have the girl get into trouble on her account.

In making her hurried exit, Nancy failed to see Emily, but Letty didn't. Her accusing finger pointed now straight at Emily.

"Emily Meriton, I am ashamed of you," Letty said in ringing

tones. She had always had a flair for the dramatic. "What have you done?"

The question was, what did Letty really know about what she had done? It would, of course, be necessary to exonerate the nurserymaid, but what more did she need to say? John had forbidden her to pester Letty about Tony. More to the point, Emily still did not know how Letty would react to word of him.

It was virtually impossible to make any guesses from Letty's present appearance as to what she might do. At the moment she looked quite mad. Her hair was tangled and falling about her shoulders, and her dress was in considerable disarray. There was a hectic flush on her cheeks. Would she return to her bed again? Refuse to speak of him? Had Letty truly returned to her senses, or had she merely put aside her inexplicable terror for the moment?

Emily could not tell, and until she could she intended to keep Tony's place in her misadventures secret.

"I don't understand, Letty. What am I supposed to have done?" she asked with a spurious air of innocence.

"You know perfectly well what I'm talking about, miss," Letty said, shaking her finger at Emily. "Don't think I can be fooled by tarradiddles like that silly girl from the nursery."

Georgy! Emily thought she had imagined hearing her friend's voice only minutes ago. She must have run straight to Letty and opened her budget about all her suspicions.

As far as Emily knew, however, those suspicions did not include a name, and Nancy had never known one.

"I do not know what you are talking about," she insisted to Letty with an air of offended virtue. "And if you are accusing me of being indiscreet in some manner, Letty, I would like to mention that you are not setting an example for discretion in your manner of going about it."

Letty suddenly became aware of how loudly she had been speaking. Putting her hands to her trembling mouth, she appeared as if she were about to weep.

Her cry of "Oh, Emily!" did much to erase the barriers of the last few weeks. Emily was on the verge of trying to comfort her old friend and find out what was wrong when Letty walked up to Emily and examined her face carefully.

The guilt Emily felt over keeping secret so much was clearly apparent. "So it's true," Letty said, to Emily's dismay. "And to think that I had to be told about this by someone else, someone outside the family!"

Letty would have to be told now, Emily realized, if only in order to rid her of whatever ridiculous fancies Georgy had evidently supplied. Resigned, Emily took her firmly by the shoulder and sat her down on the chaise longue. "Letty, I honestly do not know what you think you know," she said, searching for Letty's hartshorn. "I doubt very much whether it comes close to the truth, but I will explain what I have been doing, if you will only listen."

Instead of calming Letty, however, this provoked another storm.

"It's my fault, I know it," she proclaimed, emulating Mrs. Siddons once again and pushing aside the proffered hartshorn. "What kind of chaperon am I to let you go about unsupervised like that? Keeping assignations with bounders!"

The fact that Letty had never felt the slightest need to exert any control over Emily's actions was ignored for the present. Emily's attempt to introduce some logic or reason into the conversation was doomed to failure. Not a word could she get in edgewise.

The lament continued with a long list of *if only*s as Letty proceeded to rifle her wardrobe for apparel better suited for public occasions. If only Letty had kept an eye on her, if only Letty had left her door open for confidences, if only she hadn't been such a silly peagoose . . . "You'll be ruined," Letty wailed, "and John will blame me. And he'll be right!"

"I will not be ruined," Emily insisted, finally making herself heard.

"You will, you will," Letty answered, her voice choked with tears. She had pulled from the wardrobe a severe black gown that dated from the death of her great-aunt. It was the only dress she owned that made her look less than frivolous. Letty hated it and said she felt like a governess when she wore it.

"Letty," Emily pleaded once more for attention.

"Ruined!" As Letty whispered the word again to herself, her tears dried as if by magic. Something new had occurred to her.

"Of course, you can never marry Edward now. Even if he were willing to continue with the engagement, which I very much doubt, you would certainly have too much conscience to ruin his prospects."

The sudden flare of hope this raised in Emily's own breast frightened her. It certainly was a way out, if she wished for one. Proud as he was, Edward would not calmly accept the betrayal he would see in her behavior. If she let him know she had been helping Tony, Edward would end the engagement. She could be free—if only she were willing to cause her old friend such deep anguish.

Emily opened her mouth to protest again, but the words never came. Before she could even take a breath, a new and cataclysmic force entered the room.

"Nanny!" Letty cried. Her face went pale.

This was not the twins' nanny, Mrs. Churm, but Letty's old nanny, a woman who knew no name but her title, ancient and feared by every member of the household. Nanny had retired, nominally, many years ago. Whenever Letty was home or was ill, however, Nanny returned to take care of her charge—and none dared oppose her. John confessed himself terrified of the old woman and claimed, when he knew he could not be overheard, that she was a witch.

"Well." On Nanny's tongue it was an accusation. "Don't call for your old nurse that knows what's best for you when you be ill. Oh, no, don't do that. Let me hear it from housekeeper instead."

"But I'm not ill, Nanny. See?" As soon as she said it, Letty seemed to realize that her appearance at that moment was not like to engender confidence in her health.

"Breeding?" Nanny asked. "You don't look it to me, but that's what they say."

"No!" Evidently it had not occurred to Letty before what her supposed illness would most likely be attributed to by the general population.

"Why not?" Nanny glared at her charge for a moment.

Despite the tension of a moment ago, Emily could not help but be amused by the change in Letty's attitude. A muffled giggle on her part brought the tyrant's attention to her.

"Out," she ordered simply. Nanny was known to hold strong views on what subjects were deemed improper for the ears of young unmarried females.

Emily slipped quickly out of the room. Even without Nanny's command, she would have gone. Obviously, there would be no explaining to Letty for some little time.

But only for a little time. For Tony's sake, she had better make this explanation good.

Sitting at his usual place by the window, Tony had a few minutes' warning before the messenger arrived at his door. He recognized the livery at once, of course. He had particularly noticed the fine gold buttons on the uniform of the large footman who he had been told, would throw him bodily from the establishment.

Emily? Somehow Tony was sure Emily would find a more discreet way to contact him, assuming the matter was too important to wait until the next morning. Unless she had confided in Letty and gained her support at long last.

He counted the steps up the stairs until he finally heard the knock on his door. "Enter," he bade the man.

Despite the increased beat of his heart, Tony accepted the note coolly enough. "Are you supposed to wait for a reply?"

"Yes, sir." The footman planted himself firmly before the door. The importance of the response had evidently been made clear to him.

Tony walked over to the window and turned his face away from the observant eyes. The message was simple and blunt. "I must speak with you. Come at once." There was no signature, but he would have known Letty's hand anywhere.

There was no salutation, either. Perhaps Letty had not recognized him immediately. Perhaps she feared to meet an impostor.

But meet him she would, and within the half-hour.

Oddly, now that he was finally about to face Letty, Tony felt some misgivings. His early joyous assurance that all would be the same between them had been smashed. Only Emily's loyalty and affection for Letty gave proof that Letty had not changed past all recognition.

The question of why she should finally choose to meet him now, after so many days of hiding from him and from news of him, tickled at Tony's brain all during the short ride to the house on Grosvenor Square. If Emily had been behind Letty's action, he was sure there would have been some sign from her.

Emily had told him she thought her sister-in-law was becoming bored with her seclusion. She might simply have come to her senses. If it had been his appearance that had brought about her retreat from the world, the tension of waiting to see what would happen with his claim might have driven her at last to action.

Or she might have heard something.

In any case, he would know soon enough. The carriage stopped before the door. Remembering the last time he had approached that entrance, Tony smiled. He would have liked to stare down that arrogant butler, but the door was opened instead by a young maid.

The house seemed eerily quiet and tense. Both of the servants Tony had seen looked at him with nervous eyes, as if they expected him to turn violent any moment. There should have been more servants moving about at this hour, he realized. Letty must have ordered them to stay away until his interview was finished.

It was with some trepidation then that Tony entered the formal drawing room. Letty was sitting, her back stiff as a board, on a small spindly Queen Anne chair. Her beautiful gold hair had been pulled back into an unbecoming knot and she was dressed for a funeral. As she caught sight of him, however, her stiffness seemed to melt, and once again he saw his childhood friend playing at dress-up.

"Tony?" she said first, a little breathlessly. Her eyes squinted a little. She stood, took one step. "Tony. It is you. Oh, my dear, whatever must you think of me?" She rushed forward and took his hands in hers.

At her words the tension drained out of Tony's body as well. He smiled. "I think you are a silly goose. But then, I always did."

"So you did," she whispered, almost to herself.

"A beautiful and beloved peagoose," he reminded her, his

mind full of memories. Letty as a lovely and gullible child, hanging on his every word. Letty as a girl, even more lovely and still accepting every tall tale as truth.

"I would be afraid to ask what you see now." Letty lowered her eyes.

The habit of cheering Letty when she was low had not disappeared, Tony found. He used one hand to nudge her chin up. "I see a beautiful young hoyden . . . who has evidently convinced London society that she is a respectable matron. You look the same to me as you did when I last saw you."

That wasn't quite the truth. Time had changed the eager girl into a mature woman. Letty, like Tony himself, had changed into a very different person, but despite all changes, their old friendship remained undiminished.

"Liar," she called him. "Gallant, but nevertheless a liar. I know what the years have done to me."

"They seem to have agreed with you."

"Yes," Letty admitted. "But they haven't left me unchanged."

"Well, perhaps not," Tony said. "The years have left their mark on me, too."

He had not meant that reference as an accusation, but Letty's blush indicated she read it as such. With trembling fingers she reached up to caress the small scar on his cheek.

"And not so kindly. But I should have known you. If I had dared look at you properly, I would have. It was the voice I doubted. You sounded so cold, Tony. So threatening. It frightened me. But I am ashamed, so ashamed, that I did not come forward earlier. Come." She pulled him over to the sofa. "Sit here with me and tell me everything."

"Everything?" Tony laughed. "That would take quite some time. We've twelve years to fill in."

"Yes. You know I'm married," she said, all in a rush.

"I know. And very happy. I had been told so before, but now I can see it."

Letty looked at him earnestly, trying so hard to make him understand what he had already faced some time ago, did she but know. "John's a good man, Tony. Quiet and steady. That may not sound very romantic, but he's not just good to me, he's good for me. I love him very much."

"I understand," Tony said, smiling. "Letty, you don't have to make any apologies to me. I'm happy for you."

"Truly?"

"Truly." It would hardly be flattering to tell Letty how quickly his own affections had changed. Instead he asked, "Is this why you have been hiding in your room? Some foolish sense of guilt for not having waited for me?"

Letty bit at a fingernail. "Maybe a little. I felt as if I'd let you down again, and I didn't want to have to face you with that on my conscience. Part of me was afraid to find out that it wasn't you, too. I didn't want to have to grieve for you all over again if you were proved to have died."

"Letty—"

She would not let him continue. "No, let me admit the worst."

"And what is the worst?"

"I was afraid, too, that it was you because then I would have to come forward to help you. You see, I never told John."

Tony did not need to ask what it was she had not told her husband. "Letty, you cannot think that I would bring that up."

"I've thought and I've thought, Tony, and the one thing we know that will absolutely prove your identity is . . . you know."

"It doesn't matter. My identity can certainly be proved without doing any such thing. I'm shocked you could even think I would consider it." He gave her shoulder a playful little shake.

Letty did not look particularly relieved. "You're a fool if you don't." She sighed. "I shall have to tell John anyway, I think. If he's angry with me, I don't know how I shall bear it."

Tony paused for a moment. Comforting anxious wives was not an area in which he had much expertise. Who would ever have guessed he would have to attempt it with Letty? "There, there, Letty. If he loves you half as much as you say, I'm sure he will understand. It was, after all, a very long time ago."

"I let you down then, too, didn't I?" Letty said.

Tony thought back on all the anger he had wasted, blaming Letty for failing him. How fortunate it seemed now that she had done so. He shrugged. "Maybe this is the way it was meant to be. You and John."

"And my babies. You know I have twins?"

"Yes, I know. . . ."

With dizzying swiftness, Letty changed from morose self-condemnation to accusation. "Yes, indeed, you know. And how do you know? What have you been up to? Luring my dear sister-in-law into your clutches. . . ."

So she had found out. "My clutches? Really, Letty. Isn't that going a bit too far?"

Letty ignored him. "And using my innocent babies to cover up your clandestine meetings."

She didn't sound really angry, or distrustful. Presumably she knew Emily at least, if not him, too well to assume that anything of an improper nature had occurred between them. Until she knew it was he, the real Tony, who was meeting Emily, however, she must have worried about his intentions. The reason for her bizarre costume now became clear.

"So that's why you're rigged up like this! Just the thing to intimidate a scoundrel trying to make trouble for your family, hmmm?"

"Well, you might have been an impostor. I couldn't know. And what I was told was certainly enough to cause alarm. . . ." Her voice faded out, the sentence unfinished. Whatever she had been told evidently still troubled her.

"Then what you heard must have been grossly exaggerated," Tony assured her. "Your sister-in-law"—he dared not trust himself to say Emily's name aloud—"agreed in the interests of justice to assist me in my case. That's all." Letty's piercing gaze was beginning to make him nervous. "I hope Miss Meriton will not be chastised for her simple act of kindness."

"Kindness, is it? And what prompted you to seek her out?"

The obvious answer would be to say that it was because she was close to Letty, but oddly enough Tony didn't even think of that. Looking back to that evening when he had first glimpsed her, it seemed to him Letty had really had very little to do with his decision. It was Emily herself who had drawn his eyes. He would have noticed her even had she not been standing next to Letty and wearing his opal pin. Even if she had had no connection to Letty at all, he would still have called upon her for help, because she was the only person different enough from the rest of society to listen to him.

In the end it was only Emily's special talent that he would admit to. "She listens," he said, "to everyone."

"So she does," Letty agreed, but for some reason she sounded disappointed by his response. "I should have known that's all it would be. I certainly should have known that silly girl Georgy Parkhurst had to be mistaken."

"Miss Parkhurst?" Tony said the name with a sense of unease. "What has she to do with Miss Meriton?"

"You've obviously heard of her. I shouldn't be surprised. She manages to be the subject of far too much gossip, but she's a good girl for all that. Today she succeeded in tracking me down when I was visiting the twins and frightening me with a tale about Emily having fallen for some unscrupulous ne'er-do-well. Meaning you," Letty clarified with a laugh.

Tony laughed, too, but he was not amused. It did not seem to him, in their brief meeting, that Miss Parkhurst was a fool. What had made the girl suspect Emily? More important, what made her suspect that Emily was in love?

Oh, don't be a fool, he told himself. Romance was exactly what Miss Parkhurst would suspect, whether she had reason to or no. There was no cause for fear. Or for hope.

"She certainly roused you to action," Tony pointed out.

"And deserves thanks for that? Well, perhaps she does after all," Letty admitted. She still looked troubled, however.

"What is it, Letty? Do you still suspect me of luring your sister-in-law to ruin?" he teased.

"Oh, no," she answered with unflattering confidence. "I know you both too well for that. Isn't it terrible, though? After I got over the first shock, I almost hoped it was true."

"Letty!"

"Not really, of course. I only wanted to break off that awful engagement of hers."

As soon as the words were out of her mouth, Letty seemed to realize she had said too much. She clamped her hand over her mouth, but it was too late. The words were already out.

They cut straight to Tony's heart. "Engagement?" He got

up and walked to the window so Letty could not see his face, walked casually so she would think his question only polite curiosity. Why had Emily not told him? he demanded helplessly of himself. She should have told him.

"Please don't let anyone know I told you," Letty begged. "It is supposed to be a secret."

To Tony's amazement his reflection in the window showed no emotion at all, none at all. Perhaps it was safe to turn around.

"A secret engagement? Really, Letty, you surprise me."

"I suppose it does sound odd when you put it like that," Letty confessed, pulling at the lace of her handkerchief. "Until you reappeared it looked like a brilliant match."

"Until I reappeared." He knew then; somehow he had always known.

"I don't see why you should not be told. After all, it is your family." Letty leaned forward to explain. Obviously Letty had been dying to confide in someone. Her recent seclusion had no doubt only exacerbated the desire. Letty had always been garrulous. This time her words fell coldly on his ears, freezing what small hopes he had allowed himself.

"Ah, I see, she is betrothed to my cousin Edward," he said, as if he had only then reasoned it out.

"Exactly. You see the difficulty, Tony. It was supposed to be announced at his coming-of-age party, but, as you know, there was a rather spectacular disturbance." Her eyes twinkled at him with a merriment he could not share, although he managed some semblance of a smile.

"So I put a spoke in his wheel?" But not soon enough, he thought.

"Edward asked us to keep it quiet for the nonce. To tell the truth, I thought he was trying to hedge his bets, but as it turns out, he was right. How embarrassing to have Emily announce her betrothal to the marquess of Palin when he's not."

For the moment Tony ignored the queer feeling he had when Letty talked about Emily marrying the marquess of Palin. "You don't approve of Edward," he said, wishing he knew more much about his cousin. All he knew was that Edward was political. And that he had disappointed Emily.

"No, I do not." Letty sighed. "If she loved him, that would be another matter, but she does not."

Hope flared briefly at her words. Emily did not love Edward. The realization that it did not matter swiftly followed, however. Emily had given her pledge.

"I don't suppose you could refuse consent now that his circumstances are so changed?" he suggested without hope. Those changed circumstances would be the very thing to engage Emily's sympathies. She would never desert a friend in need.

Letty giggled. "You have not met my John yet, or you would not suggest such a thing. It seems I shall have to pray for another miracle. After all," she said, rising to embrace him, "my best friend has returned from the dead after twelve years. Anything is possible!"

Tony returned Letty's affectionate hug, but his spirits were not lifted. His title and fortune might now be assured, but all he could see was a long lonely life without Emily.

Emily couldn't seem to concentrate on anything. The prospect of the threatened interview with Letty weighed on her mind. A few times she headed for Letty's door, intending to get it over with, but each time something turned her aside. This time she did not mean to be diverted. Now, however, Letty's room was empty and the frightened maid who was clearing away the residue from Letty's explosion this morning, broken china and clothes everywhere, could only shake her head and point downstairs.

Another servant, standing at the top of the stairs, tried to prevent Emily from seeking Letty out, but she would have none of that. It was only when she was but a few steps away from the open door to the drawing room and heard a masculine voice that she was given a moment's pause. John she knew to be at his club. In another moment she recognized the familiar accents.

Tony was here. So Letty had agreed to see him at last. The voices were quiet, Letty's comforting, Tony's a little sad.

Should she join them? Emily wondered. It would certainly make the explanations easier if Tony were there with her. Letty would be less likely to tease Emily too badly in front of an audience, too. At the very least any strange misconceptions Letty entertained regarding their meetings should now be nullified.

Emily took a hesitant step forward, unwilling to interrupt them if the conversation was too private. Their reunion might very well be emotional after so long a parting. Maybe if she took a peek first.

Emily was prepared for tears, but not for this. At the edge of the doorway she could see them as they moved to embrace.

A terrible ache in the area of her heart held her immobile for a long minute. In that minute the picture before her seared itself into her memory in terrible detail. Tony's long fingers on Letty's golden hair, the stiffness of his posture, and, worst of all, the terrible blankness of his expression. When she could breathe again, Emily clutched her skirts in her trembling hands and ran, as quickly as she could, away from the scene and back to the comparative safety of her own bedchamber.

No place was safe now, however, not from her own thoughts. The powerful feelings generated by seeing Tony with his arms around Letty astonished Emily and brought painful revelation. Georgy had been right after all. She loved Tony.

What a fool she had been not to see it, not to know why she rushed so eagerly to meet him every morning! Instead, it had taken the sight of him embracing the woman he loved before she could understand why she had been so angry with Letty. So jealous.

No wonder she had been reluctant to confide in Letty. While Letty remained hidden away, Tony had belonged to her. Much as Emily wanted Tony to receive the recognition he deserved, she had dreaded in her heart the loss of their special private world. There would be no reason now for secret meetings.

And Letty didn't even love him, didn't want him! Emily was not so foolish as to see their embrace as one of lovers reunited. Well, perhaps she had, for a moment. It was not merely reason and memory that told her otherwise, however. Emily had seen her brother and sister-in-law embrace. Even their most casual expressions of affection were not so passionless as this. The way Letty had patted his back was the same way in which she soothed the twins when they were upset.

Tony's expression, however, caught in the hallway mirror,

had tortured her. Its very emptiness spoke of intolerable pain. It was the expression of a man who was saying good-bye to love.

She might as well do the same. She never had been able to compete with Letty; she could certainly not compete with a love that had endured twelve years of separation.

He mustn't ever know. That would be too terribly embarrassing. It didn't help that Tony seemed to be extraordinarily perceptive where she was concerned. Nor would it help that once Tony regained his position he would be a close neighbor. And Edward's cousin.

For the last few weeks Emily had been avoiding that one simple conclusion. She could not marry Edward, not now. It wasn't only that Edward had proved himself to be such a different person than she had believed. When she had accepted his offer her heart had been whole, if not his. Regardless of their present differences, Emily would not serve him so ill a trick as to marry him while she loved another, and that other his own cousin.

Yet how could she end the engagement without hurting Edward deeply? Their long years of friendship demanded that she assuage his pain as best she could. Hurt there would be, although not the pain of love rejected. Edward's pride would be injured enough with the reduction of his circumstances. Could she then tell him she had not only assisted his rival in presenting his claim but had then fallen in love with him?

No, she could not. Emily would have to hope Edward would agree to yet a longer delay in announcing their engagement while he settled himself as a private gentleman. Or, at the worst, she might agree to announce the betrothal and postpone the wedding another year. In time she should be able to slowly break things off. Perhaps, she thought with brief satisfaction, she could even find Edward another bride.

In the meantime she would have to smile and pretend to Tony and the rest of the world that nothing had changed.

Chapter Nine

THE MESSAGE SUMMONING Emily to join Letty and her guest came, as Emily knew it must, far too soon. She did not feel ready to face Tony now, or indeed ever. Somehow it seemed to her that her awareness of her feelings for Tony must make them more visible to everyone else, that the words of love that echoed in her heart must also shine through her eyes for all to see.

There could be no avoiding this meeting, however. The sudden desire to take to her bed as Letty had done was quickly dismissed. Even if she were willing to appear so foolish, her family would not let her get away with it. What in Letty had been considered eccentricity would in her be seen as a sign of serious illness, she thought in disgust. She was too calm, too sane and sensible for megrims.

Because she actually was too sane for such tempers, Emily answered the servant's call by immediately straightening out her gown and following the girl out of the room. A passing glance in the hallway mirror showed her to be pale, but not so much as to cause notice. Her eyes were clear and her gaze steady, showing none of the tumult within her. Everything as usual.

On the way down the stairs she tried to rehearse various greetings, blending the right combination of surprise and delight. Much would depend on how Letty decided to handle the meeting, but Emily suspected there would be no accusations, not while Tony was present. Most of Letty's worries should have been dissipated anyway by the knowledge that Emily was meeting Tony and not some impostor whose behavior was like to be improper.

Emily's frantic imagination carried her to the door of the drawing room, but failed to bring her closer to any decision on how to react. As she opened the door and faced them, her sister-in-law and the man she loved, her mind went simply blank. She stood there, silent, still wondering what to say.

Fortunately, her apparently stunned reaction proved to be exactly right. The two of them must think her astonished to find Tony not only here, but so obviously welcome. They looked at her and laughed with heartfelt amusement.

No, that was not quite true. Tony's eyes showed no amusement. He seemed still in shock himself; he would certainly not be able to notice anything odd about her. And neither of them would imagine that only minutes ago Emily had seen them in each other's arms.

Letty, still laughing, took Emily's arm and drew her into the room. "Not a word? No congratulations for having finally done what is right? I don't deserve that, I suppose. No reproaches, then, for causing you all so much worry?"

For Letty, at least, the reunion with her old friend, her old love, seemed to have brought some measure of peace. The excitement and joy Emily saw in Letty at Tony's unexpected return were real, but there was still some concern niggling at the back of her head, Emily thought.

"Oh, Letty," she said with a sigh that was not entirely free of exasperation. "We never doubted but that you would come through in the end. If we worried at all, it was for you, that you might work yourself into such a state you actually would fall ill."

Emily stole a look at Tony. He stood with his back to the window, his face in shadow. The serenity she had seen in Letty's eyes was not evident here. Even his usual grace seemed to be lacking. Had Letty somehow managed to disappoint him again?

"I very nearly did fall ill," Letty confessed. "When I think of how I overreacted this morning!"

"Hush, Letty," Emily said quickly. She did not want Letty's silly assumptions about her meetings with Tony voiced aloud, not even in jest. "Such foolishness is best forgotten."

Tony moved, a sharp, abrupt gesture. It had been involuntary, Emily was sure. The attention it drew was clearly unwelcome, yet he was able to speak with little evidence of nerves.

"Letty, you know perfectly well no one blames you for your behavior. I should like some assurance, however, that Miss Meriton will suffer no criticism for having been courageous enough to assist me."

How coldly he uttered her name! The fact that his circumspection was meant to protect her reputation was of little comfort. From now on this is the way it would be, Emily reminded herself. In private they might still be Tony and Emily, but the private moments would be very rare.

Looking up at him, Emily was surprised to catch Tony answer her gaze with one as wistful. Perhaps he, too, regretted the intrusion of the world into their friendship.

The world of society was Letty's preserve, however, and she was considering its perspective. "John," she said, "will understand. He may give me a little scold for making it necessary, but he will understand why you felt it necessary to behave in so unconventional a manner."

Something in Letty's voice distracted Emily from her covert observation of Tony. She actually sounded worried, Emily realized. And about John of all things!

"The gossips, however," Letty continued, "would not understand. So I think your early-morning assignations are best kept secret within these walls. Has anyone ever seen you together?" she demanded anxiously.

"Yes, once," Emily admitted. "Not in the park, though." She could still remember the way Tony had looked as he stood by the piano, the way he smiled at her during the dance, the feel of his shoulder beneath her hand. What a fool she had been not to realize what was happening to her! What a fool she had been, too, not to realize that once Tony began to be seen in society that meeting might not look so very innocent!

"My friend Captain von Hottendorf secured me an invitation to a waltz party at Miss Parkhurst's," Tony clarified.

His words distracted Letty so that she did not see the small private smile he gave to Emily. Emily saw, however, and was cheered a little.

"You'll have to teach us, Em," Letty was saying. "Oh, how could I let this happen? 'Silence' will roast me as it is. To have to face her without being able to waltz!"

"Letty?" Emily reproved her.

"Oh, well, I suppose someone must have noticed Tony at this gathering. . . ."

That was certainly an understatement, Emily thought. Even now, as he stood there quiet and still, his presence could never be ignored.

". . . so we had best admit he asked you to intercede with me. Once." Letty looked at Emily very pointedly. "I don't think *anyone* could take exception to that," she added.

Anyone meaning Edward, of course. Would he understand? Emily wondered. If her involvement were couched in those terms? Perhaps she could make him understand that, for good or ill, she had felt compelled to bring their uneasy situation to a resolution.

Unfortunately, she did not know how to explain kindly that the resolution no longer spelled marriage for her and Edward.

Emily looked up to find Tony's eyes on her again, a sad and almost sympathetic look. As soon as she caught him at it, however, he looked away again. He moved to lean against the side of the sofa where Letty sat.

"Having assured me, then, that my fellow conspirator shall bear no harm," Tony said, "I ask you both for advice. You know the ins and outs of this town far better than I. How do we proceed now?"

The gracious sweep of his arm included them both, but Emily was well aware her contribution would be of secondary importance now.

"I will do what I can, of course," she said, unable to refrain from giving him an encouraging smile. "But it is Letty who will do the most for your suit."

"Frankly, it terrifies me to think that my answering a few

questions from some solicitors can mean so much," Letty confessed. "You know when I get nervous I am sure to sound like a fool."

Emily smiled to hear one of the leaders of society describe herself in such terms. "I don't think anyone thinks you such a fool as to acknowledge an impostor, Letty. Perhaps the best thing you can do for Tony is simply let it be known that you recognize him. John said something the other day I think is very true. People are reluctant to be the first to come forth, but if someone else has already done so, especially someone socially prominent, others will be braver about supporting Tony."

"You have a point," Tony said. "I've thought recently there must be some old friends who are at least curious to see if they would recognize me, but would not dare take the step of seeking me out at my lodgings."

"Exactly. That would be too pointed. But if they were able to indulge their curiosity without taking specific action . . ." Emily let her voice hint at infinite possibilities.

"Of course. Yes!" Letty's eyes were shining with mischief and energy. She rubbed her hands together.

"Yes, what? What have you thought of, Letty?" Emily asked.

"There isn't time for us to plan a ball and a simple at-home won't do. What would you say is the most prestigious of the parties to which we've been invited during the next week?"

"Oh, I see." Emily nodded in understanding. "That would be tonight's ball at Devonshire's, undoubtedly."

"Perfect," Letty said with delight. "As it's a Whig affair, Edward won't be there, so we need not fear the evening will end in fisticuffs between claimants."

Emily would have to make her own explanation to Edward later, but at least she would not have to face him with Tony at her side. So intent on her plans was Letty that she seemed to have forgotten Edward entirely except as a minor irritant.

"Letty, you cannot expect me to show up without an invitation," Tony protested as he guessed the direction of her thoughts.

"Certainly not. What a shocking idea! I have no doubt, however, that if I were to ask my hostess for permission to bring you—"

"Letty, you can't." Tony's voice had a sort of horrified fascination and a familiarity that spoke of long experience of Letty's whims.

"I most certainly can and I will. You've been away from society for far too long, Tony. Why should we be embarrassed? This will probably be the making of her party."

"I've been told my problem makes a nice change from gossip about the foreign royals, but . . ." Holding his hands up as if to ward off her persuasions, Tony backed away.

"The royals! Oh, no. Emily, quick, what day is it?" Letty's expression underwent another transformation, changing again from glee to fear.

"It's Wednesday," Emily answered, confused by the speed with which Letty's thoughts and emotions varied. "The twenty-first. What of it?"

"Oh, what have I done? I hadn't realized how long I'd been hiding," Letty wailed.

"I don't understand. What is the matter, Letty?"

"But don't you see?" Letty looked first at one, then the other. With an exaggerated sigh, she threw up her hands in a gesture that declared she had lost all patience with them. "He leaves tomorrow," she explained slowly, as if to a child. "This is my last chance to see the tsar!"

Letty was right in her suppositions about her hosts, of course. The Devonshires were more than eager to open their doors, at least for this one evening, to the gentleman claiming to be Lord Palin. If their gamble proved unsuccessful and Tony were denounced as a fraud, it would be Letty who would suffer as his patron, not they. In the meantime they would have the pleasure of spiting Edward, who had allowed his political ambition to make him as many enemies among the Whigs as he had friends among the Tories.

While notes flew back and forth between the Devonshire and Meriton households, and between the Meritons' and Tony's lodgings, Emily prepared for the ball. She allowed her maid to dress her in a pale blue gown trimmed with silver lace, but without feeling the usual gratification from knowing she looked good. Despite her anxiety for the evening to be a success for Tony, she was not anticipating much pleasure from the ball.

Her sense of purpose had been lost. It was like Tony and Letty to insist she was still necessary for the prosperity of his case, but it wasn't true. From now on it would be Letty's influence and Tony's own integrity and charm of manner that would win the day. He didn't really need her anymore. Emily had not realized before how much she wanted to be needed, not merely appreciated as a willing audience.

It was pride that kept her going now, pride that insisted she look her best tonight. So she primped before the mirror, carefully arranging her hair and choosing her ornaments. As she rummaged in her jewelry box, Emily found the opal pin that Letty had given her only two weeks ago. Another lifetime ago.

It was hard to imagine now a time when she had not even known Tony's name. So much had changed since then, so much of her peace of mind lost. Yet she could not regret his entrance into her life.

Emily remembered the story Letty had told her when she gave her the pin. She remembered, too, Tony's first challenge as relayed by Captain Hottendorf. "Ask Lady Meriton if she remembers the occasion on which Tony gave her the opal brooch. . . ." It must have been a special moment for both of them, a precious memory.

Letty appeared behind her and interrupted her thoughts. "That should go beautifully with your gown. Can I give you a hand with it?"

"I was wondering if I should give it back to Tony," Emily said calmly. "After all, you only gave it to me because you believed he was dead and because you thought I would be marchioness of Palin. Everything's changed now."

Evidently Letty had not given much thought as to how Tony would regard seeing the token of his affection passed on to another. She sat on the edge of Emily's bed and answered with a carelessness Emily considered quite heartless.

"No." Letty shook her head. "I don't think you—or I, if that is what you are saying—should give it back. I think that would hurt Tony more than anything else."

"Perhaps." Emily still felt unsure. The pin had become precious to her because it reminded her of Tony, of the first time she saw him, but she could not enjoy it, thinking how it must affect him. This pin had once been the symbol of his love for Letty. How could he bear to see it on another woman?

"I think," Letty said as she began fastening the opal to Emily's gown, ignoring her objections, "Tony would be glad to see that his gift had found its way to someone who has done so much for him."

"It was not so very much," Emily protested, feeling uncomfortable.

"Not to you, perhaps, but to Tony it is a great deal. Lovely. There, now you're ready." She stepped back to take a look, then resumed her seat on Emily's bed. "Emily, I do need to talk to you about the last few weeks."

With those words, Letty finally succeeded in distracting Emily from her concern about the pin.

"Are you still upset with me, Letty?" she asked in some surprise. "I had thought that when you realized what I was doing and why, and when you realized I had not been taken in by some rogue, you would understand."

She looked at her sister-in-law's worried countenance for a moment. "It was Georgy who gave me away, wasn't it?" she hazarded. Georgy was certainly the one person who was most like to color her behavior in a troublesome light. "You had best tell me exactly what she told you."

"Georgy did come and confide her concerns about you," Letty admitted, "but in the end it was your own carelessness that gave you away." A teasing note in her voice entered her voice.

"How?" Emily demanded.

"You did not swear all your witnesses to secrecy," Letty hinted.

Emily closed her eyes a second, disgusted with her own folly. How could she have forgotten? "Oh, lud, the twins. What did they say?"

"Well, after I had heard Georgy out, I only needed to hear one word from them, and they obliged. They said 'Tony.'"

Emily covered her face with her hands.

"And thank heaven they did," Letty continued. "I know I can hardly take you to task for not confiding in me when I held myself aloof. And I am very glad that because of you Tony was not left without help."

Emily lifted her head. "But," she filled in for Letty, "you could not help wondering if there was anything behind Georgy's hints." She had her explanation ready now. "I understand. Georgy told me I glowed. If I did, it must have been because of what I was doing. I enjoyed very much the investigations I carried out for Tony. I liked the sense of accomplishment, the knowledge that justice was being served. It made me feel useful. Georgy obviously misread my pleasure as something else." Emily laughed. Yes, it sounded quite good. "If the truth be told, I suppose I also enjoyed the intrigue and the scheming. While I was arranging secret meetings with the long-lost heir, I did not feel much like a sedate maiden aunt."

Letty sighed. Yes, that seemed to have done the trick, Emily thought. Probably Letty had been hoping for a last-minute change of heart that would end Emily's engagement to Edward. Emily wished she dared confess that much to Letty, that there would be no marriage, but she was afraid that in her enthusiasm Letty would not care much what methods she used to break off the match.

"I knew it would be something like that," Letty said, looking disappointed. "No matter what I said this morning, I know you have too much sense to fall for a glib tale or throw discretion to the winds."

Oh, no, not sane, sensible Miss Meriton. Emily wondered why it was so unutterably depressing to know one was not considered a fool? Then the deeper implications of Letty's assertion of faith sunk in. If Letty had not been concerned by Emily's behavior, what had happened in the last few weeks to bring a crease to her brow?

"Letty, are you suffering agonies of remorse for some reason? Is that the problem?" she asked.

Letty lifted her head unhappily. "I cannot help but think all of us might have been spared a great deal of anxiety if I had only had the courage to face Tony in the beginning."

Sitting beside her, Emily finally gave voice to the question that had haunted them all for weeks. "Why, Letty? None of us, I believe, are angry with you or blame you. I just don't understand why you did it. What were you afraid of?"

Letty bit her lip, then admitted, hesitantly, "John. It was bad enough that I had kept a secret from him all these years. I could not bear the idea that he might be disappointed in me." Her blue eyes seemed to Emily to be pleading for understanding. She took a deep breath. "You have a right to know the truth, too. I told you Tony and I promised to marry each other and that his father was against the match. What I did not tell you was that Tony and I eloped."

Emily's first thought was how nearly Tony had been spared all the torments of prison, the loss of his love, the near loss of his very name and estates. What had gone wrong?

"You were caught?" she asked.

"No, it was very well planned. No one would have realized that we had gone until we had at least a day's advantage. We almost made it."

"What prevented you?"

"I did. I couldn't go through with it. When it came time to stop for the night, my courage failed. Not that Tony's behavior was anything less than proper, I assure you," she said earnestly. "It was just that suddenly all I could think of was what our families and friends would say and whether we would be able to show ourselves to society."

What had Tony thought? Emily wondered. He had told her once he would hate to disappoint her, having once earned her friendship. In that statement she had read a confirmation of her own creed—one did not let down one's friends. How must he have felt, being rejected because Letty could not bear to be ostracized from society?

Now Emily could see what troubled Letty. Emily's own sense of the scandalous was so eccentric that at first that aspect of their adventure had not occurred to her. Poor Letty. It was not fair to blame her for being sensible. Even now the story could do untold damage to her reputation and could make a laughingstock of John. Marriage to Tony would have been a dreadful mistake.

All the same, an inner voice whispered, he must have felt

betrayed. And Letty had done it again, albeit unintentionally, by marrying John. No wonder she had been hesitant to face Tony again.

Letty sat twisting her handkerchief tighter and tighter. "I made Tony take me back," she continued. "Between them my parents and his father were able to keep everything quiet. Old Lord Palin finally agreed to let us marry after Tony made the Grand Tour. And that was that. Tony was shuffled off to the Continent and I made my debut in London."

Emily filled in the gaps to the present. "Then, of course, Tony was arrested and was presumed to be dead. And you've been carrying this dreadful secret ever since." Poor Letty, indeed. A secret, any secret, was a burden to Letty. This one had clearly weighed on her mind for a long time. The sympathy in Emily's voice, however, was laced with mirth.

"This is serious," Letty insisted, clearly a little offended by Emily's levity. "Don't you understand? My reputation could have been ruined. It still could be. We'd all be ostracized by society. Not just me, but John, you, the twins . . ."

"But Letty, you could not have imagined Tony would ever have made your elopement public!"

"Not intentionally, no. He was such a passionate boy, though. If he had been more angry and hurt by the fact of my marriage to John, who knows what he might have said?"

Emily gave her a look that said plainly she did not believe in that possibility. How could Letty know Tony for so long and understand him so little? She had only known him a few short weeks, and she knew better.

Reluctantly Letty continued. "How could I ask him to keep silent now? This is the best proof he has. You know as well as I that Edward will claim Tony is a fraud who met the real Lord Varrieur in prison. This is the one thing that could not have been learned in such a way. Tony would never, under any circumstances, have told anyone about our elopement."

Temptation seized Emily briefly. It would be so nice to have everything settled so easily, so completely. If she felt she had to, Letty would do it. There was only one person who would not.

"Tony would not wish to win at such a price," Emily said with assurance.

"No," Letty agreed. "Although I told him he might, even before John said I must. I finally told John everything this afternoon. He was very angry with me," she added in hushed tones.

"John? Angry with you?" Emily shook her head, still dubious. "Not because of some youthful folly."

"No, because I didn't trust him enough to know he wouldn't be angry over my elopement." After a minute the humor of her statement occurred to her and she began to smile again. "Oh, I love him dearly. How fortunate I have been."

An unworthy spasm of jealousy racked Emily. It wasn't fair. She didn't begrudge Letty her loving husband and doting children, only the love Letty didn't want. Unfortunately, that love was not something that could be given away, like the opal brooch.

Emily had no time to brood, however. After Letty left to make a few repairs to her countenance, it was John's turn to stop by. Emily was beginning to feel as if her chamber were a taproom at a coaching inn, there had been so much traffic through it today. With all that had happened she had found no time to talk privately with John. Now, of course, she knew that there was a particular reason why he had been closeted so long with Letty, other than merely reconciliation and affection.

John's reaction to the news of her own behavior was something Emily had never really questioned. For a moment now, however, she wondered if she should have.

He sat down, rather gingerly, on a fragile boudoir chair. "Well, it's a queer setout, puss, make no mistake. Who would have believed it?"

Emily waited while John polished his spectacles. Sometimes he took a little while to get to the point. Her brother was not one to hurry.

"I've been talking to the fellow downstairs. Nice chap," he said approvingly. "Letty's told me what rotten luck he's had and how we should help him out. I'm glad to do it, of course, but . . ."

She wondered briefly how one word could strike such terror into a person's heart.

Her brother leaned forward and spoke in a confidential tone. "Your sister-in-law is a wonderful woman, Em, but she doesn't always see all the consequences. Now, this fellow is the rightful Lord Palin, so it's proper and just that we help him achieve his place. There's no denying, however, that your Edward is going to be hurt by it."

"I know, John," Emily said. "That has been on my mind for days now. The loss itself is going to be hard enough for Edward to bear. I am afraid he will feel we've let him down, that I have betrayed him."

"He must know you too well to believe that," John said with misplaced confidence. "It's easy to see how it happened. Here you were, anxious to get things straightened out so you could proceed with your wedding plans. So you decided to take a hand in the matter yourself. Only it didn't turn out quite the way you expected, did it?"

"No," she whispered. When she agreed to marry Edward, she had given up all hope of love. The last thing she had expected was that Tony would be her heart's Nemesis.

"Edward will realize you were only trying to help him," John assured her. "It's what we're trying to do now, presenting the chap to society, that may sit hard with him," he added in innocent understatement. "I tried to reach him today at the club to talk to him, to warn him, but I couldn't find him."

Guilt washed over Emily. She should have thought of sending Edward some sort of warning, but her head was too full of Tony. Of course, a cynical inner voice answered, messages would do little good while Edward was being so careful to avoid the least hint of intimacy with the Meritons.

"So I want you to assure him, Em," John continued, "that even if he's not the marquess of Palin, he's still a friend to this family. Any time he wants to join us and his cousin, he'll be more than welcome."

Emily had to hide her surprise behind a pretense of coughing. Even when she had held far more charitable thoughts of Edward, she would never have expected him to behave so graciously.

"I will, John," she promised. "I only hope he'll be willing to listen to me." It would solve one problem if he was not, but she was not willing to do so at the price of a long and valued friendship.

"Well, if he doesn't, he's a fool and doesn't deserve you. But I have better faith in his judgment. You've already told him his title and fortune mean nothing to you, so he must know you'll stand beside him, come what may. Tell him for me that the change in his station won't affect our attitude to the betrothal. John Meriton is not a man to stand in the way of True Love."

John enveloped her in a warm embrace, for which she was thankful because it gave her a chance to hide her burning cheeks.

Now she had a new problem. Not only did she have to find a painless way to end her betrothal with Edward, she had to find a way that would not disappoint her brother.

As a result of her unhappy thoughts, Emily had a few repairs to make to her own countenance before she joined Letty and descended the stairs to join the waiting gentlemen. John had been chatting with the man who had once run away with his wife and gave every evidence of thoroughly enjoying the encounter. This was what Emily would have expected of her brother, but she was happy to see that John's quiet dignity had made its mark on Tony. It couldn't be easy for him, Emily knew. Whatever pain Tony felt in confronting Letty's husband, however, seemed at least to be free of resentment.

As the foursome drove to the Devonshires' house, Emily could feel Tony grow more and more tense. She remembered his comment after leaving Georgy's waltz party that he felt unsure of himself in the society from which he had been isolated for so long. Could he be so unaware of the elegant figure he presented? In his evening clothes he was very much the lord of the manor, even a little intimidating.

Letty, by comparison, became more cheerful and relaxed as they approached the milieu in which she shined. Eager to catch up on all the gossip of the past weeks and to add her own contribution, her eyes glowed with enthusiasm. John, at her side, could hardly take his eyes from her.

It was a surprise then to realize that Tony's eyes were gazing thoughtfully at her, not her glittering sister-in-law. Although Emily congratulated herself on having learned to read his expression better, she could not interpret this one. For a moment she thought he was about to speak, but Letty's continuous flow of conversation made interruption difficult. The carriage pulled up at the entranceway and the moment was lost, but Emily found herself grateful for the few minutes' delay at the door to slow the rapid beating of her heart.

It was the last moment of peace she was to experience that evening. For all of two minutes after their entrance was announced there was silence in the great ballroom. Clearly their hostess had spread the intelligence throughout the room before their arrival. Would they accept Tony or turn their backs on him? Emily wondered. She felt the focus of two hundred pairs of eyes, measuring, deciding.

Letty might have carried all before her in any case, but the faithful Captain Hottendorf was also at hand to assist them. He was quick to step forward and introduce Tony to Prince Hardenburg as the man who saved his life when escaping from the French. The fact that it was necessary to shout very loudly in order to be understood by the virtually deaf prince helped spread the word more quickly.

The only mishap to mar their enjoyment, or at least Letty's enjoyment, of the evening was the fact that the tsar was not present. Letty was crushed to discover that the Russian ambassador had turned down the invitation on the tsar's behalf because of the early departure of the entourage the next day. When Lady Jersey was called away from the ball in order to bid farewell to the tsar, John commented that that alone was punishment enough for Letty's foolish behavior.

To Emily, however, it seemed that Letty's greatest sufferings must come from having to sit quietly by while the dancers took their places for the waltz. Letty's ignorance of the intricacies of the dance also meant that Emily was spared the pain of seeing Tony and her sister-in-law once again in each other's arms. Instead, when the orchestra slipped into three-quarter time, it was to her that Tony held out his hand to claim his dance.

Emily had done nothing but talk about Tony all night. Not

a person approached her but to ask either discreetly or bluntly whether Tony were indeed the old marquess's son. What Tony's inquisition had been like she feared to imagine. They had been pulled asunder almost upon their entrance. Now that she was in his arms, she found herself unable to think of anything to say to him. With Tony, however, she found that she did not need to make conversation. He, too, was quiet, but the resulting silence was companionable rather than tense or embarrassed.

The social demands of the evening had tired him, she could see. Emily had watched him throughout the evening and admired the way he carried himself. Certainly no one else would ever guess that he was nervous. While Emily wished she could be thought of as exciting or intoxicating, she was glad that Tony felt he could relax with her. His smile looked natural for the first time in many hours.

It felt very natural to be in his arms, too. Their steps matched easily, without hesitation. Tony's arm curved around her waist as if it belonged there. When he looked at her in that warm, inquiring fashion, it seemed as if it would be very easy to step closer into his embrace, to draw her fingers across the slight scar on his temple, and to raise her lips to his.

At that point the picture dissolved. Emily forced herself to face the truth. Tony's arms would not draw her closer. His eyes would register only dismay and embarrassment if she approached him in such a way. Instead of seeing the love he needed, he would only see she was not Letty.

Brutally reminding herself of all the painful facts she had confronted when she had decided to marry Edward, Emily counted them off in time to the music. She was not beautiful; she had none of the usual feminine arts to attract. To men she was the sympathetic listener, the good friend, but not a girl to love and marry. Time would not change these facts.

The only problem was that time had shown her that she could indeed love, deeply and faithfully. And she could not marry Edward.

Between exhaustion and unhappy thoughts, Emily was in no cheerful frame of mind when they returned home. The evening had shown her clearly that Tony was now public property. There would be no more opportunities for quiet conversations, no more reason for them. The only benefit Emily could see in this bleak picture was that in all the excitement no one—certainly not Tony—would notice that her heart was quietly breaking.

In such a mood the last thing Emily expected was to find cause for laughter. They were all, except for Tony, finding it a little difficult to keep their eyes open. He, on the other hand, had been left strained by the evening's entertainment. A brisk walk, he said as he escorted them in the door, was what he needed in order to relax.

Inside the door was a furious and impatient Nanny.

"Do you know what time it is?" she demanded of John. Half asleep, he jumped a full eight inches. "It's four in the morning, that's the time, and it's no time for decent people to be up and about. If you want to ruin your constitution with riotous living, that's your affair."

John tried to get a word in edgewise, to assure the aged tyrant that indeed he had meant no harm.

"No harm? No harm? Keeping my baby out among the flesh-pots, to be poisoned by the night vapors, and you say you meant no harm? Come, my little one," she said to her thirty-year-old baby, putting a firm arm around Letty's shoulders, "Nanny shall take care of you. A dose of my tonic is what you need."

Letty had been giggling behind her fan since Nanny had first accused John of riotous living, but she sobered up quickly enough at that.

"Oh, no, Nanny. I'm fine, truly I am," she protested as she was being led away. "All I need is a good night's sleep."

"And that's what you'll get, my dearie. As soon as you've had a dose of tonic." A choked sound from behind her caused her to spin around. One look and she obviously had no doubt who the guilty party was.

"So it's you," she said to Tony, shaking her gray locks in despair. "I should have known. They said as how you was dead, but I knew it weren't true. You're too troublesome to go off so easy as that." She hurried Letty away as if she were afraid of contamination and shouted back over her shoulder as she departed. "Just don't go thinking you'll lead my little girl into mischief again."

Emily had stood by silently, watching it all. They were all in shock, standing with mouths agape. After a long moment they fell into hysterical laughter.

"Too troublesome to go easy," Tony said, trying to catch his breath between peals of laughter. "I wonder if my solicitor has considered that line of reasoning?"

Emily looked at the face she had come to love, made young again by laughter and finally by a sense of security. The assurance neither she nor even Letty had been able to give him had come from the lips of one very irritable old woman.

The marquess of Palin had indeed come home.

Edward called on Emily, at long last, the next day. He was announced at a time when both John and Letty had gone to meet Tony at his solicitors, which Emily considered a fortunate circumstance. Or perhaps it was not a matter of good fortune. Edward's impeccable sense of timing owed not a little to calculation.

Although recent events had cooled much of the affection Emily had had for Edward, his unhappy harried expression demanded her sympathy. He was hurt, confused, and frightened. In trouble he turned, as he had always done, to her.

Edward brushed past the servant who opened the door to announce him, saving them both a moment of embarrassment.

"Emily, dearest," he greeted her, leaning forward to kiss her cheek. "The strangest story is making the rounds of the clubs this morning. About Letty and this impostor! I can't imagine how it got started, but I came over as soon as possible to find out the truth so I can stop these foolish rumors."

Emily could feel the pull of those old bonds of affection. Six years of friendship could not be erased in less than a month. Her own sense of guilt pleaded on Edward's behalf. She had accepted his offer knowing full well what she was doing. That bargain had included her loyalty, and she was only too well aware that she had failed to maintain her part.

Edward's voice sounded confident enough, but Emily could

see the panic in his eyes. He knew the story was true, but he didn't want to believe it.

"At least it's given me an excuse to see you without feeling conspicuous in my attentions," he said with a smile.

Emily had no heart to reprimand him for his lack of attention. There would be hurt enough in what she had to tell him. His attention, or lack of it, no longer mattered anyway.

"Have you been very lonely?" he asked.

"No, not really," she answered honestly, then tempered her denial with a smile. "There hasn't been time to be lonely in all the recent excitement."

"That's true enough," he agreed. "And it seems there was more excitement last night at the Devonshires'. Needless to say, I am not talking about Lady Jersey's visit to the tsar. They tell me the impostor attended—with your family! Can it be true?"

"He's no impostor, Edward," she said quietly, trying to take the sting out of her words. "When Letty finally began to feel better, she realized she had to see for herself if the claimant was truly her old friend or not. She has no doubts, Edward, and neither do I. He really is Lord Palin."

Denial followed swiftly, as Emily knew it must.

"But he can't be. Lady Meriton must be mistaken, or worse, duped. My cousin died in France. This man must be an impostor." Edward rose quickly and walked nervously to the fireplace. His face was pale and his hands shook very slightly.

"I cannot explain how the story of his death came about," Emily admitted, "but there is no doubt this is Lord Palin. I know, I know what you mean to say, Edward, but he knows things about the past he could never have learned from another."

Edward turned away, stiff with disbelief.

With a sigh Emily approached to stand close behind him. "There's another witness, too, one I think you must admit is impeccable."

"Who?"

"Letty's old nanny. She rushed to Letty's side to tend Letty during her illness. When she saw him she recognized him at once. Without prompting."

Emily had felt foolish that she had given no thought to the

faithful old servant. All her discussions with Tony had centered on the servants who had left his home, not those associated with Letty's household.

"An ancient woman with failing faculties . . ." Edward tried to rationalize.

"Edward, you know that isn't so."

Too late, Emily realized a note of pity had crept into her voice. She could see him begin to bristle in defense, but then his shoulders slumped. That pity, more than anything else, convinced him she was speaking the truth.

"Well, we will see what the court has to say," Edward temporized, albeit with flagging spirits. "It is the law after all that must be satisfied, not you or I or Lady Meriton or her nanny."

He was trying to remain unconcerned, but Emily could sense his fear. Since Edward had genuinely believed Tony was an impostor, he had never really considered the possibility of losing his case, of losing his title and estates. Now everywhere he looked he faced the loss of all he had once considered his own.

This was not the moment to tell him he had also lost his fiancée.

"Edward," she said, trying to be gentle, "I know this may seem poor consolation now, but I believe your cousin has a sincere sympathy for the awkwardness of your position. He seems anxious to reestablish bonds with family, if you will only let him. I think you may find him very generous."

Whether her words had reached Edward's troubled mind, Emily could not tell. He stared at the patterned carpet for a long moment. When he raised his eyes, he seemed at least to be trying to accept the facts and what they implied for his future.

"I take it Letty will continue to promote this fellow's interests as she did last night?" he asked. It was a rhetorical question. He knew very well what Letty would do.

Emily nodded.

After a minute's thought Edward seemed to come to a decision.

"Don't think too badly of me, Em," he begged. "I just don't feel I can face him, accept him as my cousin, until the courts tell me I must. Let me hope for a miracle to prove you wrong."

"Edward . . ." she began, disarmed by his wry smile, but then faltered. There was really nothing she could say to ease his pain.

"Can you forgive me for ignoring you for a little while? It won't be long. They've finally set a date for the hearing, just over a week from now. I hope by then I can come to terms with what has happened and be able to face this man you say is my cousin. Until then, however . . ."

Emily said she understood, of course. What else could she do? As she watched him leave, however, his shoulders still bowed, she wondered what she would say to him next week when he was prepared at last to announce their betrothal. While she was not.

Chapter Ten

EMILY'S PREDICTION THAT once Tony was accepted publicly by one person, others would step forward to support his claim proved quite true. While there were many who continued to view his claim with skepticism, few were confident enough to deny the possibility of his being exactly who he said he was. Certainly no one need feel shy about being seen in public with him any longer. Invitations, tendered via the Meritons, began to pour in.

One of the first to arrive was from Lady Castlereagh. The departure of the tsar had brought much relief to her household. Not only had much of the social pressure been diminished for her; much of the diplomatic pressure for her husband had gone with the Russian emperor.

Emily was happy to see her godmama, who professed herself fascinated by Tony's story, in better spirits. The gathering at the tea table was comfortable and intimate. Only the Meritons, Tony, and his friend Captain von Hottendorf had been invited. Here at least Emily felt no tension over the presentation and acceptance of Tony other than the normal anxiety that those people she liked best should also like each other.

Soon it was clear that her hosts were very impressed with Tony. Emily watched as Tony quickly fell victim to his hostess's warmth and kindness. To Lord Castlereagh he paid the tribute due that exceptional intelligence. The slight sense of social unease that Emily had detected at the ball was no longer evident.

Tony's assurance was growing by the hour. Of course, the knowledge that he was surrounded by people who believed in him must be a great support, but Emily thought there was more behind his present relaxation than that. The Castlereaghs did not care about his claim; they were interested in him.

The genuine interest shown in Tony's experiences was something that Emily appreciated as well as he. At the Devonshires' ball she had seen him patiently endure hours of silly questions and meaningless expressions of shallow sympathy. Lord Castlereagh's curiosity was not merely well informed, it was pointed. He really wanted to learn about the difficulties of *détenu* life. You could almost see him mentally file away certain pieces of information for later referral.

Emily was also aware that both Tony and the captain tacitly were avoiding subjects that might be considered too sordid for female ears. Instead of talking about mistreatment of prisoners, Tony described miraculous escapes. The question of parole inevitably arose at that point.

"Parole wasn't really a consideration for the midshipmen," Tony commented, waving aside her ladyship's offer of more tea, "since they were held in barracks. They were responsible for some of the most spectacular escapes. Some of those boys never gave up. I met a few of them more than once at Bitche."

Tony's smile faltered for a moment. Some of those stories Emily had also heard in her search for information for Tony. Failure was not the worst fate met by a prisoner attempting escape. At least one story blamed the commandant of Bitche of willful murder. Those darker memories probably outnumbered the ones that could be told in polite company.

Even in this company Emily sometimes wanted to shake his listeners and remind them that what happened to Tony was not merely a good story to tell over teacups or a bottle of port.

"For us officers, of course, it was a normal part of warfare," the captain said. "Capture, parole, exchange. Except that Napoleon did not play by the rules. It was a different matter for civilians, though."

John, who had served in the militia, set down his cup forcefully. "Detaining civilians was an unconscionable act," he agreed. "Completely against the military usage of all civilized nations. We took no French civilian prisoners," he added with pride.

"That was the point, you see," Tony interjected. "We civilians had no code for such a situation. It was the very root of all the argument behind the case of Sir Beaumont Dixie. You know the story?"

Von Hottendorf and Castlereagh were obviously familiar with the tale, but urged Tony to repeat it for the benefit of the others.

Tony leaned forward to explain, a lock of his dark hair falling forward over his brow. "Sir Beaumont was a fellow *détenu* in Verdun, living in the town on parole. He attempted to escape, but a naval officer—one of ours—who had heard of his plans turned him in to the French."

Emily was shocked, and she could see she was not alone.

"Everyone in the town took sides," he continued. "Dixie maintained that his parole had been obtained under threat, and that the French had no right to detain a civilian anyway. The officer who turned him in contended that the system of parole only worked if everyone respected it. If the French could no longer trust us to keep our word not to escape, then soon we would all be denied the opportunity to give our parole. We might all end up imprisoned in the barracks."

"A difficult question," Lord Castlereagh admitted.

John shook his head doubtfully. "But still . . . to hand the man over to the French . . ."

"There were those who agreed with the officer in principle," Tony told him, "who still felt it wrong to betray a fellow countryman. At least in this case no one could doubt the officer's motives. He really believed he was doing the right thing." Tony spoke softly in a way that sent a chill down Emily's spine. It was yet another reminder of the terrible things he had seen.

In such sympathetic company Tony had grown less circumspect about hiding his every emotion. Emily realized she was not the only one to hear that note of anger.

"The tone of your voice tells me that you know of others

who acted from less noble motives," Lord Castlereagh commented.

Tony acknowledged the older man's acuity with a toast of his teacup. "Indeed there were. I had not thought of this in years, but I remember once—it was right before I had a dreadful row with the governor and was sent to Bitche, which was what put it from my mind, I suppose—I had gone to the governor's quarters to pay a fine for being late for *appels*. When I got there, Wirion was closeted with another one of the *détenus*. The door had not been closed properly, and I could hear their conversation clearly. What I heard was one English gentleman informing on another, telling the governor of his escape plans. For money."

"No," Lady Castlereagh protested.

Letty cried, "Not for money!" at the same time.

John, too, was indignant. "Not a gentleman!" he exclaimed.

Neither Castlereagh nor the captain, however, were at all taken aback, Emily noticed.

"It was certainly a well-educated voice," Tony told the shocked Sir John. "I never saw the man's face, and I was glad of it. Had I recognized him, I should have felt obliged to denounce him."

"I see what you mean," said Emily. "It would not have been comfortable to accuse another Englishman with no evidence but your own word."

Tony smiled at her warmly, as if to say he knew she would understand. "Exactly."

"My, I don't know when I've heard so extraordinary a history," Lady Castlereagh said in placid content.

Tony's smile distracted Emily from the point she had been about to make. She prayed to heaven she was not blushing. Recovering quickly, she opened her mouth to speak, then closed it abruptly. This might be one of those subjects Tony could not bear to examine too closely, she thought. Once before she had tried to get him to consider his recent unhappy situation, but he had either misunderstood her or did not wish to hear it.

The observant Lord Castlereagh, however, had caught her momentary hesitation. "What were you about to say, Miss Meriton?" he asked.

She turned to face her host with hopeful and measuring eyes. Sitting here before her was one of the greatest brains of the nation. Perhaps he would understand and be able to explain matters to her satisfaction.

"Does it not seem to you, sir, that Lord Palin's adventures are rather too extraordinary?"

Before Lord Castlereagh could respond, Tony spoke, setting his cup down and giving her his undivided attention. "You tried to hint as much before, Em . . . Miss Meriton. What do you mean by it?"

So he did remember. Emily looked around for some sign of understanding, if not agreement, and to avoid his piercing gaze. There was no help but to blurt it all out. "I mean that what happened to you after you were sent to the punishment prison was strange, more than merely strange. You've said yourself that prisoners were never left at Bitche indefinitely—except for you."

"The commandant's spite . . ." Tony offered.

Emily shook her head. That explanation was not good enough. "And the story of your death, your funeral? Was that spite, too?"

Letty did not understand her point. "What are you saying, Emily?" she asked, confused.

Emily sighed and decided to be brave. After all, she had come this far. "I think someone wanted Tony very much out of the way. Perhaps . . . perhaps even dead. I think that someone arranged for Tony to be kept prisoner and arranged for his funeral, too."

Merely saying the words aloud made her shiver. The thought that someone had deliberately and maliciously set about ruining Tony's life terrified her, but it was a conclusion she could no longer avoid.

Someone else seemed to find her idea worth consideration, and that was Lord Castlereagh. He had gone very quiet and was listening with special attention. At least he had not laughed or dismissed the idea entirely.

"But why?" Tony insisted. "Who could want me out of the way? I'd offended no one in Verdun, except perhaps Wirion.

But he never did anything without the prospect of financial reward."

The swiftness of Tony's response told Emily he had thought about this, although not recently. He had not accepted his imprisonment with a fatalistic shrug. A new idea occurred to him now. "Enemies in England could have managed to arrange something, I suppose. Tell us, Letty, did I have any enemies?"

Letty laughed. "Don't be silly."

"Am I to suspect my cousin of scheming to get the estate? He was only a child then. My uncle Ruthven? I'd as soon suspect . . . Lord Castlereagh of villainy as he."

"Thank you," His Lordship responded. "You honor me by such a comparison. Lord Ruthven's honor is indeed beyond question."

"Whom do you suspect then?" Tony asked Emily.

"I don't suspect anyone," Emily was forced to admit with mounting frustration. "I wish I could see the reason behind all of it, but that there must be a reason I have no doubt."

"Em . . . Miss Meriton," Tony corrected himself quickly. "Don't you think I went through all this before? Believe me, I had plenty of time to consider the matter. And the answer, I am afraid, is nothing so ingenious. The answer, I think, is simply that the warden at Bitche made a mistake, an ordinary stupid mistake, and refused to admit it."

They would not listen, Emily realized in disgust. After an unbecoming amount of teasing, the conversation turned toward more frivolous matters—what had occurred between the tsar and Lady Jersey, the service of public celebration to take place at Westminster Abbey, and the plans for the celebration for the centenary of Hanoverian rule. Then Emily noticed how quiet and thoughtful her host remained.

She was therefore the only person to fully appreciate the subtle way in which the diplomat separated her and Tony from the rest of the company. His excuse was a new miniature that he wished to show them, but once they arrived in the library he made no move to bring it forth. Tony had obviously realized something was up, too.

"M'lord?"

"You do believe me!" Emily cried, grateful for his trust.

"Yes, child, I believe you," Lord Castlereagh said with a smile and indicated seats for them.

Tony contented himself with leaning against an immense desk. "With all respect, m'lord, isn't Miss Meriton's idea rather fanciful? In my experience there is usually a very prosaic explanation for even the most bizarre situation."

"Indeed there is," his lordship agreed. "And in your case I think that the answer may be that simple. Treason."

Emily could not tell if she had whispered the word aloud or not. The very word seemed ugly. Her eyes went immediately to Tony. His face, she saw, was impassive, but his posture was no longer relaxed.

"Lord Palin, the story you told me earlier . . ." Lord Castlereagh began thoughtfully. "Exactly how long before your arrest did it take place?"

"I was taken from my house late that very night," Tony answered quietly. "Wirion loved to frighten his victims by dragging them from their beds at dead of night." Now he was beginning to follow the direction of Castlereagh's question. "But, sir, all I heard was . . . a venal sort of treason, only poorly rewarded. Wirion would not have protected a minor informant like that. In any case, I could never have recognized the man."

Tony's protests seemed less fervent now. He came over to stand behind Emily's chair. The foolish thought ran through Emily's mind that he was seeking some sort of reassurance or comfort from her—as if he had any need of her now.

"If what I think is true, they could not chance it," Lord Castlereagh said. "What you overheard was, as you say, a very venal sort of treason. But the man who is willing to sell information of one kind may be willing to sell more. You see," he continued, "I happen to know that there was such a traitor in Verdun, one that we were never able to name. One easily important enough to demand favors of your General Wirion."

"But I could not identify him," Tony insisted. His hand rested on the chair by Emily's shoulder. She had a sudden urge to take it and hold it, for her own comfort. This was all beginning to be very frightening.

"Are you sure?" Castlereagh asked, leaning forward. "Remember that I am speaking of a man who cannot bear the least hint of suspicion. What if you heard a familiar voice one day? Or learned that someone else had visited the general that day? I think you could be trusted to put two and two together," he said wryly.

"Why not kill me, then? Why the elaborate charade?" The voice coming from behind her chair was still casual, yet Emily could feel the tension in Tony, even when she dared not turn to look at him.

"I do not doubt the traitor would have liked to see you dead."

Emily shivered at the cool confidence of Castlereagh's voice. This was Tony's life they were talking about.

"He, and his French masters, may have hoped Bitche would do the trick for them," Lord Castlereagh continued. "I suspect, however, that even Wirion would hesitate to murder the son of an English marquess. Your loud and troublesome friend the clergyman made it necessary for them to do something, but he also made them careful."

"That would explain why Tavvy was released," Tony said slowly. "You are right, they daren't kill me. There had just been a scandal about an officer who died under suspicious circumstances. The French said he'd killed himself, but some days previously he had sent a message to one of his lieutenants warning him not to believe any tales of suicide. After that the French had to be very cautious."

Emily's mind was racing further ahead. There was no reason for Lord Castlereagh to pull them aside to tell them this. In a minute Tony would realize it, too.

"There is more, isn't there, sir?" Emily asked.

"We never found the traitor who operated out of Verdun," Castlereagh reminded them. "Palin's tale of the venal gentleman fits in very well with what little we know or guessed of him. A gentleman *détenu* would be easily accepted by the officer class and be able to gain information from them."

Castlereagh came closer. His voice dropped, yet took on greater significance. "The *détenus* have come home now. There is very probably a traitor among them. Do not think that because Napoleon has been captured he has no use for information. If money is this man's sole ambition, there are other buyers as well. This man must still be found."

Castlereagh's words, and Emily's white, pinched features, stayed with Tony late into the evening and did little to enhance his game of whist. Across the single table in his chambers sat Gus, patiently trying to explain how he should have bid.

"You are not attending," Gus complained. "Not to me nor to the cards."

"I'm sorry, Gus. I was thinking." Tony passed the cards back to his friend to deal another hand.

"Thinking? Do you expect an excuse like that to carry weight at Sir John's club? I do not believe," he said as he shuffled the cards, "that an English gentleman is permitted to admit to such an activity. Unless it is someone as respected as Lord Castlereagh."

Tony looked up at the bland expression of his friend. The short period he and Emily had spent with the foreign minister had obviously been noticed, but this was as close as Gus had come to remarking on it.

"Gus," Tony said, "I see a brilliant career as a diplomat before you."

"Do you think so? No, after the Congress I will go home. It is time," Gus said simply.

Tony nodded. He understood well the longing for home, even though his mental images of Howe no longer brought the same comfort as before. Something was missing from that picture now, something essential.

"I'll miss you, Gus," Tony said without elaboration. The two of them had shared too much for more to be necessary.

"If you decide to brave the Continent again, you must come to see me, see how beautiful my mountains are." Picking up his cards, Gus began to study them thoughtfully. "I heard Miss Meriton might go to Vienna for the Congress. Do you think she might be persuaded to make a little detour?"

Tony froze. "I do not know," he said. Pretending concentration on his cards, he hoped his bluntness had not been too obvious.

"She looked very pretty today, I thought, in that . . . What would you call the color of her gown?"

"Gray," Tony said. Not like slate, though. It had shimmered as she walked. It reminded him of the color of her eyes when she was troubled. She had worn a silver band through her curls, too.

"Very pretty," Gus repeated while Tony moved the cards around in his hand in random order. "When I think back and realize that I doubted her remarkable quality at first, I feel like an idiot. How could a woman be so wonderful, so beloved? I wondered. It is to you I owe my thanks for sending me to seek her out, my friend."

But was it thanks Gus owed him? At first Tony had been blinded by the jealousy that seemed to hit him whenever another man so much as spoke of Emily. It was foolish to be jealous of Gus when Emily was engaged to his cousin. Tony examined his friend's face, seemingly intent only on his discard. In his own way Gus could be quite as adept as Tony in hiding his feelings.

"In fact," Gus continued, as if he had not noticed Tony's unusual silence, "this whole experience has proved very enlightening. To see such a devoted couple as Sir John and his lady . . . well, it makes one think about one's own future, about settling . . ."

Tony could take no more. He threw his cards down in disgust and walked to the window.

"It's no use, Gus. She's already promised to my cousin."

There was a moment of silence before Gus responded. "Tony, I am sorry. I had no idea. Forgive me."

Tony turned, confused. "Why should I forgive you?"

"Miss Meriton is a lovely and intelligent woman, but she is not for me. I thought she was the right woman for you, and only meant to tease you into admitting it." Gus looked appalled that his good-natured needling had done nothing but remind Tony of misery.

"Oh, you were right, my friend," Tony confessed. "She is the one. Only I have arrived too late to claim her."

"But why the secrecy? Oh, I see," Gus answered his own

question. "Until the claim to the title has been settled. If nothing has been announced, though . . ." he began to hint.

"Do you think an announcement, or lack of one, means anything to Emily when she has already given her word?"

Look at him, he was almost shouting. Tony took a deep breath and began putting away the cards. There would be no returning to the intricacies of whist after this.

"Tony," Gus said quietly, "does it mean nothing to you that that is all she has given?"

"All?" he said, allowing himself the pleasure of sarcasm. "We are talking about Miss Emily Meriton."

"We are talking about her betrothal to a man she does not love."

Tony gave his friend a beseeching look. Didn't Gus realize it was torture for him to dwell on this?

Still Gus persisted. "And who does not love her," he said, emphasizing each individual word.

Tony had thought he was beyond surprise, but these words stunned him. Even though Letty had told him she did not like Edward, it had never occurred to him that his cousin would not love Emily.

"Not love her?" he repeated, feeling thick-headed.

"I do not think he is capable of it."

That was a fairly sweeping condemnation, coming from Gus. Letty's judgment, given his experience of her changeable moods, might be called into question, but not Gus's.

"My acquaintance with my cousin, as you know, is limited to being shown the door on two occasions," Tony admitted. "I have not been able to form any opinion of his character, but the very fact that he is a valued friend to Emily must speak in his favor."

"Miss Meriton is not often wrong, I grant you. But consider, Tony—this fellow won her friendship when she was only a child, with a child's perceptions. If she were to meet him for the first time today, I do not think she would make the same mistake."

Silently considering his friend's words, Tony poured them both a glass of wine. "To try to break up a man's betrothal . . ." he said at last, unable to complete the thought.

Gus shook his head, as if in sad disapproval, but Tony noticed his eyes gleamed with mischief. ". . . would be the act of a cad, a bounder. No true gentleman would even think of such a thing," Gus agreed.

"A gentleman would stand aside and watch her marry . . ." Tony's eyes closed in pain. That thought, too, could not be finished.

Gus finished it for him. ". . . a cold fish who will value her only for the opportunities for advancement she will bring him."

"No!" Tony cried, setting his glass down with enough force to make the flimsy table shudder. "If Emily is determined to throw her life away on some undeserving fool, she might as well throw it away on me. At least I will appreciate her. And love her." He took a sip of the wine to fortify his courage. "Gentlemanly behavior be damned! She belongs with me."

"Bravo!" cried Gus.

Tony's confidence, however, did not outlive Gus's short cheer. "Lord, Gus, I don't know how to woo a girl. Letty was the friend of my childhood. I never really had to court her. What do I do? I can't even get two minutes alone with . . ." His voice trailed off for a moment. "Yes, I can," he continued with more hope in his voice, even if panic still resided in his eyes. "I can at least see her alone. For the rest I will have to trust to the fact that she has not pledged the one thing I want—her heart."

The next day Tony came to Emily with a list compiled by Lord Castlereagh of the *détenus* held at Verdun. For privacy's sake he suggested they take their discussion to the park. Emily perused the list while Tony tooled the high perch phaeton through the streets.

"What a man!" Tony exclaimed in admiration. "How he could accomplish so much in so short a time . . . !"

"I've known Lord Castlereagh for years, but I'm awed by this," Emily admitted. "It certainly is daunting, though. How can you find one man among so many?"

The sun glinted on Tony's dark hair. He had begun to acquire more color and weight these past few weeks. By the end of the summer he might be well on his way to looking brown as a gypsy again. Although he had earlier denied Emily's conjectures regarding the reasons for his imprisonment, finding the answer seemed to have given him a measure of peace, she thought. The trust placed in him by Lord Castlereagh and the task itself had cheered him. He seemed more youthful and carefree.

"We," Tony corrected her. "How can we find this man? Lord Castlereagh did not include you in our little conference by misadventure. It was your intelligence that pointed the way in the first place. I can't do without your help now."

Despite the enormity of the task, Tony seemed uncommonly cheerful. For herself, Emily had decided to enjoy these last moments together with him without allowing thoughts of the future to intrude. It would be hard to keep those thoughts at bay, however, if Tony was going to compliment her on her *intelligence*.

"If you'll notice," Tony pointed out as he neatly negotiated a corner, "some of the names have already been crossed out." There was a questioning note in his voice that told her she had better control her expression more carefully. "Castlereagh says they were aware of this fellow's activities up until about four years ago. So anyone dead, released or transferred before that time is cleared. Unfortunately, he says the cessation of activity might be due to anything."

If intelligence was what Tony wanted . . . "You mean the man might have left Verdun at that time, been released or transferred, or . . ."

"Or it may simply be that Wirion's death then changed the situation drastically. Maybe it frightened him. Wirion blew his brains out rather than face exposure and punishment for his misuse of authority," Tony said with satisfaction.

He didn't even realize how brutally he had expressed himself. Emily was glad he felt he could speak his mind to her without considering his words, but she could not help but think he would never have spoken so to Letty.

"This man may have feared his connection to the governor would leak out," he added.

"I see. In other words, to have been released before 1810 clears a person, but to have been released or moved from that time on means nothing." Keep your mind on the business at hand, she reminded herself.

"Precisely. That does not change the situation much anyway. Those who had sufficient influence to obtain release obtained it early."

Except for eighteen-year-old Tony, Lord Varrieur, who would not see English money pass into French hands. What had he been like then? Emily wondered. Sometimes there seemed to be so little of that boy in him. She looked at his profile, the little bump on his nose, the scar at his temple.

"Tony. What if he died?" That was what she was hoping. All this could be for nothing.

"He could have, I suppose, although he was not old by any means. I remember that much. Anyone who was able to elude Castlereagh and his agents must have been pretty clever, though, too clever to get involved in duels or such."

He gave her a quick smile before returning his attention to maneuvering the phaeton through heavier traffic. Had Emily thought there was little of the boy in him? Certainly Tony was approaching this matter with a great deal of youthful enthusiasm. That zeal caused a small ripple of disquiet, but Emily resolutely pushed the uncomfortable feeling aside.

If nothing else came of their discussion, it was worth it merely to be together again like this, to be able to use Tony's name without thinking twice about who would overhear. In public, even before the Castlereaghs, they had both been so very formal. Lord Palin. Miss Meriton. Tony had faltered at that, she remembered.

Unfortunately, she could not persuade herself that his behavior was due to the same sentiment as she felt. She was too *intelligent.*

"Tell me, Tony, what exactly do you recall of that conversation?" she asked, trying to keep her mind on the present.

"I remember impressions mostly. Until I realized what they were talking about my mind was concerned with my own interview with Wirion." He concentrated further. "It was the voice of a gentleman, well bred, neither young nor old."

"You said before it was one of the *détenus,* but could it not have been one of the officers?"

"No, I don't think so, at least, not regular service. Perhaps the militia. There was something too casual in his attitude for a military man." Tony made a grimace of distaste.

"What is it?"

"I remember the satisfaction in his voice. No regret at all. I wanted to believe the man desperate. The pay certainly seemed pitiful enough. Somehow, I was sure he enjoyed it."

"Someone who perhaps was not in the very highest level of society, then. Or even the next level," she guessed.

Turning to look at her, he asked, "Why do you say that?"

"Except for you, the most influential men were able to secure release. The very wealthy and well born who remained, for whatever reason, managed to support a very elegant way of life—balls, races, clubs. It sounds to me as if your man could not afford that life—and resented it." Emily turned away, embarrassed, from Tony's searching gaze. "I am only conjecturing, of course."

"I would trust your conjectures over the sworn evidence of most others. You understand people. You—" Tony broke off and returned his attention to the road. Hopefully Emily waited for him to continue, but when he spoke again it was only to return to the question of treason. "We can add another piece of information to our puzzle, obvious as it may be. It was not someone I knew well enough to recognize the voice. That clears quite a few of the clergymen and scholars who were friends of Tavvy's and who otherwise might fit your qualifications. To think I once regretted those hours of listening to Tavvy discuss philosophy and natural history with his friends!"

"Let us hope he taught you something about logical deduction as well!" she teased, then took a deep breath. "Shall I begin?"

Tony nodded and sighed.

"The Honorable Arthur Annesley . . ."

The list, much reduced by Emily's and Tony's refined criteria, was returned to Lord Castlereagh. Emily presumed her involvement would end there and wondered if she would ever know how or even if the business of discovering the traitor was concluded. For Tony's sake she hoped he at least would have the satisfaction of knowing the man who had done him so much harm would be punished. What had not occurred to her was how Tony might react to the idea of having to wait, idle and patient, for word of success.

"How can I simply let it go?" he asked. "You tell me a man is responsible for taking away ten years of my life, but don't worry, someone else will deal with it? That is not good enough for me. I admit I cannot do all that Lord Castlereagh will do, but that does not mean I have to stand by and do nothing."

It seemed very bizarre to Emily to be standing in Hatchard's lending library perusing the shelves and discussing an attempt to discover a traitor. To her right she could see old Mrs. Barres looking over a book of sermons while her two young daughters tried to sneak a look at the latest novel from Minerva Press. Around the corner Captain von Hottendorf was distracting Letty, no easy task since Letty, still hoping to displace Edward, seemed determined to push the captain in Emily's path.

Yet she had not imagined it. Tony intended to try and discover this traitor himself. No, not exactly by himself. He wanted her help.

"Tony, what is it you think we can do?"

He answered with a glowing smile. Her question was not meant to sound encouraging, but apparently it had.

"Why, listen, of course," he said, as if it were perfectly obvious. "The two advantages we have are that people talk to you, and often say more than they ever meant to."

Thinking of her recent lack of success with Mr. Neale, Emily was not so sure that was true.

"And the second?" she prompted, feeling gloomy.

"My knowledge of Verdun. If there are any discrepancies in what we're told, I will surely recognize them."

How could he sound so cheerful and enthusiastic? Did he not realize that he was talking about a dangerous man with no honor? She had already found it difficult to be persuaded that Tony was in no present danger. Both Tony and Lord Castlereagh had insisted that the traitor had more to lose than gain by any attempt against Tony now. If she and Tony were to start poking around, however, that might no longer hold true.

Emily pulled a book from the shelf and started thumbing

through the pages. The thought of danger was obviously not going to deter Tony.

"What had you planned on doing if we did discover anything?"

Taking the book out of her hands, Tony turned it right side up and gave it back to her. "Nothing. Give the information to Lord Castlereagh. He can take it from there. But at least I will have done something."

Biting her lip, Emily considered the consequences. Despite her knowledge of the seriousness of the matter, it seemed highly unlikely that she or Tony could do either harm or good. If that was true, and it would give him so much pleasure . . . The pleading look in his eyes was well-nigh irresistible.

A small voice inside whispered that they would be together again. For a while longer they would be together.

"Oh, all right," she said. It was not a gracious acceptance, but Tony did not seem to mind.

"There you are," Letty suddenly interrupted them, followed by an apologetic Captain von Hottendorf. "Found anything?" She took the book Emily had been holding. *The Natural History of Selbourne.* Are you sure this is want you want, dear?"

Emily was already regretting her decision by the time she arrived at the Parkhurst home that evening. The ball seemed destined for disaster. Since the day Georgy had offended Emily by her too-accurate intuition, there had been no chance to mend the slight rift in their friendship. Letty's determination to push poor Captain von Hottendorf in Emily's direction was becoming so embarrassing as to be humiliating.

There was a promise of pleasure to come, however. Tomorrow she and Tony would talk, just the two of them. And tonight . . . tonight for the length of one waltz, he would hold her in his arms.

When Tony came to claim his dance with her, he gave her a private smile. It was in this very house that she had first danced with him. She could still remember how he looked when she saw him standing by the piano. Business, however, still seemed to be the order of the day, now as before.

"There is one thing I don't understand," Tony admitted quietly as they strolled in search of refreshment afterward. He carefully steered her away from a matron who looked ready to intercept them. "Someone told me one of the fellows on the list—Neale—is actually on Lord Castlereagh's staff. Surely His Lordship knows the man well enough to discount him?"

"I think His Lordship was merely being scrupulously fair. He would not offer his own judgment of the man as evidence. The only thing that might be considered suspicious about the man is that he is in a position where he might"—Emily paused as another couple passed by within hearing—"do the same sort of work."

"I see what you mean." Tony was quick to pick up on the nuances in her voice. "You don't like him, do you?"

"No," she conceded. "But that is only because he has had the bad taste to deny your claim. When I first met him, I thought him quite attractive."

Tony raised an eyebrow at this, but all he said was, "Well, if the gentleman is one of my detractors, then we must certainly hope he is the villain, regardless of His Lordship's good opinion."

This was said in so good-natured a tone as to make Emily wonder. "Sometimes you speak so calmly of the man who caused you so much pain. You have said you want to catch the fellow, but do you have no longing for vengeance? No desire to make this man, whoever he may be, pay for what he did to you, all he cost you?"

Emily herself, gentle as she had always been, felt a red-hot rage against the traitor when she thought of Tony's needless anguish. There was no torture so painful or so lengthy that it could satisfy her longing for revenge.

"How can I explain?" Tony asked, obviously struggling for the right words. "Do I want to make this man pay? Yes, for every minute I spent in that dungeon, I'd like to inflict the same on him. I want him to pay for every soldier and sailor he betrayed," he said with deep-seated anger. "And yet . . ."

"Yet . . . ?" she asked, looking up at him.

Tony's eyes were thoughtful as he answered her.

"You spoke of what he cost me, and, you see, that's the point. It has taken me a long time to realize it, but I haven't lost much, and I've gained . . . oh, such pompous words, but yes, wisdom and strength."

Emily did not think his words pompous. Perhaps it was true that much of what she admired in Tony had been the result of learning to survive the unendurable. Nevertheless, she could not believe there had been no losses. One in particular easily came to mind.

Her eyes wandered to where her brother and Letty sat talking with friends. Before she blamed herself for being too obvious, Tony followed the direction of her gaze. He spoke quietly, but with surprising emphasis, in her ear. "You're wrong, you know. Letty and I were friends first. That hasn't been lost. In fact, it has been saved from the folly our marriage would have been. It was not easy to admit, but my father was right. We were too young. And she belongs with your brother."

Emily halted and turned back to face him. His eyes looked a little sad as they met hers, but they were perfectly sincere. The admission itself must have cost him dearly, but it was the truth. Was it possible that someday his heart might recover completely, that he might even be able to love again?

"Only think, Emily," he said in a more lighthearted vein, "if this traitor had never plotted against me, we might never have met. Now, that would have been a loss indeed."

It was only flattery of a very conventional type, Emily tried to persuade herself. Over the years she had had more foolish and extravagant compliments whispered in her ear. None of them, however, had ever caused the slightest change in her pulse or had left her in such a state of confusion.

Be sensible, Emily told herself. Tony did not indulge in meaningless flirtation. If his phrase had not been meaningless, however, neither had it been flirtation. He had only paid a compliment to her much as he would to Captain Hottendorf. Once again she was the faithful friend, the good listener.

When he needed help, she was the person to whom he turned; that in itself was a delicate compliment. Restraining a sigh, Emily risked another look at his open, friendly face as they walked. Oh, yes, he turned to her. If he was ever able to love again, he would surely bring all his hopes and anxieties over another woman to her, too.

Soon they rejoined John and Letty. Tony was immediately drawn into a discussion of farming procedures. The conversation would seem deadly dull to most, but Tony listened eagerly and bombarded the other men with questions. In society such as this, Tony seemed completely at ease.

She realized in despair that as soon as his concerns were taken care of, Tony would be going home to his estate. Once there he was not like to leave it again—unless he considered it his duty to take a bride and provide the estate with an heir. In that case Emily would hardly see him again but for a few weeks in the summer when they went to visit Letty's old home.

Lost in such unpleasant thoughts, Emily failed to notice the approach of a friend.

It was Alan Johnstone, one of the gentlemen who had been present when Mr. Davies had so surprisingly provided Emily with an account of Tony's athletic prowess—when Emily had ingenuously denied any knowledge of Tony.

Due to the excellence of Mr. Parkhurst's cellar, Mr. Johnstone was very slightly foxed. The finger he waved in front of Emily's nose, she noticed, was less than steady as he asked in ringing tones, "Emily Meriton, you little deceiver, what have you been up to?"

Chapter Eleven

MR. JOHNSTONE'S VOICE was definitely louder than it needed to be. Suddenly Emily was alerted to the possibility that she had not been discreet enough. She had never known what it was to be the subject of gossip, but she was afraid she was about to find out what it was like.

"What have I been up to?" she repeated, trying to make his question appear no more than a conventionally polite inquiry. "The usual. I had tea with my godmama the other day. Today Lady Meriton and I spent the afternoon at the lending library. And you?"

It was no use. "You know what I mean," he insisted, without moderating his voice. Mr. Johnstone was beginning to attract a little attention. "A few days ago you were unable to des . . . describe that fellow there," he said, pointing to Tony. "But I saw you . . . I saw you here at Georgy's days before that. With him. So I want to know: What are you up to?"

It looked like a few other people were interested in knowing, too. While Emily's reputation was in many ways protection against just such conjecture as was now being made, she also realized that it encouraged in some a greater desire to find some stain, anything, against her good name.

When it came to the point, Emily did not know what to say in answer. Considering the man's mildly inebriated state, she doubted a simple denial would have much effect. Deep in conversation, Letty had not noticed the danger in time. Someone else, however, had.

"Shouldn't you be asking me what I have been up to instead?" Georgy asked appearing behind Emily's shoulder. "Emily, it may be kind of you to try to protect my reputation, but it is also foolish. You should know by now it's a wasted effort."

"Georgy . . ." Emily started to protest, but their befuddled friend with the exceptional memory was before her.

"You said you hadn't seen him, either, Georgy Parkhurst," he accused.

"Really, you could hardly expect me to admit to knowing him before someone had recognized him publicly, now could you?" she asked reasonably. "Captain von Hottendorf was so persuasive, however, that I agreed to give him a chance to beg Emily for Lady Meriton's assistance. Why not? Doesn't everyone come to Emily when in need?"

Mr. Johnstone, who had in the past poured his troubles into Emily's ear, was duly convinced, as no doubt were any other interested onlookers. Georgy came in for a little good-natured teasing, but she handled it with the ease of long practice.

When the gentleman at last departed, Georgy did not allow Emily time for thanks.

"I certainly could not allow anyone to think I had been hoodwinked into entertaining his lordship without knowing who he was," she whispered with a twinkle in her eye. "And to think you chided me for not keeping a closer eye on my guest list."

"Oh, Georgy, I am sorry for having deceived you," Emily said, contrite and grateful. Whether a little gossip would have done her much harm, she did not know, but it would certainly have hurt Edward deeply, and that she did not want. Such generous behavior was a pointed reminder of what a good friend Georgy could be. The memory of their last parting hung over her.

"I'm sorry, too, that I was so angry with you when you last visited. Even then I knew you meant well," Emily admitted, holding out her hands for forgiveness.

"Meant well?" Georgy said as if revolted. "My dear Emily,

if you say unkind things like that aloud, you really will destroy my reputation."

The brittle words and voice did not fool Emily. She could only hope that behind her mask Georgy realized how much Emily regretted their quarrel. Clearly neither thanks nor apologies would be allowed.

"Tell me instead," Georgy demanded, "how things have been with you?"

"Well," Emily said, a little tongue-in-cheek, "your last conversation with Letty roused her to a state of hysteria. That was the last moment of calm our household has known."

Georgy looked over to where the cause of all the excitement stood talking to a former acquaintance. At the time Emily's inebriated friend had made his disturbance, Tony was too far away to hear. When Georgy appeared, Tony had been about to return, but obviously the sight of her made him hesitate.

His tall elegant presence easily dominated the room. As if he could feel Emily's eyes on him, he looked up and, seeing her, gave her a warm smile.

"So I see," Georgy said, leaving Emily in no doubt but that she saw a good deal more.

Emily tensed, expecting further inquiry, but Georgy surprised her by merely giving her a brief hug.

"No, dear, I'll not tease you again. Let me simply remind you that when the time comes that *you* need someone to listen, I'm all ears."

No, clearly Georgy was not fooled. She knew that there was more to Emily's meeting with Tony than intrigue, had known it before Emily even realized the truth. Perhaps Emily ought to be grateful at least that the revelation of Tony's identity had soothed Georgy's fears that she was about to elope with a scoundrel.

The fear that her feelings were clearly visible for all to see set her nerves on edge. It was not the frame of mind she would have chosen in which to meet one of the gentlemen from Lord Castlereagh's list. Clever maneuvering on her part had gained her a waltz with Mr. John Stanhope, but now she felt unready for the encounter.

Stanhope seemed a pleasant enough fellow, although more

suited to the hunting field than the ballroom. Emily's reputation as a "good sort" had evidently comforted him. He admitted to her that he found the most beautiful society women made him nervous. Since he seemed quite at ease with her, Emily wondered what he thought of her looks.

"Never know what to say to 'em," he confessed. "Oops, was that your toe?"

"No," Emily lied stoically. "You have been away from society, too, have you not? I'm sure I should have remembered if I had seen you in London before." Her feet certainly would never forget him.

"You're right on that account, Miss Meriton. Until last year I was a prisoner of the French. It was only March of last year that I finally managed to escape."

"Escape? My, how brave." Emily had heard he'd escaped as his release came through.

Obviously this story had given Mr. Stanhope far more success with the ladies than his usual hunting stories had done. His chest puffed up with pride. This caused him to nearly miss his step again.

"Haven't quite got the hang of this waltz thing. All this going round in circles makes a man dizzy." He laughed.

"If you would rather sit . . ." Emily offered hopefully.

"No, no, wouldn't want to deprive you of your pleasure. I could see how much you like to dance. We danced in Verdun, of course, but nothing like this."

"Verdun?" Emily exclaimed with real enthusiasm. "Why, then, you must have known Lord Palin. I daresay you will be speaking for him at his hearing."

"Eh? Palin? Oh, yes, Varrieur that was. No, not really, only by reputation."

He did not seem to have reacted to Tony's name, but perhaps she had missed something while she had been protecting the hem of her gown. She would persevere.

"Oh, but you must. He was detained in Verdun, too. If you could remember anything about him, I know your evidence would be much appreciated."

Stanhope was counting one-two-three under his breath. "No, sorry, can't say I recall him at all."

"Are you sure? My sister-in-law is acquainted with him, you know. It occurs to me now that you must be the Mr. Stanhope he mentioned when he was speaking of his adventures."

"He mentioned me?" Mr. Stanhope tried to appear nonchalant, even dubious, but Emily thought he sounded nervous now. "Do . . . do you remember what he said?"

"Let me see." Emily bit her lip in feigned concentration. Oh, yes, he was definitely nervous. If his dancing deteriorated any further, she would need a Bath chair to get around. "I know. He was telling us about your racehorse. Evidently there's quite a story behind one particular race."

She smiled up at him encouragingly and watched him turn from beefy red to ghostly white. All Tony had said was that he thought he remembered Stanhope as horse-mad and that the fellow had owned a spectacular racer. What was there in her poor attempt at flattery to cause such a reaction?

"Perhaps we might sit the rest of this dance out after all," Stanhope suggested. All his clumsy energy had disappeared.

"Certainly." Emily was now as curious as she was relieved. She led her unresisting partner to a secluded alcove she had seen Georgy leave earlier in the evening. Stanhope seemed barely conscious of her presence.

"I always knew it would come out," he whispered, as if to himself. "All these years nobody suspected a thing."

Could it be true? Could their search end so easily? Emily would not have thought this fox-hunting squire had the intelligence to conduct espionage.

"So you were responsible. . . ."

"I had to do it!" he cried, pleading for sympathy. "My silly boasting . . . Wirion told me he'd bet five hundred pounds on my horse. If the horse lost, Wirion would still get his winnings—by taking them from me! I couldn't afford a loss like that, especially after the amount I'd paid for the beast. Do you understand? I was facing complete ruin."

"So you—"

"I had the other horse hobbled. It was despicable, I know. You cannot think less of me than I do myself."

Emily was hard put not to laugh. Oh, Stanhope was a traitor, all right—a traitor to the strict code of honor of the sporting gentleman—but he had not sold information to the French and he had not send Tony to prison.

Who had?

Emily described the scene to Tony the next day when he came to call. They were not alone in the comfortable morning room, but at least they could be private. Had Letty and her friend Lady Soames chanced to look up, they would have seen the two of them apparently engrossed in a picture book showing aquatints of the Lake District. As it happened, neither Letty nor her friend could be distracted from their discussion of their respective children's virtues and achievements.

This was fortunate because neither Emily nor Tony was able to restrain their laughter, and they doubted that the Lake District could be considered that amusing.

"I felt so bad, Tony. This poor man was practically weeping. All I could think was how silly it all sounded compared to what we had suspected of him."

"The poor man indeed. Emily, do you realize Stanhope probably thought you were trying to blackmail him?"

"To do what?" The way Tony's eyes crinkled when he laughed distracted her.

"He thought you were trying to obtain money with menaces," Tony explained patiently. "Or rather that you were trying to threaten him to speak on my behalf." The thought of Emily as a blackmailer set him off again, and he had to try to cover his laughter with a cough.

"Oh. Oh, no!"

Tony smiled at her horrified expression. "Oh, yes. He's probably on his way to the Americas by now."

She put her hand to her mouth. "If he doesn't ruin our case by making up stories about how well he knows you. I'm so embarrassed, Tony. What can I ever say to this man?"

"I think you've said quite enough already. I would not advise you to try to set the record straight."

"My apologies, Mr. Stanhope, I was merely trying to see if you might be a traitor." She rehearsed other versions in her head. None of them was any good. "No, I suppose I cannot explain that very well."

Tony shifted his position a little as he turned the page. He was sitting very close to her. While they had been laughing together, Emily had almost been able to suppress her awareness of him. Now she had to restrain herself from pushing aside the lock of hair that swung obstinately over his brow. She remembered seeing Letty sit with John like this on the sofa, but with her head resting comfortably on his shoulder. How shocked Tony would be if he knew she longed to do the same with him.

A slight nudge of his foot against hers brought her back to an awareness of what they had been discussing—Stanhope's misdeeds.

"Ouch," she said, glad to have an excuse for her automatic start. "I'd feel more guilty if I did not think the man deserved to suffer for crimes committed on the dance floor."

"That bad?" he asked.

"Bruised from heel to knee. It was that made me suspect he might be guilty of more vicious acts."

Tony smiled in appreciation, but his next words revealed his mind was still concerned with what they had learned about Stanhope.

"I can't help but feel sorry for him," he said. "It was a terrible thing to do, but I can understand why he broke. Wirion was an expert at that sort of extortion." In a more teasing note he added, "Perhaps that experience explains why Stanhope was quick to suspect the same of you."

"More likely his guilty conscience."

Tony became pensive. This thoughtfulness was not like the times when Emily suspected him of dwelling on the past. The wheels were turning.

"Guilty conscience. It's true," he admitted. "When you've done something you would rather not have bruited about, you do become especially sensitive about it. Sort of as if you had the secret emblazoned across your forehead."

"Yes," Emily agreed, her voice quiet. That was precisely how she felt about her love for Tony. Could he not see it? Or was he simply too much of a gentleman to acknowledge it?

"I was thinking . . ." He certainly was. She could almost see the wheels turning. "No," he continued, "that would be a filthy

thing to do. Pretend to know more than one really did and subtly threaten exposure."

Shocked, Emily turned to him. "Tony! That would be das-
tardly." Her voice had risen enough to finally attract a warning
glance from Letty. "Worse, it would be dangerous," she hissed
at him.

"Well, one would have to be very careful. Especially if the
person happened to be a man of impeccable virtue. We'd look
pretty silly threatening exposure to someone like my uncle, who
lived like a saint."

Somehow Emily did not think that Tony was properly attending to what she was saying. "No! You can't really
intend . . ." To deliberately intimate greater knowledge than
one possessed in order to precipitate an intense reaction, if not
an actual confession, seemed foolhardy in the extreme.

"We won't say anything that would offend the clear conscience," he said in a voice that was meant to soothe, but failed
to do so. "I'm simply suggesting we continue as you have so
ably begun. As you said, only someone who really had a guilty
secret on his conscience would read anything more into our curiosity."

Emily did not think she had said anything of the kind, but
there was too little time to protest. In a minute Tony would
have to leave. Whether she chose to implement his plan or not,
she could see that he wanted to give it a try.

"We'll see," she said in a damping tone she had learned from
Letty's nanny.

"Your brother is taking me to his club later this afternoon.
I'm hoping for a chance to see Underwood there." Tony
seemed to become aware of her disapproval. "Emily, you could
show a little trust. I'm hardly like to embarrass your brother
when he has been so generous to me."

That was indisputable. Emily's fears seemed foolish in that
context, until she remembered who and what it was they
sought. She'd treated the manner blithely enough the night before, perhaps because John Stanhope was obviously not a man
who could be taken seriously as a villain. The real traitor was
a man who had left Tony to rot in prison for almost ten years

merely to avoid the slight chance of recognition. What would he not do now to avoid discovery?

Emily shivered. There was no point in reminding Tony that this was not a game. The traitor had left him in a position of helplessness, robbing him of the opportunity to play any part in the late war. She could not blame him for refusing to be deprived of his chance for action now.

"That leaves de Crespigny and Neale," she said. "I suppose I might as well take Neale. He is like to avoid you, and he knows me. I hope you recognize my generosity in doing this. Of them all, he must be the least probable."

"True," Tony said slowly, "but if there is anything to be learned from him, I think it is more likely to be elicited from him by surprise, by the unexpected."

"Yes, and the last time we spoke he was very uncommunicative, a novel experience for me. The tsar's visit must have had him running in circles. Very well, I'll take de Crespigny."

Emily was not happy with the program Tony had planned for them. While they sat there, laughing and talking in Letty's charming drawing room, none of it seemed real. But there was a real traitor behind all this. Unlike Tony, however, she could not so easily put aside her fears, even though she understood his determination.

Smiling, Tony took her hand in his. "Until this evening then," he said.

For that promise, Emily closed her eyes to danger. She persuaded herself the traitor was dead or abroad. Nothing mattered but that she would see Tony again, tonight.

As he promised, Tony joined Emily at the theater. He and Captain von Hottendorf were not Letty's only guests, however. Emily's hopes for quiet conversation and a good performance were dashed when Lady Soames and family were suddenly added to the party. Although Emily and Tony shared the same box, with so many conversations floating around them it was impossible to discuss anything privately.

It hardly helped matters that Letty had almost forcibly set Emily next to the captain. Or that Lady Soames's eldest daughter, enjoying her first season, was flirting with Tony with dogged determination. The girl's behavior made Emily long to take a stick to her.

She had, luckily, found an opportunity to speak to Philip de Crespigny earlier in the evening while they had been sauntering through the gallery. It had not been pleasant. Everything about de Crespigny made her cringe. For the first time in her life Emily thought she was going to be the victim of a man's unwelcome attentions, and that in spite of the fact that her family stood mere steps away where Tony kept them distracted.

The fact that the man was overbearing and a loose fish, however, did not make him a traitor, she reminded herself.

Tony, she noticed, had managed to keep a close eye on them throughout the interview, even while he kept John's and Letty's attention elsewhere. It was a little annoying to think that he had not trusted her to be able to handle the situation, but it was also lovely to think he cared.

When they had been interrupted for the third time in one intermission, Tony shrugged in resignation. Much as Emily hated to admit it, she was beginning to think they would have to wait until the next day to speak together. Already this break had ended and the farce was about to begin, when Letty gave them the opportunity they had been waiting for.

"Oh, dear, there's old Lady Selena beckoning to me. She'll never give up and she'll never let me go if once she gets hold of me. Emily, be a dear, you handle her so well. Make my apologies and tell her I cannot escape from my guests. You weren't interested in the farce, were you, dear?"

Emily tried to look nonchalant. "No, not particularly."

"John will escort you," Letty added, to her disappointment.

"I will not," her gentle husband said with some force. "Do you mean to send me to the wolves?"

"Oh, very well," Letty said. "Captain, do you mind terribly . . . ?" She asked with becoming hesitance, as if, Emily thought, she weren't quite sure of getting her own way. Very soon, Emily promised herself, she would have to talk to her sister-in-law about this obvious maneuvering to throw the captain in her direction. It was becoming quite embarrassing.

Tony was obviously thinking faster than she. Before the captain could even respond, Tony was already on his feet.

"No, no, don't disturb yourself, Gus. I'll go," he offered with alacrity. "Miss Meriton?"

Emily took his arm and hurried out of the box before Letty could think of a new strategy. Once outside they both breathed a sigh of relief.

"Who is this Lady Selena who strikes such terror into everyone's hearts?" Tony asked as they walked, very slowly, around the gallery.

"An old great aunt of Letty's. She's quite nice, actually, but she insists on bringing Letty *au courant* with everything that has happened to the family, each aunt, uncle, cousin, and cousin's cousin, every time they meet. As I'm not related by blood, I only get a few questions about the twins."

"Whew, that's a relief. So, tell me, how did you fare with de Crespigny?" His voice was a little tense. Perhaps he felt guilty for leaving the rake to her.

"No, you first," she insisted. "After all, you saw most of what happened with de Crespigny. Tell me what you learned of Underwood."

Tony halted and turned to her. "I begin to think everyone in the world must carry around some dreadful secret of which they are heartily ashamed." Resuming their walk, he admitted, "But his is not treason. It was much more human, and he would understandably prefer to keep his new wife in ignorance of that part of his past."

"Ah," said Emily in comprehension. What a pity Tony would never tell her the exact details.

"Not a bad fellow, I think. Merely foolish."

Now it was her turn. "Well, de Crespigny is a bad fellow. Oddly enough, that's the very reason why I think he cannot be the man we're looking for. A man wishing to avoid any notice of his activities does not flaunt a reputation as a rake." While Tony considered that, she added, "Besides, when you hint you have heard of something awful from his past, he cannot think which of his misdeeds you mean. I don't know where he'd find time for treason among all his other vices."

"You may be right," Tony admitted with regret. "There would be too many officers who would have nothing to do with one of his sort."

Emily was a little disappointed, too. "It's too bad. I really would have liked it to be him."

"I'd certainly have liked to black his eye this evening," Tony said with fervor. "If I ever see him come near you again, I may still do so."

Her breath stopped a moment before she realized that Tony would feel the same about any girl he saw being accosted in such a manner. His violent attitude probably denoted a brotherly affection on his part, rather like the way John would feel. How dispiriting.

Their slow perambulations had finally brought them to their destination. "This is Lady Selena's box," she told him.

"Wait," he asked. "Emily, are you terribly disappointed by our results?"

She must endeavor to appear more cheerful or at least to hide her thoughts better. "No, not at all," she said. "*Frightened* would be a better word. Tony, are you sure we're doing the right thing?"

Tony looked down at her, his expression an odd mixture of suppressed excitement and passionate resolution. "Oh, yes," he said. "This is definitely the right thing. I am sure of it."

Emily was restless after they returned home from the theater. Of course, every meeting with Tony was bittersweet, because she realized that all too soon they would end. They had shared something very special while she was the only person to believe in him; now they had a very private secret to bind them together. Once their small part in Lord Castlereagh's investigation was finished, however, she knew it would never be the same between them.

They would be friends, of course, but only in the same way that she was friends with all the other fellows who brought her their troubles. It seemed painfully shallow after the closeness they had known.

Finally Emily gave up pacing her bedchamber, snuffed out the candle, and went to bed. But not to sleep. It was not, for once, her sorrow at the inevitable loss of Tony that was keeping her wakeful.

She reviewed the events of the evening to find the source of her discomfort. Most of the time she had spent trying to figure out a way to talk to Tony privately. When their chance had finally come, they had not talked of personal matters but of the hunt for the man who had betrayed him, and their disappointing results.

Clearly their clumsy attempt at intrigue was almost over, but she had long realized it would be only a brief reunion for them.

Emily turned over and tried to beat her pillow into a more comfortable position. Could it be that she was worried now for Tony himself? For what he might attempt in trying to discover the traitor? He had revealed a reckless daring regarding their investigations that seemed odd when contrasted with his lack of bitterness.

There was only Neale left, she reminded herself. Lord Castlereagh was not likely to ask them to do more. Once the traitor had been found, the foreign minister might ask Tony to confirm some information, she supposed, but no more. What was there to worry about?

There was only Neale left, and Neale was a member of Lord Castlereagh's staff. It seemed impossible that a man of Castlereagh's caliber could be fooled by a traitor.

That was assuming the man had continued his treasonous activities while in the foreign minister's service.

That was also assuming Castlereagh believed the man innocent.

Once you took away the assumption that Neale must be innocent, he began to look very suspicious indeed. Tony would confront the man expecting the same sort of reaction the others had displayed. He would not be prepared for the desperation of a condemned man.

Her chances of stopping him were slim, she realized, but she could at least forewarn him to be careful. At least he would know enough to carry some weapon, to arrange his interview in a public place, to protect himself somehow. She threw off the covers and jumped out of bed.

A hurried search first for a light, then for pen and paper ensued. The reasoning that had led Emily to suspect Neale was still clear in her mind, and she was able to transfer it to paper without too much difficulty. As she sanded and sealed the note, the distant gong of the grandfather clock in the hall told her it was four o'clock.

The servants would be up in a few hours. Tony would surely sleep longer, she told herself, and would not seek Neale out until much later in the day. Even if the note were not delivered before noon, he would still have plenty of time to plan a course of action. She knew it.

Why, then, could she not go back to sleep?

Returned to his lodgings, Tony settled himself into his favorite space by the open window, a glass of wine near his hand. The lovely view of the starlit sky failed to work its magic tonight as he mentally reviewed the events of the evening, and of the last few days.

It had been wonderful to finally be able to join Emily in her box at the theater rather than seek out a glimpse of her from the stalls. If the physical distance had disappeared, however, there were times when a troubling emotional distance had taken its place.

Not always. There were times when she would look to him—look first to him, before any other—to share a moment of laughter or sympathy. Unfortunately, there were also times when he felt he could not say anything right to her.

Had he been too fulsome in his compliment telling her that never to have met her would be too great a loss? Had he sounded too jealous when he revealed a desire to plant the pawing rake a facer?

He would at least prefer to think it was his social ineptitude that caused Emily to look glum every time he assayed gallantry. The alternative—that she was well aware of what his pathetic wooing implied and did not care for it—was unbearable.

Perhaps, another alternative, Emily was merely oversensitive to the awkwardness of her situation. After all, she was still engaged to his cousin, however she now felt about it. And he was not supposed to know about it.

The boy Edward was more of a threat to his love than he had ever been to his title, Tony thought in despair. Tony had hoped that by his politicking for the title, Edward had damaged his chances beyond repair. There was no doubt that for a while

Edward had been in danger of losing all Emily's respect. Tony was not sure if it mattered that Emily did not love Edward, but he knew it would matter if she had no respect for him.

It did not help, he realized, that in their present rivalry it was now Edward who would get all Emily's sympathy. Letty had been right when she prophesied Emily could never reject a fellow who had just lost everything he owned.

Could that be part of Emily's recent low spirits? Tony thought with a surge of hope. Once the hearing was over and things were decided, there was no reason to continue the secrecy surrounding her betrothal. If Emily had any doubts about the wisdom of marrying Edward, she might be torn between the desire to express those doubts before matters became public, and the wish to comfort the boy.

Tony took a sip of wine. All his conjecture did not take into account the fact that Emily and Edward appeared to be on very good terms when last they met. What Letty had told him had not been encouraging. She had even seen Emily bestow a chaste kiss upon Edward in parting. While chaste kisses were not precisely what Tony wanted from Emily, he had to reluctantly admit that they represented extraordinary affection on her part.

Damn! He could not seem to stop his mind from covering the same ground again and again. The only person who could answer these nagging questions was Emily.

Yet knowing that was not sufficient to make the nagging questions and doubts disappear. A glance at his pocket watch told him it was almost four in the morning, a suitable hour for unhappy soul-searching. An hour when it was difficult to find distraction from painful thoughts.

His ploy to stay close to Emily had not worked as well as he had hoped. Obviously, he had not given enough thought to how he might charm, impress, and woo her when all they did was talk about other men. Tonight's episode with de Crespigny showed, too, that he had not given enough thought to the problems their questioning might cause. He had assumed because Emily would only meet these gentlemen in public, she ran no risk of being hurt. Risk of another kind, however, there certainly had been, despite his precautions. He would have to be more careful.

What he should have done was let Emily tackle this Mr. Neale and then he could have dealt with de Crespigny. Jealousy, clearly, was bad for judgment. Simply because Emily had once said she thought the man attractive, he had overreacted, and had not been able to keep in perspective her later claim that she no longer liked the fellow.

Now that he thought of it, that was odd. Emily had never professed a dislike for anyone, not that he could recall, not even de Crespigny. It was odd, too, that Mr. Neale had not succumbed to Emily's blandishments. There was something about Emily that called forth confidences, yet Dominic Neale had not confided in her.

Tony was surprised to find after some thought that he considered much about the gentleman suspicious. For one thing, Neale fit Emily's description of the traitor marvelously well—a man of modest means living on the fringe of fashionable society. A quiet, unobtrusive man.

He had stepped forward, however, to present evidence against Tony. So much Tony had eventually learned from Emily. Neale had been the first, too, to publicize the story of his death and funeral. Tony did not think he was being spiteful when he remarked that the man who had had him imprisoned could hardly be pleased to see him restored to his honors.

What Tony felt most needed explanation, however, was the fact that Neale had been released four years ago. As Tony had said so many times, it took influence and money—and lots of it—to win release. Yet Neale had no patron, no important friends in either the political or scientific arenas. His attachment to Castlereagh's staff had begun only after his release.

Could it be that Neale's patron had not been English, but French?

In a few short hours Gus would arrive. They had planned to go to a prizefight tomorrow—today. Perhaps, Tony considered, it was time to recruit someone else into his little game. Someone who knew how to handle a gun or a saber.

In the end Tony had paid little attention to the prizefight. Now, a few hours later, he would be at a loss to tell anyone who had won. He and Gus had perfected their plan on the way back, and now here he stood at dusk, before Neale's apartment at the Albany, wondering if he were insane to do this.

A sudden urge to give it up and take all his deductions to Lord Castlereagh assailed him. Nevertheless, he raised his hand and knocked at the door with apparent confidence. Already Gus would be at the back of the building trying to gain entry through one of the windows. There could be no turning back now.

Tony had been expecting a servant to respond, so he was a little surprised to find the door opened by a man who could only be Neale himself. He was comfortably attired in a handsome silk dressing gown and carried a pipe in one hand.

"Yes?" he said, apparently only a little annoyed at having his moment of relaxation disrupted by the arrival of a stranger.

"Mr. Neale," Tony said with more assurance than he felt. "I apologize for disturbing you so late at night, but I thought it more discreet to approach at a time when we may be private and unobserved. My name is Palin."

Neale had recognized him at once, he was sure. The air of surprise and distaste was more studied than natural. It occurred to him now that Neale could simply slam the door in his face, making all his concerns about how to handle the interview completely irrelevant.

Discretion evidently was important to Mr. Neale, however. Tony smiled to himself. He really was an unknown quantity to the older man. Tony's capacity for public display, or perhaps even violence, could not be assessed. The risk of being embarrassed in front of one's neighbors was too great. Neale admitted him into the sitting room.

"I am acquainted with young Lord Palin, and you are not he," Neale challenged. "You are, I assume, the person presently contesting the title."

"You know very well who I am," Tony answered. There was no point in backing down now.

Neale shrugged, neither agreeing nor disagreeing. "What I do not know," he said, "and cannot guess, is why you should seek me out."

"I would have thought that was obvious." Tony had not been offered a seat, but he took one. The room, he noticed, was tastefully furnished, nothing ostentatious but everything of the best quality. It revealed a clear appreciation of the little elegances of life.

Neale also sat down and puffed on his pipe while sizing up his opponent. "My dear sir, if you have come to persuade me to speak on your behalf at your hearing, you are doomed to disappointment. If you have come to threaten"—he paused and glanced meaningfully at Tony—"for the same purpose, you will remain disappointed. I am not a man to be threatened."

Perhaps not, but Tony thought he was afraid nonetheless. That might be merely due to the oddness of the conversation and the fact that Tony was taller, stronger, and younger than Mr. Neale.

Or it might be due to a guilty conscience.

"You mistake me," Tony said, listening intently for signs that Gus had been successful in making his illicit entry into the apartment.

"I hope so. I should hate very much to have to inform the court at your hearing that you had tried to suborn a witness." Neale's voice had a distinct edge to it.

"I repeat, sir, you mistake me," Tony said soothingly. In the same gentle tone he continued. "And you lie."

Neale jumped to his feet.

"You would like nothing better than to destroy my efforts to prove my identity." Neither Tony's voice nor his casual pose changed. Inside, however, he was beginning to feel a tingle of excitement. This man actively disliked him. That was an unusual enough occurrence among Tony's acquaintances to be worthy of notice, but as far as Tony knew they had never been acquainted.

"It is you who mistake me, sir," Neale said, taking his seat once more. "I have no particular interest in your case but the interests of justice. The evidence I will present at your hearing is simple enough and might be given by any one of a hundred fellows who were in Verdun at the time. If you feel that my evidence is damaging to your case, I suggest you find an explanation for such facts that will act in your favor. The facts themselves you cannot change."

The words were reasonable enough, yet Tony felt more sure than ever that the man was lying.

"The facts will speak in my favor, Mr. Neale. By now I think even my redoubtable cousin has been forced to admit to himself that I am who I have always said I was. And I will win my case, no matter what you do or do not say at the hearing. I do not need your assistance. And you cannot do me any harm. Not anymore."

Neale's head snapped up at those last two words. "What do you mean, 'Not anymore'?"

He must have realized his reaction was too pronounced because he then made a show of distraction upon finding that his pipe had gone out. A few minutes were wasted in trying to relight the pipe as he paced the room, failing, and finally setting the pipe aside. It did not fool Tony. With that one reaction the diplomat had given himself away.

How odd it felt to know that the man in front of you had robbed you of freedom and changed your life irrevocably, Tony thought. How much odder still to sit and discuss the whole matter rationally!

Neale, he hoped, would be wondering precisely how vengeful he felt.

"You see, Mr. Neale, there is an explanation for what happened to me in France. There was a traitor in Verdun who thought I could identify him, so he had me sent to Bitche and left there."

The traitor was at his desk now. He leaned against it, threw back his head and laughed. "You are certainly imaginative, whoever you are. Why not simply kill you?"

"I've wondered about that myself," Tony admitted, with more assurance. A slight movement from the inner room showed him where Gus was hidden. "Why didn't you?"

Neale looked at him, as if measuring his chances of persuading Tony of his innocence. "Oh, I wanted to," he finally confessed. As he turned around, Tony could see that he now had a gun in his hand, a gun pointed directly at him. "It would have saved me the trouble of doing so now. I was afraid this might be necessary. For a while it seemed so unlikely you would be recognized. Then I hesitated because you were too visible. It does not matter anymore." He shrugged. "I really could not allow you to spread rumors about me, however foolish, at this late date."

Would Neale be willing to rouse all the neighbors by firing the gun here? Even if Neale made a good story of self-defense, Tony thought, it would certainly attract notice. And Neale would have to do it himself. There was a difference between selling secrets that resulted in men losing their lives and actually shooting a man oneself. Perhaps it was shock, but he could not bring himself to be terrified.

"You're too late for that, Neale," Tony said quickly, fearing that Gus might move too soon. "Murdering me might afford you some small satisfaction, but will hardly help your case."

"Oh, yes. Young Miss Meriton with her great silver eyes and her interminable questions. I would not put too much faith in her abilities."

Emily might not mean anything to Neale, but the mere mention of her name in such a tone called forth a deep anger in Tony that he would never feel on his own account. Something of that rage glittered in his eyes and made Neale step back.

"You are foolish to dismiss Miss Meriton," Tony said. "It was she who insisted that there must have been someone behind my misfortunes." With some difficulty, Tony tried to hide his disdain for Neale. That might be the very thing that would goad Neale to action. Still quiet and calm, he uttered Neale's death sentence. "However, we could not see a reason behind it—until it was pointed out to us by Lord Castlereagh."

The name of his employer hit Neale like a sword thrust to the heart. He paled and faltered.

"Castlereagh?" Neale tried to make a recovery, to deny the truth. "Your imagination is indeed impressive. But . . . a wasted effort."

"The husband of Miss Meriton's godmama, the woman for whom she was named," Tony reminded him. "Family connections are so important, don't you agree?"

"Oh, yes, I know too well what it is to make your way in the world without powerful connections." Neale sat down, slumped forward, but still holding the gun in his hand. "I managed to make my own way, find my own patrons. Wirion was far from perfect, but his own fear of being spied upon seemed a good guarantee of freedom from discovery." He laughed, but it was a harsh sound, devoid of real amusement.

"And then one day . . ." Tony began.

"A door with a faulty lock slipped open, and we never noticed, until it was too late," Neale remembered. "From the moment I learned it was you who had been in the anteroom, I knew somehow, someday, you'd expose me. You, with your strict sense of honor, the one nobleman who refused to bribe his way through or out of Verdun. You, with all your friends among the naval prisoners. You spelled ruin."

Keep him talking, Tony told himself. "But the French would not risk the murder of an English marquess's son," he prompted.

"No. Even Wirion, even the commandant at Bitche refused to go that far." Neale became pensive. "Wirion would have done better to have killed you and moderated his greed. I would have done better to have stayed in France, I suppose. You would have done better to have stayed home tonight." He looked Tony in the eye.

"Do you really think it would have made any difference?" Tony asked, watching him warily.

"Anything can make a difference. I keep remembering Wirion lately, wondering if he might have saved himself somehow. You might be wondering the same thing about yourself about now. As for me, I don't wonder. I know."

Neale smiled and raised the gun. Seeing the intent in his eyes, Tony lunged with Gus following from behind a half-second later. Too late.

Dominic Neale had followed Wirion's example and escaped exposure of his crimes.

Chapter Twelve

WHEN THE FOOTMAN had told Emily that Tony was out and that it had been necessary to leave her note in the hands of his landlord, she had tried to persuade herself that the short delay did not matter. She did not succeed.

As the hours passed with deadly slowness, her anxiety grew until it was nearly unbearable. Finally she was obliged to claim a migraine in order to avoid accompanying Letty and John to a dinner party. Thus, she was alone when Tony at last came to call.

One look at Tony told Emily that it was all over. Whatever she had feared had already happened. He was pale, rumpled, haggard from exhaustion, and there were stains on his blue tailcoat that Emily feared were blood, but he was alive and apparently unhurt. Relief threatened to undo her.

"I hoped to be here before the news," he said. "Have I failed?"

"What news? Oh, Tony, what has happened? Are you all right?" Without thought she reached out to touch him, to assure herself he was solid, real.

"I'm fine. Is it my appearance that frightened you? I'm sorry." He took her hand in both of his. "I thought it would be better to tell you first rather than go back to my lodgings to make myself respectable."

He looked ready to drop. Emily could see it took every ounce of concentration for him to speak.

"Tell me," she urged. "You went to see Neale, didn't you?"

He laughed. "I should have known you'd be ahead of me. Yes, I saw him. You had already realized he must be the traitor, hadn't you?"

"I suspected him," Emily admitted. "You will find a note from me at home warning you to take care. It appears I was too late."

"I thank you for the concern nonetheless."

His voice and smile warmed her. "You still haven't told me what happened, though."

"There's not much to say. I had Gus sneak in the back and hide in the apartment as a sort of protection. As we talked, Neale said something that pretty much gave him away. Eventually he confessed. When I told him Castlereagh was on to him, he caved in. He killed himself."

And Tony had been there when he did. What a horrible thing to have to see. Yet part of Emily was glad, glad Neale had paid for hurting Tony, glad there would be no more danger, glad most of all that the guessing and the worrying were done. Now Tony could finally put this behind him.

"I sent for Castlereagh, and he's keeping everything quiet. He's calling it an accident."

"I see." There was more to it than that, she was sure, but Tony either would not or could not tell her. He could hardly concentrate as it was. Emily's messenger had said Tony had gone out at the crack of dawn. It was near midnight now and Tony said he had not been home yet.

"You're exhausted, aren't you?" she said, ignoring her own sleepless night. "Go home and go to sleep. You've done your duty, and I won't worry anymore."

He hesitated a moment. "As I can't keep my eyes open, I had better go. I'll see you soon," he promised.

"Of course you will," Emily said, feeling herself a liar. Walking him to the door, she took one last look at the dear features, the beautiful dark eyes trying to stay open, his hair mussed from running his hands through it, and said good-bye.

*   *   *

That good-bye weighed on Emily's heart. Already it seemed final, only a last memory of Tony to cherish. She saw very little of him now that the date of his hearing approached. If anyone noticed any signs of unhappiness in the next few days, however, no one said anything. There was, after all, a perfectly valid reason for her to be concerned.

Even Letty was not so heartless as to fail to appreciate Edward's position, however little she liked him. It was Emily who felt heartless. Since she had met Tony, Edward had taken up less and less of her thoughts. Now, when she did think of him, it was generally to worry how she would ever be able to break off their engagement.

Poor Edward. It was not his fault he was not Tony—not the marquess of Palin, and not the man she loved. Neither he nor the bargain he had offered her almost a month ago had changed in any essential.

It was she who had changed. A month ago she had thought herself very lucky indeed to accept a second-best sort of love. When the genuine article came along, however, second-best loves looked very poor and tawdry.

None of which could she explain to Edward, still smarting from the loss of title and fortune.

She had gone over all this before and still she had no answer. For the sake of long friendship, Edward deserved better of her, deserved some kindness and consideration. How could she hurt him so by rejecting him now? Yet how could she let him believe a lie? Or let him make the lie public? Was that even a kindness, when Emily knew she would not, could not ever marry him?

She should have talked to John, she realized. Even without mentioning Tony's part in her change of heart, John would have understood the delicacy of the situation. Since Letty had at last come to her senses, however, she and John had hardly left each other's side, acting most unfashionably like a pair of lovebirds.

She was no closer to an answer when the day of the hearing finally arrived. The sound of laughter as everyone returned told her everything had gone well. In a minute they joined her in the morning room to tell her all about it.

Tony was with them. She had distinguished his voice immediately and was prepared then to see him again. Relief, and the joy of success, had smoothed the lines on his face. His blank, shielded look was gone forever. He looked years younger and very happy.

"A rout, a veritable rout, Emily," Letty announced. "I wish you had been there to see it."

That much kindness Emily thought she owed Edward, not to come and gawk at the spectacle, especially not to come and sit with the foremost supporters of his rival.

"Tell me what happened," she demanded.

"The number of people who spoke on Palin's account was very impressive," John said.

"All those people you helped me find, Emily," Tony added. "They all came forth and talked about Verdun and Bitche."

"Lord Castlereagh came to show his support, even though he had no evidence," Letty told her. "And then Edward's lawyer tried to confuse us and make us admit to lying, but, of course, he couldn't."

"And you? What about your testimony?"

"Oh, in the end I was not nervous at all. But the star was really Nanny. She was marvelous." Letty laughed. "I thought she was going to tell Edward's lawyer to go to bed without supper."

Tony took up the story. "Then they had me answer questions from the people my cousin had found, people I had either not seen or who did not believe me. I had been a little worried about that, because no one remembers everything from the past. Letty remembers things we did as children that I don't, and I remember things she doesn't. In the end everything was all right, however. I was able to answer their questions."

"And he was able to show that he remembered far more than he might have learned either in prison or from us," John added.

"You don't mean they suggested that we prompted Tony?" Emily said.

"They did," Letty answered. "And everyone laughed out loud!" A thought suddenly occurred to her. "Do you think they were laughing because they thought I hadn't the intelligence to do it?"

John's soothing reassurance was cut off by the appearance of the butler.

Withers was clearly somewhat at a loss how to announce the new arrival. He hesitated over the name. "Mr., er . . . Edward . . . Howe, ma'am."

Tony immediately cast an anguished glance toward Letty. He obviously doubted whether his cousin was ready to see him.

"I'll see what Edward wants," Emily offered. He had probably come to see her anyway. "Bring him to the larger drawing room, Withers," she said, then excused herself from the company.

Tony rose politely as she left the room. She thought for a moment that he had been about to stop her, to say something. His eyes looked sad again, no longer brimming with enthusiasm and joy. How like him, she thought, to feel compassion for Edward at such a time.

In the drawing room Edward waited, hat in hand, looking rather embarrassed. As he turned to greet her at her entrance, Emily noticed with relief that he seemed to be bearing his loss better than she expected. When they had last met and talked, he had appeared utterly devastated by her news. It seemed he had used his time wisely to accustom himself to the change in his status.

"You've heard the news. Ah, well, you told me how it would be anyway," he said.

"Yes, I heard," she said. "I'm sorry that you should be so hurt in this, Edward. It seems unfair the innocent should suffer so in this case."

"Yes, well, I daresay it will take some getting used to, but I think I'm ready to face it now. I haven't had the courage to face my cousin yet, but you were right. Uncle tells me that he's offered to make a very generous settlement on me."

Emily drew him to the sofa. "What will you do now?"

"For the time being I will make my home with Uncle. I'd like to get into the House of Commons, now that I'm no longer a peer. Some friends are looking about for a possible seat for me."

Emily nodded. While she was glad for him, she could not

help but think that Edward would be settled, and ready for a wife, quite soon.

He must have been thinking the same thing. "Emily, about us . . . My situation is very changed from what it was last month. . . ."

"Edward, you know the title never mattered to me, or the fortune," Emily said automatically, without considering the implications.

"It mattered to me, Emily."

"I know you're very disappointed, Edward, but—"

"You don't understand, Emily. I'm not asking you if you want to release me from our betrothal. I'm telling you I can no longer go through with it."

Emily stared at him, stunned. The last thing she had expected was that Edward would feel he did not need her anymore. If she had not been so relieved to be free, she might have felt insulted.

Misunderstanding her shock, Edward continued to explain. And then she did feel insulted.

"I'm sorry it has to be this way, truly I am, Emily. But you knew from the beginning what sort of life I had planned. While I was marquess of Palin and master of a considerable fortune, you provided exactly the sort of wife I needed to make my way in political circles. All that is changed now. Without fortune behind me, no amount of family connections can help advance me in the world."

"You're saying you can't afford me anymore," Emily said slowly. "You need a rich wife now."

"To put it bluntly, yes." His voice took on a wheedling tone. "You've always been a good friend to me, Emily. Be a good sport now. Let me go so I can make a better life for myself."

There was so much Emily would have liked to tell him. She would have liked to say that she had found something better herself. She would have liked to have challenged his sureness that she would let him go without a fuss. Oddly enough his rejection had hurt her in a way. Nothing he had done over the last month could have destroyed their friendship as this had. If he had told her he loved another, she would have congratulated him and wished him well. To be told he loved money and position better was intolerable.

"If that is what you want, Edward, then certainly I will let you go. I can see how wise you were to have us keep the betrothal a secret. Neither of us will be embarrassed now to have it end."

Relief at having the matter so easily concluded made Emily generous. She would not waste time or effort in telling Edward what she thought of him. Obviously, he would never have understood anyway.

He rose from the sofa. Now that he had accomplished what he had come to do, he was anxious to get away. Part of him recognized that he had behaved badly, Emily knew, and she would always be the uncomfortable reminder of it. Henceforth he would avoid her like the plague.

"I knew you would be reasonable. Thank you, Emily, for everything. I wish you all the best."

"I hope you find what you want," Emily said, well aware her wish was less generous than his.

He opened the door and then paused a moment, discomfited. "There is one thing more, Emily. If you would let your brother and sister-in-law believe that it was you who had a change of heart . . . ? I can't tell my uncle it was I who broke off the engagement. He isn't understanding like you. Sir John and Lady Meriton would never blame you for changing your mind. What do you care if my uncle thinks you were too afraid to stand by me?"

"I care," a voice behind Edward spoke. "Am I to understand, cousin, that not only have you jilted Miss Meriton, but you have the audacity to ask her to take the blame for it?"

"My discussion with Miss Meriton, cousin, is private," Edward said angrily. "I do not have to explain myself to you."

"No," Tony agreed, "but evidently you do expect to have to make an explanation to Lord Ruthven. Well, explain this."

It all happened so quickly Emily could hardly follow it. One moment Tony and Edward were trying to stare each other down, and the next moment Edward was trying to pick himself up off the floor.

"I think you've broken my nose," he whined, still dazed and sitting on the floor.

"Oh, I doubt it," Tony answered. "Just drew a little claret. You'll have a wonderful black eye by tomorrow, though."

Satisfaction at having bested his opponent seemed to war with some other emotion. Did he think too badly of her, Emily wondered, for ever having agreed to marry such a poor specimen?

Edward picked himself off the floor. "How am I going to explain that?"

"You walked into a door?" Tony suggested, offering his cousin a handkerchief. "Just be very sure that Miss Meriton's name does not figure into your explanation at all. Unless you care to tell the truth? I thought not. Good-bye, cousin." He escorted Edward to the drawing-room door and then shut it behind him.

"You knew," Emily accused from her seat on the sofa.

"Yes, Letty told me about you and Edward."

"After such a scene as that I must seem a prize fool. He wasn't always like that," she tried to explain. "Or if he was, he managed to hide it from me. We used to be such good friends." The oddity of Tony's sudden appearance finally occurred to her. "What brought you here, Tony? Did you know what he would do?"

"No, I had no idea he could be that foolish. I was afraid you were going to marry him after all." He came and sat by her on the sofa, but did not look at her. "I meant to stop it, if I could."

All at once the room had become incredibly still. Emily answered him very quietly. "No, I would not have married him—although I do not know whether I would have told him so today."

"Because you no longer respected him?"

"That, too, but mostly because I realized that when it comes to love, only the real thing will do—at least for me. You can't settle for less when it comes to love."

"Oh." He sounded disappointed. "You see, I was hoping that if you were looking for a fellow you liked very much and who was a good friend to spend your life with, you might spend it with me."

Emily tried to sense what lay behind this offer, but he kept his face turned away. This was the offer she had dreamed of, but was he offering for the same foolish reasons that had led her to accept Edward?

"Second best won't do, though, will it?" Tony asked.

"You would find that out soon enough yourself," Emily said, close to tears. "Especially with Letty by to remind you of what might have been yours. Perhaps in time you will find someone whom you will love better than you loved Letty."

"I already have," Tony said, finally turning to face her. "You're not second best, Emily. You never could be. Letty and I were children, too young to know what love really is. I know now—and it's you I love. I can't think of a single reason why you would look twice at me, but if you think in time you might . . ."

Emily felt as though her heart would burst. Tears lodged in her throat made it impossible to speak.

"No?" he said with a sad smile and then prepared to rise.

"Yes!" Emily cried, her voice sounding unnaturally loud. For too long she had allowed only the outer shell of her emotions to be shown. She could do so no longer, not with Tony. "I mean, I don't need time, Tony—and I do love you, and if you want me . . ."

Now Emily understood what Georgy had meant when she said she glowed. Tony looked lit up from the inside. She probably did, too, albeit a little damp. The tears had started to flow.

Tony rose and pulled her up after him. "If I want you . . . ? Oh, I want you. What's this? This is no time for tears." He pulled her into his embrace.

"I always cry when I'm happy," Emily said.

"But you have to stop for a moment," Tony insisted, "so I can kiss you properly."

Emily stopped crying at once and lifted her face to his. She was, after all, a very sensible girl. Yet, as Tony had once so astutely commented, she was also quite capable of throwing proper behavior to the winds for someone she truly loved.

On July 7, 1814, the day set aside for public thanksgiving for the allied victory, crowds filled St. Paul's Cathedral to pray, to admire each other's toilettes, and to gawk at whatever royal visitors might be left in town. Wellington was home, and that in itself seemed reason for celebration.

On a more private note the *Gazette* noted the betrothal of Miss Emily Meriton to the marquess of Palin. Miss Meriton herself later remarked to her betrothed that really it felt very odd to have so much happen in one's life and end up where one started, still engaged to Lord Palin.